What the critics said about *Louisiana Fever*:

"Delivers . . . genuinely heart-stopping suspense."

—*PUBLISHERS WEEKLY*

"Sleek, fast moving."

—*KIRKUS*

"Broussard tracks the virus . . . with a winning combination of common sense and epidemiologic legerdemain."

—*NEW ORLEANS TIMES-PICAYUNE*

"This series has carved a solid place for itself. Broussard makes a terrific counterpoint to the Dave Robicheaux ragin' Cajun school of mystery heroes."

—*BOOKLIST*

"A dazzling tour de force . . . sheer pulse-pounding reading excitement."

—*THE CLARION-LEDGER* (Jackson, MS)

"A novel of . . . terrifying force. . . . utterly fascinating . . . His best work yet."

—*THE COMMERCIAL APPEAL* (Memphis)

"The autopsies are detailed enough to make Patricia Cornwell fans move farther south for their forensic fixes. . . . splendidly eccentric local denizens, authentic New Orleans and bayou backgrounds . . . a very suspenseful tale."

—*LOS ANGELES TIMES*

"A fast moving, . . . suspenseful story. Andy and Kit are quite likeable leads . . . The other attraction is the solid medical background against which their story plays out."

—*DEADLY PLEASURES*

"If your skin doesn't crawl with the step-by-step description of the work of the (medical) examiner and his assistants, it certainly will when Donaldson reveals the carrier of the fever."

—*KNOXVILLE NEWS-SENTINEL*

"Keep(s) the reader on the edge of his chair and likely to finish in one sitting."

—*BENTON COURIER* (Arkansas)

"Exciting reading . . . well planned . . . fast paced."

—*MYSTERY NEWS*

"Tight and well-paced . . . Andy (Broussard) is a hugely engaging character . . . (the) writing is frequently inspired."

—*THE ARMCHAIR DETECTIVE*

What the critics said about *Sleeping with the Crawfish*:

"Streamlined thrills and gripping forensic detail."

—*KIRKUS*

"Action-packed, cleverly plotted topnotch thriller. Another fine entry in a consistently outstanding series."

—*BOOKLIST*

"With each book, Donaldson peels away a few more layers of these characters and we find ourselves loving the involvement."

—*THE COMMERCIAL APPEAL* (Memphis)

"The pace is pell-mell."

—*SAN ANTONIO EXPRESS-NEWS*

"Exciting and . . . realistic. Donaldson . . . starts his action early and sustains it until the final pages."

—*BENTON COURIER* (Arkansas)

"A roller-coaster ride . . . Thoroughly enjoyable."

—*BRAZOSPORT FACTS*

"The latest outing of a fine series which never disappoints."

—*MERITORIOUS MYSTERIES*

What the critics said about *New Orleans Requiem*:

"Lots of Louisiana color, pinpoint plotting and two highly likable characters . . . smart, convincing solution."

—*PUBLISHERS WEEKLY* (starred review)

"An . . . accomplished forensic mystery. His New Orleans is worth the trip."

—*NEW ORLEANS TIMES-PICAYUNE*

"Andy and Kit are a match made in mystery heaven."

—*THE CLARION-LEDGER* (Jackson, MS)

"Nicely drawn characters, plenty of action, and an engaging . . . storytelling style."

—*THE COMMERCIAL APPEAL* (Memphis)

"Donaldson has established himself as a master of the Gothic mystery."

—*BOOKLIST*

"The tension will keep even the most reluctant young adult readers turning the pages . . ."

—*SCHOOL LIBRARY JOURNAL*

LOUISIANA FEVER

D.J. Donaldson

This is a work of fiction. All characters and events portrayed in this novel are either fictitious or are used fictitiously.

LOUISIANA FEVER

Astor + Blue Editions

 Published in the United States by:

Astor + Blue Editions
New York, NY 10003
www.astorandblue.com

Publisher's Cataloging-In-Publication Data

Donaldson, D.J. Louisiana Fever—3rd ed.
Originally publishing in 1996 by St. Martin's Press

ISBN: 978-1-938231-35-3 (paperback)
ISBN: 978-1-938231-34-6 (epdf)
ISBN: 978-1-938231-33-9 (epub)

1. Detective Duo—Murder Mystery—Fiction 2. Fiction 3. Police forensic mystery—Fiction 4. —Fiction 5. Court Case—Fiction 6. —Fiction 7. American Murder and Suspense Story I. Title

Book Design: Bookmasters
Jacket Cover Design: Ervin Serrano

Acknowledgments

This story would never have gotten off the ground without the advice of Dr. O.C. Smith, assistant medical examiner of Shelby County, Tennessee, who, with his usual sharp instincts, suggested exactly the right virus for the book in our first brief conversation about it. Thanks also to Dr. Jerry Francisco, medical examiner for Shelby County, Tennessee, who, along with Dr. Smith, read and commented upon the final manuscript. For the scenes in Dr. Blackledge's laboratory involving ticks, I'm indebted to Dr. Lew Coons, who showed me those things in his own lab and who, in conjunction with Dr. Bill Lamoreaux, taught me what I needed to know about those odd creatures. I'm grateful as well to Dr. Bob Craven and Dr. Roy Campbell of the CDC for background information on tropical viruses, and to Dawne Orgeron for advice on emergency medical procedures. Thanks also to: Angie Baker, Eunice Steimke, Dr. David Smalley, Amanda Durbin, Bert Price, Dr. Harold Dundee, Vernon Foret, Dr. Joan Chesney, Kristy Cupples, Jeff Schryver, Ellen Karle, and Paul Sheffield. Apologies to anyone I've forgotten. If I've erred anywhere, it's my fault.

Introduction to this Edition

This book marks the second Andy Broussard-Kit Franklyn mystery reissued by Astor + Blue. The first was *New Orleans Requiem*. It's always thrilling to see one of my books get a second life, because it moves Andy and Kit back into the light. And that feels like something I owe them.

In this one, they both suffer through some events I'm sure each of them would rather forget. In Kit's case, her trials include discovering a secret about herself that will forever change her life. Broussard suffers, too, but in the process learns a huge lesson about someone he doesn't like. On a personal note, sometimes people blame me for the bad things that happen to Andy and Kit. But these same people don't blame ESPN when their favorite team loses a game, nor do they hold the weatherman (or woman) responsible when it rains . . . unless it was supposed to be dry. What I'm trying to say is, I'm just the messenger here. Sure, Andy and Kit get into a lot of jams . . . but it's the nature of their work. So please . . . before you send someone over to my house to toilet paper my trees, think about what I've just said.

—D.J. Donaldson

Prologue

Walter Baldwin rubbed his eyes and looked again, praying that everything would be back to normal. It wasn't.

The traffic signs and the words on the buildings were still gibberish and he still had no idea where he was or how he'd gotten there.

He'd lived all his life in New Orleans and knew each block of every major street. He was a salesman who drove them daily, for God's sake. He knew them . . . he did. But today, he might as well have been on Pluto. He took a shaky breath to calm his rising panic and felt something warm run into his mouth.

Shifting in his seat, he looked at himself in the rearview mirror. Christ, now he had a nosebleed.

He pulled to the curb and grabbed a Kleenex from the glove compartment. Adjusting the seat so he could lie back, he stuffed a crumpled tissue into his left nostril. In this new position, his headache percolated from his forehead to the back of his skull.

What the hell was happening?

He lay there reciting his name, his address, his place of employment, looking for other gaps in the familiar and exchanging tissues until one came away with just a small amount of blood on it. He raised his seat back and watched himself in the mirror until he was satisfied the flow had nearly stopped.

It had been several minutes since he'd looked out the window. Slowly, he shifted his gaze from the mirror to a sign a few yards in front of the car. NO PARKING HERE TO CURB.

NO PARKING. . . . He could read it.

Eagerly, he checked the buildings lining the street. He knew where he was. My God, it was less than a mile from home, a place he passed at least once a day.

Elation at this return to normality was instantly pushed aside by the fear that he was losing his mind. He pictured his mother crawling around the floor of the mental hospital, sweeping imaginary tobacco into her hand.

Mental illness . . . it runs in families they say. Was that where he was headed? Was the blood even real?

He looked at the pile of bloody Kleenex in the wastebasket straddling the hump between seats. It seemed real enough. The thought that he might be going the way of his mother sucked at him until he felt withered and dry inside. Then the pain from his headache pushed through, demanding attention.

Knowing there was a K and B drugstore five blocks from where he sat, he checked for approaching traffic and pulled from the curb. The fan on the ventilation system was already on its highest setting, but the car was so hot.

He rolled his window all the way up and turned on the air conditioning, even though outside it was cool enough for a long-sleeved shirt. A mental ward . . . confinement . . . God, no.

Two minutes later, the first stirring of nausea began. It escalated quickly, converting his stomach to a churning cesspool. The white line in the road began to undulate like a snake. He pulled to the curb, closed his eyes, and hugged the steering wheel.

His vision soon cleared, but he still felt dangerously close to vomiting.

Home . . . must go home.

Sweat pearling from his forehead, blood again trickling from his nose, he lurched from the curb. A horn blared. Brakes squealed. Oblivious to the electrical-supply truck that had almost hit him, Walter drove on.

Somehow, he made it to the parking lot of his apartment house without vomiting. Though he was now as sick as he'd ever been, he remembered to grab his briefcase off the seat next to him.

The steps to the building felt rubbery as he hurried to the front entrance. He was definitely going to throw up, but he was determined to do it in private.

Blood dripping from his chin onto his tie where it lay on his paunch, he hit the button to the elevators and saw through heavy-lidded eyes, a dark spot on the back of his hand that seemed to be spreading as he watched, further evidence of his escalating madness.

He wiped at his nose with his arm—the blood that came away on his white shirt, a stark statement.

After an eternity, the elevator arrived and he staggered on. Turning to face the front, he saw a familiar briefcase sitting back by the front entrance. He glanced at his own briefcase and saw that his hand was empty.

The mental ward beckoned . . . a long finger that brought tears to his eyes. Stifling a cry, he reeled from the elevator and made his way back to the entrance, where he snatched up the briefcase and clutched it to his chest, now whimpering aloud.

Thankfully, the elevator was still waiting for him and he was soon at his apartment door. He stabbed at the lock with his key, but the aperture danced away. The pressure built in his throat, a dam about to break. Finally, his key slid home.

Inside, he slammed the door, dropped the briefcase, and ran for the bathroom. But it was too late. His body was ripped with a massive peristaltic convulsion and he emptied himself.

The great contraction was followed by a succession of smaller sisters that kept him on his knees. When he was eventually able to open his eyes, a fist grabbed his heart. The carpet was soaked with a thick black liquid tinged with red. Though he didn't know it, he'd also delivered a substantial portion of the tissue lining his stomach.

Help . . . he needed help.

But he was confused. Where would he find it? Then he vomited again, this time less black and more red, and more of his stomach.

Walter's problem was simple. In his travels that week, he'd picked up a tiny passenger that, without Walter's knowledge, had conducted some commerce with him—taking something and giving something in return. And now, Walter was teeming with the progeny of what he'd been given.

1

Like the others, the single long-stemmed yellow rose had been waiting for her in the wicker basket under the mail drop when she'd arrived home from work. It was the third day in a row this had happened. Like the others, the rose was resting in white gift tissue in a slim white box tied with yellow ribbon. Unlike the others, the latest one had come with a note, neatly printed on a general-occasion card: "If you want to meet the one who's been sending the roses, come to Grandma O's restaurant at 1:00 P.M. tomorrow. Don't worry about a description. You'll know who I am."

There was, of course, no question she'd go. The mystery was far too tantalizing to ignore. And there was absolutely no danger involved, because the designated rendezvous was a restaurant where she ate lunch practically five days a week.

As Kit neared the restaurant, she'd just about decided this was a prank being played on her by Teddy LaBiche. How he'd managed it was a puzzle, though, because he lived 125 miles away in Bayou Coteau, where he had his alligator farm, and had been in Europe for the last three weeks, lining up buyers for his skins.

Kit paused in front of a mirrored window and dug in her purse. She applied a fresh coat of lip gloss and reset the faux tortoiseshell combs that kept her long auburn hair out of her eyes. She lingered a moment longer, appreciating how the spray of freckles across the bridge of her nose was less obvious in the cool seasons. Then it hit her. Grandma O . . . That's how he could have done it, she thought, beginning to walk again. . . . And Bubba, her grandson. She smiled. . . . A conspiracy. Teddy had arranged it with Grandma O and was now back a few days early, waiting for her inside.

She detoured around a wad of gum on the sidewalk and hurried to the restaurant's front door, her heart high in her chest.

Most of the noon to 1:00 P.M. lunch crowd had already left, but there was a small queue of laggards at the register, where Grandma O was trying to get them out as quickly as possible.

The place was still about half-full, so it took Kit a moment to scan the occupied tables. Her eyes paused briefly at one in the back, where an older man dressed in jeans and a khaki-colored shirt with epaulets seemed unusually interested in her, then she moved on, still looking for Teddy.

But he wasn't there.

Her eyes went back to the man in the khaki shirt and she now saw that he was holding a long-stemmed yellow rose.

Disappointed that Teddy wasn't at the bottom of this, she crossed the room. As she approached the man's table, he rose to greet her.

"Kit . . ."

He spoke her name and hesitated, taking her in. He looked to be around sixty years old—disheveled white hair, heavy salt-and-pepper eyebrows shielding deep-set eyes, skin with a texture that looked as though it had seen a lot of sun and wind but that now had a pasty color. And there was a sheen of perspiration at his hairline, though the restaurant wasn't hot. Suddenly, his eyes glazed, and his mouth froze in an O.

His right hand came up and grabbed Kit's wrist as his knees buckled. He went down, yawing to the left, and hit the edge of the table, rocking it off its pedestal, pulling Kit after him.

Kit saw him slide down the tilted table in slow motion, pursued by the container of sugar and artificial sweetener and the napkin dispenser. Her own face was heading for the tabletop. A scant second before she hit it, she turned her head.

A megawatt arc light went on inside her skull. Then her mains blew.

She was out only briefly, and when her eyes opened, the world was clad in blue-and-white stripes.

She was sliding sideways.

The stripes began moving, slipping past her eyes until they abruptly changed direction, to run perpendicular to their original course.

A shirt cuff.

"Are you all right?" a voice said.

She turned onto her back and looked up into a face sporting a mustache with bread crumbs caught in it.

"I think so. . . ."

Behind him, she caught a glimpse of Grandma O's worried face, her dark eyes glittering. Then she disappeared.

"Maybe you shouldn't get up."

"No . . . I can manage."

"You sure?"

"Yes."

And she wasn't just being optimistic, because, with the man's help, she was soon on her feet, her hold on consciousness unwavering.

"Doesn't look like *he's* doing well," the man said, looking behind her.

Grandma O rarely wore anything but black taffeta, which magnified her already-considerable bulk and made her sound as though she was passing through a field of dry weeds wherever she went. When Kit turned, she saw her draped over the fallen man like a great bat, performing CPR.

"Has anyone called nine-one-one?" Kit asked.

"On the way," Grandma O said, bending to give the man another breath.

Though the stricken man had said only one word to her, Kit felt a pang of responsibility for him, and here she was standing by, doing nothing to help. . . . But what was there to do? And so she did all she could, silently urging the man to breathe on his own.

The minutes inched by without any encouraging signs. Finally, in the distance, a siren, then closer . . . a green-and-white ambulance outside.

A female white-shirted medic in blue pants charged through the door, her male partner close behind, pulling a stretcher loaded with equipment.

"We'll take over now," the female said, helping Grandma O to her feet. "How long's he been out?"

"Maybe ten minutes," Grandma O said.

"He eaten anything?"

Learning that he hadn't, the medic grabbed a shoulder bag from the stretcher and dropped to her knees beside the victim's head. In seconds, she had a mask strapped to his face. While she gave him air by squeezing a blue bag attached to the mask, her partner grabbed a shoulder bag and a cardiac monitor from the stretcher and hurried to the victim's other side. He pushed the fallen table away with his foot, knelt, and ripped the victim's shirt open. He turned on the monitor and clapped two paddles to the exposed skin.

The monitor showed only a flat line, a permanent copy of the bad news issuing from the monitor on a paper tongue.

The medic gave it a name. "He's in fine v. fib."

He removed the paddles from the victim's chest, rubbed a jelly onto their contact surface, and slapped them back against the victim's skin. He nudged a dial on one of the paddles and pushed a button. The paddles gave off a barely audible buzz that gradually grew louder. A tiny red light on each paddle flicked on.

"Clear."

The victim bucked under the jolt of current and the air was filled with the smell of burning hair. Seeing the same flat line on the screen, the medic nudged the dial on his paddle. The buzz returned, escalated, and the red lights winked on.

"Clear."

The victim bucked again, more violently, but the heart refused to kick in.

Another nudge of the dial.

A third, even more powerful shock, lifted the victim off the floor, but still the heart resisted. By now, the smell of singed hair was so sickening, most of the bystanders had moved back. Having smelled far worse odors at crime scenes she'd attended with her boss, and feeling linked to the victim, Kit held her ground. The medic looked up at her, holding out an IV bag. "Take this and stand right here."

Happy to be helping, Kit moved closer and took the bag from him.

"I need somebody to do chest compression," the female medic announced, her voice filled with urgency.

Grandma O and a man who wouldn't take up nearly as much space at the victim's side as she would stepped forward simultaneously. The medic chose the man, her decision generating a hard look from Grandma O.

The medic working the monitor slipped a needle into a vein in the front of the victim's elbow. He attached the IV tube and taped it in place. He then discharged the contents of a preloaded syringe into a port on the downstream side of the bag. The heart shock paddles had also been serving as temporary leads conveying the victim's heart rhythms to the monitor. The medic now switched to the regular leads, sticking them to the victim's chest.

The monitor showed only the same flat line as before. Continuing to stare at the pattern that wasn't changing, the male medic said, "Anyone know this man?"

No one spoke up, so Kit said, "We were talking, but I didn't really know him."

"What happened?"

"When I approached the table, he stood up, said my name . . . then dropped."

"You wouldn't know, then, if he's had heart trouble or what kind of medication he might be taking?"

"No, I wouldn't."

Precious seconds passed, their flight marked by the rubbery squish of the ventilator bag and the volunteer counting off each chest compression. Yet the medic just stared at the monitor. Mesmerized by the struggle playing out before them, no one in the crowd moved. Finally, when Kit was about to suggest he do something, the medic shocked the heart again, still without success.

On the opposite side, the female medic removed the victim's face mask and passed a long plastic tube into his mouth. She attached the blue bag to that and ventilated him twice while listening to his chest. Apparently satisfied that the tube was properly placed, she taped the tube to the victim's face and signaled for her volunteer to resume chest compression.

The medic at the monitor emptied another syringe into the IV port. He waited a short time, then shocked the heart again. Despite Kit's wishes, the line on the monitor remained infuriatingly flat. The medic produced a radio.

"Charity Med Control. This is Unit Six-two-oh-one, on the scene. Patient is a white male, approximately sixty years of age, found in full arrest. ACLS protocols implemented and IV going. Patient remains in fine v. fib. Any further orders?"

"Load and go."

"En route. ETA three to five minutes."

The medics strapped their patient to a stiff slab of yellow plastic and loaded him onto the stretcher. They put the IV bag Kit had been holding under his head, thanked everybody for their help, and whisked him away.

Kit was ashamed of the relief she felt at his departure.

The knot of people who'd been watching broke up and went back to their tables, buzzing about what they'd seen—all of them except for a woman in a green cotton jogging outfit that, given her age and shape, likely hadn't been doing much jogging. She came over and shook her finger at Grandma O.

"That was very foolish of you . . . giving that man CPR with your mouth on his. You don't know what he's been doing with that mouth or what bugs he might have."

"Well, it's like dis," Grandma O said. "Ah lef' mah face mask an' ventilator bag in mah other purse an' Ah jus' los' mah head. Besides, ain't no bug got the nerve to try anything on me."

From the look on the woman's face, she didn't know what to make of Grandma O. But then, few people did. As the woman moved off, Grandma O turned to Kit.

"When he came in, he said he was waitin' for somebody, but Ah didn't know it was you."

"Someone sent me a yellow rose on Monday with no note attached. The same thing happened Tuesday. Yesterday, one came with a message that the sender would be here today if I wanted to meet him."

"He looked too old for you. Now, if he'd sent *me* dose roses . . ."

"But like I told the medic, I've never even seen the man before."

"Child, dis can't be da first time a man you'd never noticed tried to get your attention."

"No . . . but this one seemed different."

"'Cause of his age?"

"More than that."

"Ah don' guess anybody ever died on you like dat before."

"You . . . don't think he'll make it?"

Grandma O walked over and picked up the yellow rose Kit's mysterious admirer had dropped. She came back and handed it to her. "Ah hope Ah'm wrong, but Ah think dis is da las' rose he'll ever buy."

2

Having no appetite for lunch, yet too keyed up to go back to her office in Charity Hospital, Kit lingered at the restaurant, wanting to talk more with Grandma O about what had happened. But Grandma O had customers to deal with. So instead, Kit carried the yellow rose down to the river and watched the ship and barge traffic for a while from a bench in front of the aquarium, spending most of that time reliving those awful moments at the restaurant and wondering what it all meant.

Finally, deciding that enough time had passed for the mystery man to get to the hospital and be checked in, she headed back to her office to see what she could find out about his condition.

Twenty minutes later, as she got off the elevator on her floor, she ran into her boss, Andy Broussard, chief medical examiner of Orleans Parish, waiting to get on.

Because he was so overweight, if you saw him coming down the street and didn't know him, you'd probably think he wasn't very healthy. But when he got close and you could see that above his gray beard, his skin had a robust glow, you might reconsider. And if you'd ever seen him climb a ladder to rescue the odd cat that had become stuck in a tree in his yard or to put a baby bird back in its nest, you'd know you were wrong. Kit hadn't actually seen one of those ladder rescues firsthand, but Charlie Franks, the deputy ME, had slides of him doing it, so Kit didn't believe Broussard's denials that he ever did such things. Aside from his surprising agility, the most remarkable thing about him was his mind, which was so sharp, Kit was still intimidated by him, though she'd played a major role in solving more than one case since she'd arrived.

"Heard you had some excitement," he said.

"Who told you that?"

"Grandma O."

Ignoring what he'd probably been told, Kit poured out her own version of the story, finishing by saying, ". . . and when they took him away, it didn't look like he was going to make it."

Broussard tilted his chin and examined her through the tops of his glasses. "He didn't."

"How do you know?"

"He's downstairs, in the morgue."

"Who is he?"

Broussard shrugged. "Beats me. I haven't actually seen him yet, but Guy said he had no ID on him. I told Phillip about the situation. . . ."

Kit briefly wondered which Phillip he meant, then realized it had to be Phil Gatlin, Broussard's longtime friend in Homicide.

"He went over to the restaurant to see if the victim had come by car, thinkin' he might get a line on his identity that way, but he just called sayin' every car in the lot was accounted for."

"Jesus, you two work fast."

"We're old, but we're good. I'm on my way downstairs now to see what killed this fellow."

"I'd like to know that myself," Kit said. "Will you let me know when you find out?"

He nodded and slipped a lemon ball into his mouth from the linty cache in the pocket of his lab coat. He offered her a wrapped one from the other pocket, a ritual that had become so commonplace, the transfer was made without comment. “Should take about an hour and a half.”

Kit went to her office and put the yellow rose in a badly chipped bud vase she’d been meaning to replace for months. She then tried to pick up the project she’d been working on that morning, construction of a psychological autopsy on a nineteen-year-old male who’d shot himself in the head in front of his buddy. They’d bought the gun, a .38 Smith & Wesson, at a pawnshop because his buddy’d had his car hijacked at gunpoint and felt he needed protection to keep it from happening again. The victim had loaded the gun, pointed it at his head, said, “Life sucks,” and pulled the trigger.

But nothing else about the guy sounded like a potential suicide. He had plans for the future and hadn’t been depressed. Something wasn’t right.

She looked at the police report in front of her. Except for an empty chamber at the nine o’clock position, the gun had been fully loaded. Why the empty chamber when there were extra rounds still in the box?

Her concentration wavered as she saw again the pallid complexion of the man stricken at Grandma O’s—his surprised expression before he went down, the flat line on the cardiac monitor.

As Broussard left the elevator, he felt a twinge around the knife scar on his side. It’d been a little over a year since that dreadful affair, and except for an occasional sad thought about the cause of it all and an ache in the scar just before a rain, he’d fully recovered.

When he entered the morgue, he found that Guy Minoux and Natalie D’Souza, his two assistants, had already stripped the body. Except for their facial protection, which they hadn’t put on yet, they were each fully turned out in a disposable front-zippered jumpsuit covered by a disposable surgical gown with a Velcro fastener and tie at the back and elastic closures on the sleeves. They had protective booties on their shoes, two pairs of rubber gloves taped at the wrist to the gown, and a disposable hood tied under the chin. This was a bit much for Broussard. After all, there was such a thing as style.

"Afternoon, Your Honor," Minoux said, bowing. "He's ready for inspection."

"Nice to get a clean one once in awhile," D'Souza added, referring to the fact many of their customers came in bloodied and had to be washed before much could be done.

"We're gonna need a set of prints," Broussard said, going to the dressing alcove.

"Already done," Minoux said, beaming at his own efficiency.

D'Souza stepped over to the stereo. "What'll it be today—Tchaikovsky, Mozart?"

While he occasionally liked Tchaikovsky during an autopsy, Broussard generally viewed him as a composer better suited to microscopic work. Mozart was a different matter—*that* was an autopsy composer. "Mozart, disc three."

She nudged the select button on the stereo, using the knuckle of her gloved hand, then pushed play, warming the cool room with the opening strains of *The Magic Flute.*

"Delivery crew said he keeled over at Grandma O's," Minoux said. "That's not gonna be good for business."

"He hadn't had anything to eat, so I don't think we can blame her," Broussard replied, slipping a pair of booties over his mesh shoes. While Broussard donned his plastic apron, on which someone had long ago written THE BOSS with a permanent black marker, the two assistants each put on a mask and a plastic visor. Broussard added two pairs of rubber gloves to his meager outfit, walked over to the body, and reached for a Polaroid camera on a nearby bench.

Though he had seen thousands of cadavers, the tenuous nature of life had never ceased to fascinate him. A single puncture wound in the right place and it was gone. . . Constrict the airway for a few minutes, it was gone—an irrevocable loss far too easy to achieve.

And even when it happened without external intervention, as apparently this one had—a death by so-called natural causes—it seemed no less deplorable.

Whenever an endotracheal tube is inserted during attempts at life support and then the patient dies, the tube is left in place so the ME can determine if it was properly placed. That tube and the tape securing it now obscured the man's features. Even so, it was easy to see he wasn't young. The gray scalp hair, eyebrows, chest, and pubic hair alone indicated that.

He took a picture of the face with the tube in place, then motioned to Minoux, who cut the end of the tube off with a big pair of scissors and tucked the protruding remains behind the cadaver's teeth. Broussard photographed the face again and traded the camera for a clipboard holding a sheet of paper depicting front and back views of a sexless human.

He began his superficial exam, starting at the head. After a few seconds of general inspection, he asked Minoux to spread the eyelids, which were half-closed. Using a penlight, he saw that each eye exhibited arcus senilis, a thin white line of deposited lipid circling the cornea near its junction with the sclera—an indicator of heart disease. He noted this on the form.

The next feature of interest was a tattoo lettered on the right wrist, crudely done, like those often acquired in jail. The sentiment expressed, "Think Free," supported that notion. "Mark it," he said, noting its location on the diagram.

D'Souza tacked a small adhesive-tape ruler to the skin under the tattoo.

Broussard turned to Minoux and made a twisting motion with his hand. Responding, Minoux rotated the arm so Broussard could examine its posterior surface, the absence of rigor making the task easier than it otherwise might have been.

On the back of that hand, amid a cluster of freckles, Broussard noted a small ecchymosis—a hemorrhage under the skin—probably an injury suffered during his fall in the restaurant. D'Souza also marked that.

Minoux then rotated the arm at the shoulder so Broussard could inspect the axilla, which was unremarkable.

There were two more ecchymoses on the back of the body's left hand. He found patches of brawny edema on both legs, collections of tissue fluid that felt rubbery rather than yielding and soft as in the other major type of edema, further evidence the man was plagued with vascular disease. His sparse leg hair also supported that diagnosis.

"Okay, let's get him over."

The two assistants rolled the body onto an adjacent wheeled table and Broussard examined its posterior surface, finding only one item of interest, and that, hardly worth noting—a small reddish brown nodule on the right calf.

D'Souza marked the nodule and Broussard noted it on the diagram. He traded the clipboard for the camera and took a close-up of the nodule. "Time to roll him again."

The two assistants grappled with the body and returned it to the first table so it again lay on its back. Broussard photographed all the marked areas, then reached for a large syringe. "Let's get our fluids."

While Broussard plunged the massive needle on his syringe into the right subclavian vein, Minoux slipped a much smaller needle into the left eye and sucked out the jellylike material that occupied most of the globe, collapsing it. Restoring the eye to full turgor would be a job for the funeral home.

With a syringe and needle the equal of Broussard's, D'Souza penetrated the skin just above the pubic hair and drove her needle into the bladder.

"I'll be wantin' a purple top and a gray," Broussard said as his syringe filled with dark blood.

D'Souza emptied the contents of her syringe into a plastic bottle and capped it. She then gave Broussard two plastic tubes sealed with colored rubber tops. The tube with the purple top contained EDTA, a chemical that keeps the blood from clotting, allowing this sample to be used for ABO and other antigen typing. Blood in the gray top would be sent to Toxicology, any cocaine in the sample kept intact by the sodium fluoride in the tube.

"Want us to get some dental X-rays?" Minoux asked.

"Eventually, but I'd like to finish the post first," Broussard replied.

The two assistants moved the body to the autopsy alcove and transferred it to a long stainless-steel platform welded to a stainless sink.

"It'll be a while before you'll be needing me again," Minoux said. "I've got something next door I have to clean up. I'll be back."

Broussard nodded in agreement, allowing Minoux to leave.

D'Souza picked up a disposable scalpel and drew the blade deeply through the cadaver's skin in a long Y that began at the tip of each shoulder and ended at the pubic bone. On the chest, the cut revealed dark red muscle. On the belly, it exposed gobs of bright orange-yellow fat and the glistening gray serpent of intestine. With the penetration of the abdomen, a cloying visceral perfume seeped into the air.

"Well, he liked his veggies," D'Souza said, remarking on the bright color of the fat. Broussard said nothing, concentrating on the long, thin knife he was stropping on an oilstone.

D'Souza began dissecting the skin flaps off the chest, the flashing strokes of her scalpel quickly separating them from the underlying white connective tissue. She did the side flaps first, then moved to the upper one, her swift movements rapidly carrying her dissection to the arch of the mandible, where she draped the loosened skin over the face and cut through the muscles attached to the mandible, thereby entering the mouth. She freed the tongue and pulled it forward, her scalpel slashing at the restraining tissue, liberating the trachea and esophagus.

Broussard had finished sharpening the long knife he would use to section the organs and had begun arranging the perforated plastic sample containers on his cutting board at the shallow sink under the data blackboard when he heard D'Souza say, "Oh, shit."

Turning, he saw her tearing at the tape holding her gloves to her wrists. Obviously, she'd cut herself.

She pulled off her gloves and Broussard saw that her left index finger was bleeding heavily. To a degree, that was good, as it would wash any potentially infectious organisms out of the wound.

"How bad is it?"

"Not deep enough to hit any tendons or need sewing up," she replied behind her mask.

"Good. Now get out of here and let it bleed under water for five minutes, then put some Betadine and peroxide on it. When you feel up to it, fill out an incident report."

Behind her visor, her eyes were filled with worry. "I'd like to hear that speech again about how unlikely it is to acquire a disease from something like this."

"First of all, sudden deaths like this one aren't caused by infectious disease," Broussard said. "It's likely he had a coronary. And even if he did have somethin' infectious, your chances of acquirin' it are about like your chances of bein' struck by lightnin' today."

"Even if he's HIV-positive?"

"Even then."

"I feel better."

"But just to be on the safe side, we're gonna have the lab check him out. And you're gonna need to give some blood for a baseline. So, when I'm through here, you can take his samples up to the lab and let 'em draw yours. Now, go on . . . take care of your finger. . . . You're gonna be fine."

As she went into the adjoining room to disinfect her wound, Broussard hailed Minoux on the intercom. "Guy, Natalie's cut herself. I need you."

Broussard then got out a large syringe and five test tubes—three red tops, which contained no chemicals, and two tubes containing viral transport medium. To his test tube collection, he added a bottle containing aerobic and one containing anaerobic bacterial transport medium. Returning to the body, he inserted the needle into the right subclavian vein and drew enough blood to fill the red tops and inoculate the medium in the other containers. The samples would be sent to the Department of Laboratory Medicine, where they would be parceled out to Immunology, Microbiology, and Virology to determine if the deceased was harboring any infectious agents. He really believed what he'd told D'Souza about there being no cause for worry. Still, it was always better not to cut yourself.

Rather than do nothing while waiting for Minoux, he picked up the dissection where D'Souza had left it. To determine just how far she'd progressed, he checked along the mandible to see if all the tissue had been freed there. Finding that it had, he caught a glimpse of the roof of the mouth, which, to his surprise, was dotted with what appeared to be small hemorrhages, a finding associated with strangulation or choking. But if he'd choked, the scleras should also have shown them.

Puzzling.

Could they be Koplik's spots? He was kind of old for measles, though. And these didn't have white centers.

Maybe he did choke. It's not always possible to tell at the scene whether there's an obstruction in the airway. But Kit said the deceased hadn't eaten anything and he hadn't grabbed at his throat or appeared to gag. Odd . . .

He pulled the tongue forward to see if the ET tube was in the trachea and not the esophagus. It was.

After removing the tube, he cut through both sternoclavicular joints, then severed each rib through its cartilage attachment to the sternum, pleased that he didn't encounter enough ossification to call for the saw. With that done, he was able to remove the breast plate, revealing the lungs, which cupped the heart in pinkish gray angel wings.

His scalpel stopped moving.

He pressed on one lung with a forward motion to see more of it.

Puzzled at what he saw, he did the same with the other lung. Both were studded with small hemorrhages.

Very peculiar . . .

He cut the major vessels entering and leaving the heart, noting there was copious blood flow from them, something commonly seen in heart-attack victims. He removed the tongue, trachea, esophagus, lungs, and heart as a block and dropped them into a stainless pan as Guy Minoux stepped up to the table.

"Take over, will you, while I work at the sink?"

Minoux nodded and picked up the scalpel Broussard left for him.

Broussard took his pan to the sink under the blackboard, poured the contents onto his cutting board, and began separating the organs, prior to close inspection of each one.

He first examined the tongue, noting there was no indication the deceased had bitten it. With the long knife in one hand and the other pressing on the upper surface of the tongue, he halved it horizontally in the same way he'd slice a bagel. When he separated the two halves, he saw more tiny hemorrhages.

This was becoming a major mystery, as the emerging pattern of affected organs fit nothing he'd ever seen.

He took a few thin slices across the long axis of the tongue, trimmed them, and put them in a sample container that he dropped into a waiting bottle of formalin.

Next, he slit the esophagus, inspected it, then opened the airway and examined the gray lining of the larynx. Close inspection showed there was an area just above the vocal cords in which the small vessels were blanched and devoid of blood, an indication the small balloon used to seal the airway around the ET tube had been inflated properly.

The heart was in very poor condition, enlarged and with fibrotic streaks all through the muscle. And the coronary arteries were almost completely blocked. Broussard weighed the heart on the hanging pan to his right and chalked the results in the appropriate space on the blackboard.

Minoux stepped up and put another pan containing the abdominal viscera in the sink. He then went back to the cadaver, slit the scalp from ear to ear across the top of the head, and peeled the skin forward and backward as if husking an ear of corn.

At the sink, Broussard continued to prowl through the deceased's organs, weighing, slicing, and adding more sample containers to the jar of formalin, concentrating so intensely he barely heard the sharp whine of the Stryker saw as Minoux turned it on. Nor did he notice the way the sound became labored and dull as the saw cut through the skullcap, throwing bony sawdust and bits of flesh into a thin plume of friction smoke.

Out of a habit arising from the knowledge that defense attorneys often try to make MEs look careless by asking if the victim had an appendix, a totally irrelevant fact, Broussard noted that one was present. Less than a minute later, Minoux plopped the cadaver's brain into Broussard's sink and returned to the body to aspirate the blood from its cavities and wash them out.

As for Broussard, he continued to find hemorrhages—in the lungs, the kidneys, the pancreas . . . and in the brain, where they seemed particularly prevalent in the upper part of the postcentral gyrus. Most likely if this had progressed much farther, the deceased would have experienced sensory deficits in his hands and arms.

Broussard cut small pieces from several of the affected organs and parceled them out to bacterial and viral transport media. He then sliced the brain into sections like a loaf of bread, chose a few to trim and add to the formalin jar, and he was finished. He photographed the data on the blackboard and carried all the pictures he'd taken and the fingerprint cards to the old desk in the adjacent room, where he filled out the various autopsy and lab forms, then called the dictaphone upstairs and recited his report, drawing no conclusions about the widely disseminated hemorrhages he'd found, because he didn't know what they meant. Death was surely caused by his bad heart and those blocked coronaries. The other . . . who knows?

His failure to understand the hemorrhages was like an alligator in a chicken coop. It disturbed things. And he did not enjoy being disturbed.

He gathered up all the samples for the lab, labeled them with the case number, and put them on the desk alongside the form that would accompany their delivery.

"Guy, Natalie's gonna take care of everything from this case that needs to go to Laboratory Medicine. When you finish in there, would you see that the rest gets on its way? I'll leave the forms on the desk."

"Sure thing."

"I'd also appreciate it if you'd take care of those X-rays and let Dr. French know that we need the teeth charted."

On the desk was a grocery bag and a big tan envelope stamped with the case number of the individual they'd been working on. After changing out of his autopsy gear, Broussard picked those items up along with the autopsy photos and the fingerprint cards and went into the hallway. Before going to the office, he stepped into the room where the morgue assistants each had a desk. D'Souza was at hers, filling out the incident report required when anyone cut themselves or was injured, which fortunately didn't happen often.

"How's your finger?"

She looked up. "It throbs, but it's on my left hand, so that's good. You didn't find any signs he was suffering from some horrible infectious disease, did you?"

Broussard hesitated before answering. He didn't know what he'd found, so it was hard to answer. And without knowing what was going on, there wasn't anything she could do until the tests on the blood came back. They'd just have to wait. Most likely, it was some kind of physical deterioration unrelated to any causal organism.

"Looks like he died of a weak heart."

"I'm glad—not that he died. I mean . . ."

"I know. The samples for the lab are on the desk in the next room. Be sure and give Margaret that report when you're finished."

Reaching the office, he called Kit, then emptied the bag of clothing he'd brought up from the morgue onto his desk. Half a minute later, he heard Kit's knock, and she came in.

"So what was it?" she said. "Bad heart?"

Broussard leaned back in his chair and laced his fingers over his belly. "Pretty bad. Is that for me?" He was referring to the file folder in Kit's hand.

"Yeah . . . my report on that kid who shot himself." She put the folder in front of him.

"Suicide?" he asked.

She shook her head. "Misadventure. The gun was a recently purchased Smith & Wesson thirty-eight, fully loaded except for an empty chamber two to the left of the spent round under the hammer. The victim had owned a Colt thirty-eight for several years. . . ."

"Ha." Broussard rocked forward. "Misadventure. I agree."

"You don't even want to hear my reasons?"

Broussard shrugged. "The Colt cylinder rotates clockwise, the Smith counterclockwise. I assume the deceased was known to play pranks from time to time. . . ."

"Yes," Kit said, unable to keep exasperation out of her voice.

"This was meant to be another one," Broussard said. "He loaded the Smith with an empty chamber just to the left of the firin' position, thinkin' the cylinder was gonna rotate the empty chamber under the hammer and he'd have a good laugh on his friend. But it rotated the other way. . . ."

Kit was hugely disappointed. She knew little about guns and had developed this explanation on instinct and a call to the police firing range. And, damn it, that called for a "Well done." Obviously, today wasn't going to be the day she'd hear that phrase for the first time from him. But someday . . .

"Okay, let's talk about the man downstairs," Broussard said. "These are his clothes—expensive labels and so new, they still smell like it." He opened the manila envelope he'd also brought up, then dumped out its contents—a ring, a wristwatch, a wallet, some coins, and a pocketknife. Kit pulled one of the visitor's chairs closer, sat down, and leaned forward, her folded arms on the desk.

Broussard picked up one of the coins and examined it through the bifocal part of his glasses. "African, if I'm not mistaken," he said, passing it to Kit.

He briefly looked at the watch, front and back. "Hmm, expensive, and not very old." He passed the watch to Kit and picked up the ring, whose primary feature was a large stone of black onyx. Inside, where the thin gold surface had worn away, he could see silver beneath. Though it was a cheap ring, Broussard valued it highly, for it bore an inscription.

"If this ring has always belonged to him, we've got his first name," he said, handing Kit the ring.

Inside the band she read, "To Jack, with affection."

"So he's now *Jack* Doe," Broussard said.

Broussard opened Jack Doe's wallet, checked the money compartment, and whistled. Minoux had said the guy was loaded, but Broussard wasn't expecting this. He pulled out a sheaf of crisp new hundreds and counted them. ". . . thirteen, fourteen, fifteen. That's a lot of walkin'-around money." He put the bills back in the wallet and looked into the pocket for credit cards, but he found nothing. He moved on to the plastic photo sleeves and his shaggy eyebrows lifted. "Look at this . . ."

He turned the wallet, and Kit saw one of those photos of a pretty young woman that come with a new wallet.

"What's that?" Kit said, pointing to a folded piece of paper in the opposite sleeve.

Broussard extracted the paper and unfolded it. He looked at it and handed it over.

In a scrawled hand, written in ink, was the cryptic message: "Schrader, Wed., 11:00 A.M."

"Well . . ."

Kit looked up to see what else Broussard had found.

"This fellow's clothes are new; the watch is new; the wallet is new . . . Here's somethin' that isn't."

He slipped a worn photograph free and passed it to Kit, who looked at it and felt her jaw drop.

It was a photograph of her parents and herself when she was a teenager, coming out of their house in Speculator, New York.

3

The man in the morgue and the picture they'd found in his wallet remained center stage in Kit's consciousness the rest of the afternoon. It was still there as she pulled up to the wrought-iron gates on Dauphine Street in the French Quarter and signaled for them to slide open.

Her life had certainly taken some unexpected turns lately. Who could have predicted that shortly after she'd bought a great little house uptown, she'd find the skeleton of a murdered young woman buried in the backyard, then be attacked in her own bedroom? She shuddered when she thought of it. There was no way she could have remained there after that.

And then this opportunity: a rich friend of Teddy's looking for someone to occupy and care for his house for three years, rent-free, while he supervised construction of a series of desalination plants somewhere in the Middle East. That was a godsend. Three years in which she could get back on her feet financially after the beating she'd taken on the sale of her place.

And what a house this new one was . . . She guided the car through the gates and came to a stop a few inches from the back wall of the detached brick alcove that gave the house privacy from the street. She signaled the gates to close, then got out and gathered up the mail from its wicker basket under the mail drop.

It was all throwaway stuff—a waste of a tree.

Between the portico and the house was a wonderful courtyard floored with gray brick. On each side of the patio the brick was interrupted by a small rectangular pool. The pools were connected by a narrow channel, open except for a short section that ran under the brick, allowing easy access to the front door.

Everywhere, there were signs of spring. On the winter-darkened ivy covering the concrete lady at the bubbling origin of the pools, hundreds of bright green accents had appeared almost overnight. In the pools, snow-white flowers with a blush of pink on their tips poked bravely between the lily pads, their perfection coaxing the eye from the pool edges, where long green stems with furled leaves thrust upward from taller water plants that were growing inches a day. The tree hibiscuses populating the large flower beds fronting the house and against the portico struggled under a load of deep red blooms with yellow tongues, clusters of yellow irises and clumps of yellow pincushions at their feet. From the side walls of the courtyard, which were formed by neighboring houses, a million jasmine blossoms poured their heady perfume into the air.

All this renewal caused Kit to reflect more deeply on the death of Jack Doe. She might also have thought about the young man who'd accidentally shot himself, but her name hadn't been the last word he'd ever speak. Nor did he possess a photograph of her and her parents.

The house was a two-story gray stone Italianate villa with Palladian windows and life-size stone figures strategically placed along a stone balustrade on the roof. She crossed to the front door and put her key in the lock, kicking off a sensor that turned on all the lights inside. She hadn't lived there nearly long enough to be immune to the dazzling interior. Stretching before her were two huge high-ceilinged rooms joined by a columned portal that framed against the far wall an English painted leather screen behind a gilded nineteenth-century Russian settee upholstered in black leather. Leading the eye to this focal point were splashes of color and surprising blends of Chippendale and Georgian—gleaming woods and bright fabrics, accents that drew the eye—an orange pillow with zebra striping, African masks of hammered copper, glided mirrors and sconces, flashes of glistening oak floor between Chinese and Indian carpets, every piece, every pillow, every chair in just the right place, facing exactly the correct direction—leather and gold, velvet and chintz.

When her three years were up, it was going to be very difficult to leave. She thought briefly of her own few furnishings safely stored in the attic, then crossed to the phone and called her parents in Speculator for the third time that day, having tried the first two times from the office.

Still no answer.

She hung up and went to the kitchen, where the gleaming black counters and white cabinets once again almost made her feel like learning how to cook.

What made this whole arrangement even more astonishing was the willingness of the owner to accept her dog, Lucky, in the deal. True, he'd had to audition for the owner's lawyer and she'd had to agree that he'd never be left alone in the house, and then it was hers—for three years, anyway.

She opened the door to the small courtyard in the rear and saw Lucky lying on his belly, watching a black butterfly slowly flexing its wings.

"Lucky . . . Here, boy."

The little dog's head jerked her way and there was a brief moment of hesitation while his brain seemed to be checking out alternate responses. But then he gave the one she'd never tired of seeing. He jumped up, threw his head back in sheer joy, and came running.

"What a good boy." She knelt and gave him a brisk rub-down, then lifted him onto his hind legs and scratched his chin as his big brown eyes rolled upward in ecstasy.

They went inside and she gave Lucky his dinner before putting a Lean Cuisine in the microwave for herself.

Lucky finished his meal in about the time it took hers to heat and he began pushing his bowl across the floor.

"Grape?"

Lucky's ears went up and he stared at her, poised for action.

She got three grapes from the fridge and held one up for Lucky to see. Then she rolled the grape across the floor, sending Lucky scrambling after it. When he caught it, he threw it up in the air and went after it again.

He tossed it a few more times, then took it to the carpet by the sink and ate it. He was only a three-grape dog, so that he chased the second one as fast as the first but tossed it only once before carrying it to the carpet. He went after the third with much less enthusiasm and ate it on the spot.

With the grape game over, Kit took her dinner and a glass of wine to her favorite room in the house, a small octagonal conservatory bay with five tall windows through which she could look out onto the front courtyard. There, she pulled a fan-back wicker chair over to the carved black lacquer table in the center of the room and had her dinner, Lucky lying at her feet.

As she ate, her mind drifted back to the conversation she'd had with Broussard about Jack Doe, particularly about him having a bad heart. It felt so strange. She'd spoken to the man around one o'clock. By three, his heart was in Broussard's hands.

Suddenly, the sliced beef on her plate seemed too . . . *organic* to be edible. She pushed it away and returned to the telephone.

This time, it was answered.

"Hi, it's me."

"Me who?" her father said, never tiring of this little game.

"Where've you been? I called earlier, and you were out."

"VFW hall. Tonight is steak night. Should have stayed home, though. Meat was so tough, I could have made shoes with it."

"Is Mom there?"

"Yes, dear," her mother said. "And you shouldn't believe a word your father says. He ate all of his and some of mine."

"Say, something peculiar happened to me today. . . ."

"You're not hurt?" her father said.

"No, I'm fine. I met a man in a restaurant today who seemed to know me, but I didn't know him. Barely after we began talking, he collapsed and died . . . of a heart attack. He was taken to the morgue. . . "

"I wish you wouldn't use that word," her mother said.

"What should I call it? Never mind. We were looking through his belongings, trying to learn who he was, but he had no identification. In his wallet, there was a picture of you two and me in my junior varsity cheerleading outfit. We were coming out of our old house on Claybrook."

"How odd," her mother said.

"He stood around six feet tall, was probably sixty years old, and had deep-set eyes, a straight Roman nose, and a little cleft in the center of his chin. There was a crude tattoo on his right wrist that said 'Think Free,' and we believe his first name was Jack. Does that sound like anyone you know?"

"Nobody I know," her father said.

"No . . . not at all," her mother added. "I wonder where he got that picture? How very strange."

"It is, isn't it? I'd hoped you could tell me who he is. It's driving me crazy."

"I'm not surprised," her mother said.

"There's a chance we'll find out his identity tomorrow," Kit said. On the other end of the line, she heard the phone bump something.

"Mother . . . Daddy . . . Are you there?"

There was a pause and her father said, "Yes, Kitten, we're here. Go on, you were saying . . ."

"They've sent his prints to every identification network there is. If he was ever printed for the service or was ever in jail—and we think that tattoo suggests he was—we should find him."

"And you say you'll hear tomorrow about that?" her mother said.

"Probably late afternoon."

"Call us and tell us the results, will you?" she asked.

"Of course. Well, you've heard my news. How are you two?"

"We're both fine," her mother said. "Aren't we, Howard?"

"Oh yes. Couldn't be better. Had a light sprinkling of snow this morning. Didn't last, though, and didn't stick. Probably be seeing some signs of spring here in a few weeks. Yes . . . both fine."

"Good to hear your voices, even if you couldn't help me."

"You, too," her father said.

"Be sure and call us tomorrow," her mother said.

"I will. Talk to you then."

Kit hung up and sat staring at the phone. She couldn't remember the last time a question about her parents' health had not brought forth a detailed account of her father's troubles with his blood pressure or her mother's latest migraine. And there had been something in her mother's voice. . . . If they weren't her parents, she'd almost think they'd lied to her.

KIT SPENT MOST OF the next day investigating the death of a punter for the Saints, who'd been found with toxic levels of cocaine in his blood. After talking with his friends and family, she concluded that, like the gunshot death, this one, too, was an accident. All through the day, below the surface, her mind picked at her meeting with Jack Doe, his death, and the odd feeling she'd had when talking to her parents about it.

A little after three o'clock, Broussard called with the news that none of the computers they'd fed Jack Doe's prints to had found a match. As promised, Kit passed this information along to her parents, who were home this time on her first try.

At 4:15, as the last page of her report on the cocaine case hummed from her laser printer, she realized she'd made a decision. Tucking her report into a clean file folder, she headed down the hall to Broussard's office, where, for a moment, the absence of light behind the frosted glass panel in his door made her think he was out. But then the room grew brighter.

She knocked and stuck her head inside, to see Charlie Franks, the deputy medical examiner, standing by a slide projector. On the wall across the room was an image that at first she couldn't decipher. Then she realized it was the right shoulder of a corpse—and not a very fresh one. Broussard was rocked back in his chair, which was turned to the image, his fingers laced over his belly. The two men looked her way.

"I can see you're busy. I'll come back later."

As she withdrew, Broussard said, "C'mon in. Charlie's just showin' me a couple of slides he's thinkin' of usin' in his talk on body identification at the University of Florida next week. You might find the information interestin' considerin' our conversation yesterday."

"Hi, Kit. By all means, join us," Franks said.

"Orient her," Broussard added.

"This is a photograph of the right shoulder of a body found three weeks after death," Franks said. "We knew who lived in the house, but the face was so bloated, it was unrecognizable. Fingerprints were also useless, and there were no dental records available. A relative said the occupant of the house had a tattoo of an American flag on his right shoulder, but, as you can see, the decomposition pigments produced by the reaction of bacterial hydrogen sulfide with erythrocyte hemoglobin have produced such discoloration, it's impossible to tell if he even *has* a tattoo. But look what application of a gauze pad containing three percent hydrogen peroxide for ten minutes does."

He pressed the advance button on the projector and another image appeared on the wall. In this one, a flag tattoo was clearly visible.

This was a downside of working for Broussard—never knowing what grisly thing he'd want to show you. She was much better now at handling it than when she first came, but it was definitely not a perk of the position.

Both men were looking at her, beaming with pride, waiting for her reaction.

"Amazing," she said. Then, fearing a one-word response might seem unappreciative, she added, "And so easy."

Broussard smiled happily.

Franks chuckled. "That's the beauty of it. Simple and effective."

Franks showed a couple more examples and Broussard suggested he eliminate the final one, which wasn't quite as impressive as the others. Franks then unplugged the projector and excused himself, flicking on the lights as he left.

"Now," Broussard said, rocking forward in his chair. "What can I do for you?"

She put her report on his desk. "The punter . . . an accidental overdose in my opinion."

"Then it'll be my opinion, too." He looked at her for a moment, then said, "I don't believe I ever told you this, but . . ."

At last, Kit thought. He was going to say it . . . She was doing a good job. There was no doubt in her mind he'd always believed that, but, damn it, he wouldn't say it. The closest he'd ever come was when he began buying wrapped lemon balls just for her when he saw she was reluctant to take the naked ones he carried for himself. This need she had for his approval was something she tried to fight, but it was always there. . . Why? She had no idea.

She was competent and she knew it. That should be enough. But it wasn't. So she felt her pulse quicken as she waited for him to finish his thought.

He hesitated, teetering on the edge.

She leaned forward in anticipation.

Then, above his short beard, his face flushed and she saw retreat in his eyes.

"I . . . think it's time we get your office repainted."

"That'd be nice," she said, making sure her disappointment stayed hidden. "Speaking of our conversation yesterday, I've decided to try my hand at figuring out who that man is—or was—on my own time, of course. . . ."

"No reason to do it off the clock. It's somethin' I need to know, too. Better we turn the body over to relatives than to strangers who'll just want to get him buried as cheaply as possible."

"In any event, tomorrow is Saturday and Teddy will be back from his trip. I thought he and I would start on it then. Any ideas where we should begin?" It was a question she would have asked even if her search was to be a purely personal activity. He was simply uncanny when it came to solving puzzles, and it was highly unlikely he hadn't already set his mind to work on this one.

In reply, Broussard reached under the table behind him and put the bag containing Jack Doe's clothing on the desk. From the bag, he withdrew one shoe, turned it sole up, and handed it to her. It was covered with dark stains and there was a kind of sludge in the treads.

"His shoes are new, but he went somewhere in 'em that got him into some old grease. I found strands of hemp in that grease, along with these. . . ."

He handed her a photograph. Looking at it, she saw several dozen golden objects against a black background—some shaped like clams, some like flowers, some like figure eights. Others resembled triangles filled with pebbles.

She looked up, her brow furrowed.

"Diatoms," Broussard said happily. "One-celled algae with silica shells. I found 'em in the grease. Every body of water has 'em, and in every location there are distinct types. Most of those are typical of the kind found around Pensacola."

"So he's from there?"

"I don't think so. I also found a couple typical of the Caribbean and a few common to the middle of the Atlantic."

"I'm lost."

"No you're not. Where in New Orleans might you find hemp and diatoms from several bodies of water?"

Kit thought a moment. "Hemp . . . isn't that used to make rope?" Then it hit her. "He was on a ship. . . . The docks . . ."

"That's where *I'd* start." He opened a drawer in his desk and took out a stack of Polaroid photos, sifted through them, and handed one to her. It was a morgue photo of Jack Doe's face.

"Take that along. Maybe it'll jog someone's memory."

After Kit left, Broussard sat for a moment wondering why he couldn't just tell her how impressed he was with her and that he didn't see how he'd functioned all those years before she'd come. It seemed a simple-enough statement. But every time he was about to say it, it came out as something else. Paint her office—where had *that* come from? Ah well . . .

He got up, turned on the stereo, and as the room filled with the opening passage of Tchaikovsky's "Dance of the Sugar-Plum Fairy," he went to his microscope, sat down, and removed his glasses, letting them dangle against his shirt from the lanyard at the temples. He selected a slide from the tray to his right and put it on the stage of the microscope. This would be the first look he'd had at the cellular detail of Jack Doe's organs.

The slide was of the kidney, a maze of tubules that looked perfectly normal at low power. He moved the slide to the cortex of the organ and switched to a higher power. Immediately, he saw numerous necrotic foci—cells whose nuclei had become shrunken and black and whose cytoplasm was fragmenting.

He turned to a higher power and saw in many places the extensive capillary network was blocked by small blood clots. He returned that slide to the tray and chose another—this time of the liver. Here, too, many of the smaller vessels were blocked by clots. Slide after slide showed the same thing—the brain, the adrenals, every organ was involved. Had the victim not succumbed to a heart attack, he would soon have died of multiple organ failure or bled to death internally as the tiny clots used up his clotting factors and the tissue served by the blocked vessels died.

Disseminated intravascular coagulation—DIC. Not an uncommon condition, except when it occurred, it was usually in people with cancer or someone suffering from complications of pregnancy, neither of which applied here.

He sat back, folded his arms, and closed his eyes. Stroking the bristly hairs on the end of his nose, he thought of all the other conditions associated with DIC—burns, transplant rejection, heatstroke, mismatched transfusions—but none of those was appropriate, either. That left—

His eyes popped open. . . . Some type of infection.

With alarm, he remembered Natalie cutting herself.

He put on his glasses, went to the phone, and called Laboratory Medicine, where Jack Doe's blood and tissue samples were being tested for disease.

"Hello. . . . This is Dr. Broussard, the medical examiner. I sent a blood sample to you yesterday—John Doe number six. We know anything yet?"

He was put on hold while the person who answered went to check on things. She came back a minute later with the news that the immunology report was on the way up to his office and that they'd found nothing. Micro and Virology had likewise found nothing, but they needed a few more days for a definitive result.

Broussard broke the connection with his finger and stood motionless, staring at the phone.

Kit was wrong in her belief that he loved puzzles. Rather, he hated intellectual disorder. And questions without answers were the most nettlesome example of that. What had caused Jack Doe's organs to be filled with microscopic blood clots? What, what, what?

When his mind was unsettled like this, everything felt out of kilter, as if somebody had moved every piece of furniture in his office a few inches from its normal position. Water from the fountain in the hall didn't taste quite right, the air-handler noise in the hall sounded louder, and his clothes no longer seemed to fit. He ran his finger around the inside of his collar, trying to stretch the fabric. At the same time, he became aware of his belt constricting his belly and his socks squeezing his calves. By God, he needed an answer.

But first . . .

He entered the number of the morgue assistants' ready room and got Guy Minoux.

"Guy, this is Andy. Is Natalie there? No . . . don't get her. Just give her a message for me. Tell her they've found no evidence of disease in that body she was workin' on when she cut herself, but I want her to get a gamma globulin shot anyway." Then, remembering that Grandma O had given Jack Doe mouth-to-mouth during her CPR attempts, he called the restaurant and advised her to get the shot, as well.

Having done all he could in that quarter, he hung up and loosened his belt a notch.

On the way to her car, Kit was about to cross Tulane Avenue when she heard a voice call her name. Looking in that direction, she saw, behind a green Chrysler stopped for the light, a familiar red sports car with the top down. The driver beckoned her.

Somewhat less reluctantly than she acted, she walked back to the car.

"I've been meaning to call you," Nick Lawson said, tilting his sunglasses onto the top of his head.

Lawson was a crime reporter for the *Times-Picayune*. For some reason, he considered himself a real ladies' man. But in Kit's opinion, any guy who wore his hair in a ponytail and regularly risked his life engaging in dangerous sports had a lot of growing up to do. She pointed at his sunglasses. "Doesn't that get oil from your hair on the lenses?"

"Yeah, but it's worth it for the look," Lawson said, grinning. "I thought the last time we spoke, you were gonna let me know when you were ready for our date."

Kit feigned a puzzled look. "Has there been a cold spell in hell that hasn't made the papers?"

"You didn't mean that."

Kit arched one eyebrow. "No?"

"You're just trying to make me yearn for the unattainable."

"That's partly right."

"I thought so."

"The unattainable part."

The light changed and the car in front of Lawson's sped away. Exercising his obligation as a native New Orleanian, the driver behind Lawson immediately leaned on his horn.

"Even the highest apple in the tree eventually falls to earth," Lawson said, pulling away.

She was about to fire a retort at his back but realized it would only encourage him. Everything seemed to encourage him. Harboring a tiny smile she wouldn't even let herself see, she walked back to the crossing and waited for the light to change.

4

Kit usually saw Teddy LaBiche only on weekends, when he'd drive to New Orleans Saturday morning and go back early Monday. Sometimes Kit found that arrangement entirely acceptable. At other times, she wanted him around more frequently. His trip to Europe had meant two weekends without his company, so as she waited for his arrival this Saturday morning, she was fidgeting like a schoolgirl about to go on her first date.

Teddy had the trip down to an art form, always arriving between 7:00 A.M. and 7:05. She looked at her watch: 7:02. Suddenly, Lucky began to bark. Teddy had his own control for the gates and Lucky always heard them open.

Kit checked her hair in the antique Federal mirror by the door and stepped into the courtyard. When Teddy came out of the parking alcove, all she could see of him were his alligator boots and a couple of inches of denim. The rest was hidden behind a huge rectangular white box tied with a pink ribbon and a giant pink bow.

"What on earth is that?" Kit said.

Teddy shifted the big box to the side and peeked out from behind it.

At first, she wasn't sure it was Teddy. Instead of his usual rakish straw hat, he was wearing a beret. And under his nose was a thin black mustache.

"Eh bien, ma chère . . ."

Meeting her where the little courtyard canal went under the brickwork, Teddy put the big box down, took Kit in his arms, and kissed her, his new mustache velvet against the skin above her lip. He broke the kiss and whispered in her ear. "I missed you."

"Me, too," Kit whispered.

At Teddy's feet, Lucky clamored for attention, bouncing on his hind legs, his paws windmilling on Teddy's jeans.

Teddy picked the little dog up and looked into his eyes. "Did you miss me, too, partner?"

In reply, Lucky licked his face. Surprisingly, Lucky's tongue plucked off Teddy's mustache.

"It's a fake," Kit exclaimed as Teddy waited for Lucky's tongue to reappear. When it did, it was without the mustache.

"I think he swallowed it," Teddy said.

"He's eaten worse than that and it didn't hurt him," Kit replied. "Besides, I'm glad it's gone. Can we get rid of the beret as easily?"

"I don't know." He looked at Lucky. "You feel like eating a beret, boy?"

Lucky cocked his head in doggy puzzlement.

"Maybe I'll just stow it in my truck," Teddy said, putting Lucky down.

"I'd like that."

He went back into the alcove and came out the old Teddy, with something behind his back.

"The big box is for you," he said, "but I didn't forget Lucky." Kneeling, he brought out a green alligator hand puppet and began grabbing Lucky's nose with its pink-lined mouth. Always ready for a game, Lucky backed off a few inches and charged, clamping his teeth onto the alligator's lips, or whatever alligators have in place of lips.

Abruptly, Teddy let out an alligator roar so realistic Lucky bolted into the nearby flower bed and cowered behind a clump of irises.

"Sorry," Teddy said sheepishly. "I didn't think it'd scare him like that." He shucked the puppet from his hand and put it on the bricks.

"I hope you won't react that way to *your* gift."

"Let's find out."

Teddy helped her work the ribbon off and they laid the big box down and removed the lid. Inside was a stuffed white rabbit with extraordinarily long, drooping ears. It was wearing a tiara of fabric roses and a purple velvet dress trimmed in handmade lace and more fabric roses.

"What do you think?" Teddy asked, obviously concerned.

"I absolutely love it," Kit said, lifting it out of the box. The rabbit was supported by a metal pole at its back that led under its dress to a circular metal platform with three short legs that allowed it to stand upright.

"It doesn't really *do* anything," Teddy said.

"Of course not—it's for decoration." She leaned over and kissed him on the cheek. "Thank you. It was a perfect choice."

At their feet, Lucky had the alligator by the mouth, mercilessly whipping it on the bricks.

"I hope he's not doing that to anything in the house," Teddy said.

"Man, dat's some big rabbit," a voice said from the alcove.

It was Bubba Oustellette, Grandma O's grandson. Bubba worked at the police department's vehicle-impoundment station and also kept Broussard's fleet of '57 T-Birds running. But he was more than just a mechanic. He was Broussard's friend, and Kit's too. He'd come over this morning to fix the speedometer on Kit's car.

Bubba was a minimalist when it came to clothing, agreeing with his grandmother that when you find something that works, you stick with it. In Bubba's case, it was navy coveralls over a navy T-shirt, brown work shoes, and a green Tulane baseball cap—or at least it *used* to be. Whatever had motivated Teddy to buy a beret seemed to have affected Bubba, too. For he was now wearing brown coveralls over a brown T-shirt. And perched on his head was a purple Saint's baseball cap.

After trading greetings with Kit in English, Bubba shook Teddy's hand and they exchanged a few words in Cajun French.

"You look different today," Kit said to Bubba.

Above his thick black beard, his face reddened and he hunched his shoulders. "Las' week, Ah read an article in *Cosmo* dat said da biggest roadblock to personal growth was resistance to change. Dat got me to thinkin'. An' it didn't take long to see where Ah needed some growth. So . . . dis is it. It still feels kinda funny, but Ah 'spect Ah'll get used to it."

"How many pairs of brown coveralls did you buy?" Kit asked.

"Ten . . . an' fifteen brown T-shirts. So Ah'm set for a while." He looked at the gift box and then pointed at the rabbit. "I guess dat's new?"

"Teddy gave it to me just now."

Bubba walked over to the rabbit, which was a couple of inches taller than he was, and pointed at the side of its face. "You got a seam comin' loose here."

Teddy came around and looked for himself. "He's right." Teddy took his hat off and hit his thigh with it. "Nuts. I wanted this to be perfect. I'd take it back, except I bought it in Belgium."

"Ah got some big upholstery needles at home," Bubba said. "An' Ah'm sure Ah could fin' some thread to match. How about when Ah leave, Ah take da rabbit with me an' fix it?"

Kit hesitated. She liked the rabbit so much, she didn't want to let go of it, even for a little while.

"Ah won't get any grease on it."

"Okay, do it," Kit said.

"Dat was sure some excitement you had las' week at da restaurant. You tell Teddy about dat?"

"I was just about to bring it up." She then related all that had happened. Even though he'd apparently heard it from Grandma O or Broussard, Bubba listened as intently as Teddy.

"What kind of man goes around without any identification?" Teddy asked when she paused in her tale.

"Somebody up to no good," Bubba suggested.

"He did have a tattoo that made Andy think he might have spent some time in jail."

"See . . . what Ah tol' you," Bubba said.

"I thought my parents might know who he was, but they didn't recognize the description I gave them over the phone. I had the feeling, though, they were holding something back."

Teddy eyed her suspiciously. "This doesn't sound like something you could walk away from . . ."

"It isn't. Andy found hemp and algae cells from different regions of the ocean caught in some grease on the man's shoes, suggesting he'd recently been down on the docks."

"And that's where we're going today," Teddy said.

Kit turned to Bubba. "He's such an intelligent man."

"Ah jus' hope you don' fin' somethin' you don' want," Bubba said, his brown eyes crinkling at the corners in concern.

"Why do you say that?" Kit asked. Lucky had pulled one of the alligator's eyes loose and Kit picked it up to keep him from eating it.

"Gramma O say she got a bad feelin' from dat fella when she gave him mouth-to-mouth. An' at night in a dream, she saw the groun' covered with feathers, an' dey was movin' like somethin' small was under 'em. An' den it began to rain blood."

Kit was aware that from time to time, Grandma O showed certain abilities difficult to explain. So she didn't dismiss this as simply the ramblings of an old woman. But neither was she prepared to let it change her plans.

"Thanks for the warning. We'll be careful." She bent down and picked up the alligator's other eye, then looked at Teddy. "Bubba's here to work on my car."

"You don' min' if Ah put da rabbit in da box and take both of 'em, do you?"

"Not at all. Let me help."

Teddy and Kit laid the rabbit in the box and slipped the bow over the box to secure it.

"My truck's out on da street," Bubba said, pointing. "But don't worry, Ah won't put da rabbit in it 'til Ah'm ready to leave."

"Bubba, would you like a cup of tea before you start on my car? I could put some cinnamon rolls in the microwave."

He shook his head. "No thanks. Ah had eggs an' *boudin* this mornin' at home."

"We'll leave you to it, then. When you're finished, shut the gates with the control that's on the front seat of my car. Then just put the control in the mail drop."

Bubba picked up the box and headed for the parking alcove.

Kit looked at Teddy. "You hungry?"

His eyes danced. "For you."

"Shhh," she whispered. "Bubba'll hear you. I was referring to something to eat."

"So was I."

"Business first, LaBiche. Then we'll see."

"Okay . . . sure. I could use some food. Our usual place?"

"I don't think so. There are two sets of docks for freighters, one upriver and one at the foot of Esplanade. I thought we'd work the near one first. And if we do that, there's no point going way out on St. Charles for breakfast. So, why don't we just have some of those cinnamon rolls?"

"Are they homemade?"

"Of course. I was up all *night* baking."

"Ah, my little hausfrau . . . what a jewel you are. Cinnamon rolls, by all means."

THE FRENCH QUARTER EXTENDS from Canal Street to Esplanade Avenue, two streets that couldn't be more different. Where Canal is a typical bustling city thoroughfare lined with high-rise hotels, department stores, fast-food joints, and electronic shops, Esplanade, just thirteen blocks away, is another state of mind in a different century. Esplanade is divided by a wide median planted along each edge with a row of twisted old oaks whose graceful curled limbs arch across each half of the street, their leafy fingers gently caressing the balconied sitting areas of the adjacent old houses. When the sun is out, as it was that day, its rays falling through the leaves make the pavement a dappled carpet.

A breeze blowing from the river nudged dried oak leaves from the edges of the sidewalk and they crunched underfoot, mixing with soft purple petals drifting down from a wisteria climbing a nearby balcony support. Through an open window behind a faded green shutter, Kit heard the squeaky bedspring chatter of zebra finches. It was a glorious day, and with Teddy beside her, Kit found herself unable to maintain a somber frame of mind consistent with the business at hand.

A few yards ahead a man stepped from a doorway onto the sidewalk and came toward them. He was dressed in ordinary clothing—pale green twills and a green-and-white plaid shirt. In one hand, he was carrying a tux on a hanger; in the other, a large galvanized bucket. His features were concealed behind a heavy layer of white mime makeup.

As he passed, Teddy said, "Good morning."

The fellow put his bucket down, tipped an imaginary hat, picked up his bucket, and continued on his way.

"Just your typical New Orleans pedestrian," Teddy remarked. "By the way, what did this guy we're investigating look like?"

Kit reached into the outside pocket of her bag and handed him the picture Broussard had given her.

"Boy," Teddy said, glancing at it. "He looks awful."

"He should. He was dead when it was taken."

Teddy made a sour face and handed the picture back, holding it by the tip of his index finger and thumb. "You know, since it's

Saturday, a lot of people who would normally be down on the docks won't be there."

"Maybe those who are can help."

A few minutes later, to the accompaniment of "Lady of Spain" being played on a riverboat calliope, they passed the imposing old orange-bricked U.S. Mint building, crossed N. Peters Street, and went through the Esplanade portal in the wall screening the riverfront.

The change was like jumping from a sauna into a snow-bank. In front of them, up on a cement slab four feet above ground level and across five sets of train tracks, a huge corrugated-metal warehouse ran for at least a quarter of a mile along the river. The relatively short section to their right proudly sported a fresh coat of green paint. To their left, its poor yellow country cousin stretched downriver, dented and rusting, sadly waiting for the painter's return. Over the warehouse roof, Kit and Teddy could see the superstructure of several freighters.

"Might as well begin here," Kit said, leading the way across the tracks toward three eighteen-wheelers backed up to a loading dock in the green section.

None of the truck drivers recognized the man in the picture.

Kit and Teddy then went up a cement ramp and ducked into the warehouse through a door beside a sign that warned them against trespassing. In the gloomy interior, they were greeted by bales of cotton stacked fifteen feet high and the smell of exhaust fumes from forklifts that scurried here and there, making a disproportionate amount of noise for their size and drowning out the riverboat calliope.

None of the forklift operators wanted to shut off their machine, so Kit had to question them at the top of her lungs, getting for her trouble nothing but a slight headache.

"What now?" Teddy asked over the departing sound of the last forklift they'd stopped.

Just as it appeared on the outside, the inside of the warehouse was one long, continuous space. Seeing no activity in the shorter section toward Jackson Square, Kit motioned for Teddy to follow and she headed downriver, where a hundred yards away, she saw more forklifts.

For most of that distance, they passed between mountains of white plastic sacks that spilled a fine granular material from the occasional ruptured seam. Whatever it was, the sparrows nesting in hidden alcoves near the ceiling liked it very much and darted down for a quick peck or two before flashing back to safety. As Kit and Teddy neared their destination, the granular litter on the floor was replaced by corn.

The purpose of all the bustle that had drawn Kit in this direction was the stacking of sacks on wooden pallets, which were then forklifted out to the wharf, where through a huge doorway, the side of a massive freighter blocked all view of the river.

It took about ten minutes to canvass the forklift operators and the sweating men loading sacks onto the pallets. For all the good it did, they could have saved themselves the trouble.

Farther downriver, the warehouse angled to the right, so they couldn't see if there was any point in going that way. Kit, therefore, headed instead for the dock, nearly getting run over by a forklift coming in for another load.

She knew the ship at dockside was big, but she still wasn't prepared for the way it dwarfed its surroundings, its gray hull rising into the sky like a canyon wall. And it stretched along the wharf an astonishingly long way. Leaning over, she tried to see the river between the ship and the dock, but there was no space between them.

Teddy, too, was impressed, and he let his eyes linger on the bow, speculating on the weight of the massive anchor snugged against the hull. Then he studied the lettering on the bow, trying to figure out what language it was. Turning to ask Kit's opinion, he found her gone.

Sweeping the dock with his eyes, he saw her halfway up the metal steps leading from the dock to the ship's deck. Hurrying after her, he discovered that those steps were angled in an odd way, as though they were folded up, so you had to walk on their front edges. This produced such precarious footing, he didn't catch up to her until she was already on deck, where he found her staring into the cargo hold.

This view was even more impressive than their first look from the dock. The hold was so deep the men guiding the pallets of cargo being lowered on steel cables attached to the boom of a giant onboard crane looked like dolls. Suddenly, from Kit's left, they heard a voice.

Turning, they saw a small man in jeans, a blue T-shirt, and a hard hat. Clearly, he found their presence on deck surprising. He spoke again, and Teddy was sure it was Russian.

"English?" Kit said, making sure she could be heard over the grind of the crane engine. "Speak English?"

The man shook his head. "No English." He motioned for them to follow. "Chief mate . . . please . . ."

He opened a small oval door in the ship's superstructure, ducked his head, and went inside. Going in after him, Kit was so concerned about knocking her head on the low opening, she stumbled over the threshold, which was about three inches high. Seeing her trouble, Teddy did much better.

They found themselves in a hot, gloomy hallway paneled in Formica intended to resemble bleached wood. Hard Hat opened the door to a tiny elevator paneled in the same Formica and waved them on. Three was the maximum number the little elevator could hold, so they formed quite an intimate group as the elevator carried them sluggishly up two floors. The decor there was no different from that below, and they were led to a small cabin sparsely equipped with a desk, a chair, a small green sofa, a TV, and an antique VCR. On the wall Kit saw a chess set with flat chessmen hanging on little hooks and she wondered if Russian sailors played standing up. There were windows here that admitted a welcome breeze.

Hard Hat suddenly called out in Russian, making Kit jump in surprise. At first, she thought she'd committed some shipboard sin, but then she saw a tall, angular fellow come out of a doorway behind the desk, and she knew that Hard Hat had merely announced their arrival.

Hard Hat explained what was going on, and the other man, apparently the chief mate, looked at Kit and Teddy with a friendly expression. "What can we do for you?" he said, with an accent just like Natasha in the Rocky and Bullwinkle cartoons Kit used to watch as a kid.

"I'm Kit Franklyn, and this is Teddy LaBiche. . . ."

"Believe it or not, my name is Boris," the chief mate said.

His smile was tentative and restrained, as though he was embarrassed at the condition of his teeth.

"We're trying to locate anyone who knew this man."

Kit produced the photo and gave it to him. He winced when he looked at it. "He looks very sick."

"He died, and no one knows who he was."

"A man should not leave this earth in such a way. But I do not know him. Why do you come here with your picture?"

"We have reason to believe he had recently visited the docks, maybe boarding a ship. How long have you been in port?"

"Since late Tuesday."

"Would you mind if we showed the picture to the members of your crew?"

"If he had been on board, I would have known," he said, his manner stiffening. Then he relented. "But of course you may ask." He rattled off something in Russian to Hard Hat, then said, "This is Victor. He will take you around. Unfortunately, I'm presently engaged and cannot help you myself. Victor speaks no English, nor does crew. So if you find someone you wish to question beyond showing them your picture, bring him here and I will interpret . . . yes?"

Kit thanked him and they followed Victor into the hall.

They questioned two crewmen swimming in a pool that appeared to have a fuzzy green growth on its bottom and spoke to two more lifting weights in a miniature gymnasium. In the galley, they interrupted a man shredding lettuce into a big enamel bowl and bothered another one cutting up a pile of chickens. Both were sweating heavily into their green sleeveless T-shirts.

Neither recognized the man in the picture. But the one cutting up chickens pointed at Teddy's hat with his cleaver and said, "Clint Eastwood." Then he laughed. "Wait . . ." He put the cleaver down, washed his hands, and ducked out a door at the end of the galley, to reappear a few seconds later with a furry Russian hat, which he held up to Teddy. "Trade?" He pointed at Teddy's hat.

"Sure," Teddy said, removing his hat and giving it to the man. He took the Russian hat and, despite the heat, put it on. It looked as ridiculous as the beret he'd worn earlier.

The Russian donned Teddy's hat, laughed, and patted Teddy's shoulder.

Kit subsequently showed the picture to another fifteen men, including the captain, who was on the bridge, but got no positive responses.

"No more," Victor said, shrugging.

"Chief mate?" Kit said.

Nodding, Victor took them back to Boris's cabin, where he was studying a chart spread out on the desk.

"We didn't find anyone who recognized the picture," she said. "But what about the man working the crane and the ones down in the hold?"

"Those are not crew," Boris said. "Longshoremen . . . U.S. citizens. You want to talk to them, they eat lunch at noon on dock." He pointed at Teddy's hat. "You picked up souvenir?"

Teddy nodded.

"Lady must have souvenir also." He disappeared through the door behind the desk and came back with a sparkling white cap with AMAEPMA lettered across the front, the name on the ship's bow.

"It is perhaps not as fine a souvenir as fur hat, but is thought that counts in gift, yes?"

"Absolutely," Kit said, accepting the cap. She thanked him for that and his hospitality, and as Victor was showing them from the cabin, Boris said, "Tell me . . ."

They turned.

"Either of you ever meet Dolly Parton?"

Back on the dock, Kit donned the cap Boris had given her, and Teddy was awed at how attractive she looked in it. "If you tell me how good I look in *my* hat, I'll return the favor," he said.

Kit studied him, stroking her chin. "Sorry, I still prefer the straw model."

"Well, you look super."

Kit didn't reply, but Teddy could tell she was pleased.

She glanced downriver, where the wharf made a slight right turn, so they couldn't see beyond the stern of the *Amaepma*. "There's another ship down there," she said, pointing. "Let's try that one."

They picked their way past old crates and piles of empty pallets and walked about seventy-five yards down to the ship Kit had seen from the deck of the *Amaepma*. She certainly wouldn't have described the *Amaepma* as sleek, but the ship downriver was a major clunker—bigger, boxier, and with a towering superstructure that rose skyward like a gargantuan white box of generic breakfast cereal with holes cut in it for windows.

At first, she thought the hull was covered in rust. But as they drew nearer, she saw it was merely rust-colored paint.

"I don't think this one has a chance for the America's Cup," she said, glancing at Teddy. When she turned back to the ship, her eyes fell on the name lettered across the bow and she stopped walking.

The SCHRADER . . .

There was something about that. . . "The note in his wallet," she said, looking at Teddy.

"What note? What wallet?"

"The dead man. He had a note in his wallet that said, 'Schrader, Wednesday, eleven A.M.' This is it."

5

Broussard woke Monday precisely at 6:00 A.M. without benefit of an alarm, as he did every morning, if he hadn't already been called out to a murder scene. It was a talent. Come daylight saving time, he'd make the hour adjustment mentally and still hit six on the nose.

He lay for a moment, wiggling his feet, enjoying the buttery feel of his Portuguese cotton flannel sheets against his bare toes. Withdrawing his arms from under the bedclothes, he let them rest on top, where his eiderdown comforter supported them ever so gently, and the flannel duvet covering the comforter felt so creamy he couldn't imagine why Charlie Franks thought sleeping was a waste of time.

But there was work to do.

He threw the comforter back and swung his feet over the side of the bed. On cue, Princess, his Abyssinian cat, trotted from the doorway, where she'd been watching him, and jumped into his lap. In the morning, but no other time, she liked to have Broussard rub her head hard with his knuckles, which he did now for exactly nineteen seconds. Any more and she'd nip at him. Then a couple of scratches under her chin and she jumped to the floor and trotted to the kitchen to await breakfast.

Broussard showered, brushed his teeth, shaved, and dressed, taking a moment to rub some Curél into the soles of both feet, which for some reason were always dry and cracked this time of year.

In the kitchen, he fed Princess, then took some freshly roasted Meru beans out of the freezer and poured them into the coffee grinder. He pressed the button to start the machine and sent his mind on ahead to the quail eggs à la chatelaine he was planning to whip up in just a few minutes, a trip so riveting, he barely heard the whine and rattle of bean against blade or the sound of the telephone.

Eventually, the latter got through and he answered it.

"Broussard."

"Had your breakfast yet?" the voice of Phil Gatlin, ranking Homicide detective on the NOPD, asked.

"No. Have I missed my chance?"

"Might be better that way. I got a stiff here making me sorry *I* ate."

Broussard did not like other people interpreting murder scenes for him before he saw them himself. But he always had to weigh that dislike against the relative inconvenience of the time the call came in and the judgment of the detective working the case. Life was too short to throw on your clothes in the middle of the night and dash off to a run-of-the-mill murder that presented no unique or puzzling features. True, he hadn't eaten yet, but he *was* already dressed. And if Gatlin wanted him, that was good enough.

"Where are you?"

He jotted the address down on the little spiral pad he kept taped to the counter.

"I'm on my way."

He tore the page out of the pad, stuffed it in his shirt pocket, and grabbed his bag, which always sat by the back door. He went into the garage, set the timer for the light at five minutes, and paused for a moment on the top step, admiring the sight before him—six 1957 Thunderbirds, all of them in mint condition.

It was a dazzling display—each a different color, their spotless paint reflecting the garage lights like great jewels. The Russians had Fabergé and his eggs; the English, Grinling Gibbons and his picture frames; the French, Falconet and his bronzes. But the United States had Henry Ford, and Broussard had six examples of his finest work, one for every day of the week . . . well, almost every day. He had long believed that six cars was abundance and that seven would be eccentricity. Still . . . there *was* room for another.

A few minutes later, he backed out of the garage in the white one and headed for the Mississippi River bridge. For neckwear, Broussard owned only bow ties, mostly because the long kind had a tendency to fall into his work when he bent over. Then, too, there really wasn't enough clearance between the T-Bird's steering wheel and his shirt for any extra fabric.

The sun was a cool sphere low in the sky and he reached over and flipped the passenger visor down to keep it out of his eyes. After so many years as ME, he rarely encountered any big surprises, but he still found drama in death and his blood still sang in his veins on his way to a scene. When that was no longer true, he'd retire.

As he turned onto the West Bank Expressway a short while later, his stomach rumbled mightily in protest over his missed breakfast. To calm it, he unbuttoned the flap on his shirt pocket, fished two lemon balls out, and slipped one into each cheek.

The address he'd been given turned out to be a five-story apartment house displaying a large green canvas awning over the entrance, with the street number stenciled on its end in large gold numerals. Beside each metal pole supporting the awning was a huge concrete urn predictably planted with a conical evergreen. Sitting on the rim of one of the planters was Phil Gatlin, sucking on a cigarette.

Broussard saw Gatlin's Pontiac nearby and one police cruiser, but no other official vehicles, which was odd. Normally, a murder worthy of his appearance at the scene would generate more interest.

He parked, grabbed his bag off the passenger seat, and shed the car. At his approach, Gatlin stubbed his cigarette out on the planter, felt the tip of the butt for heat, and put it in the pocket of his suit coat.

"Savin' it for later?" Broussard asked.

"Killing myself with them is bad enough. No need to litter, too."

Gatlin stood about six inches taller than Broussard but was about the same age. Over the years, Broussard had watched Gatlin's features soften and round, until he'd turned into someone the occasional felon would mistakenly think could be bested in a footrace or relieved of his weapon. And of course, Broussard hadn't changed at all.

"Where is everybody?" Broussard asked.

Gatlin wiped his big mitt over his face, fuzzing his eyebrows. "I'm not sure what we got, so we're taking it slow right now."

This piqued Broussard's interest. "Show me."

"We gotta go upstairs . . . third floor." He gestured at Broussard's bag. "You haven't got a couple of gas masks in there, have you?"

"There's an odor?"

"Oh yeah."

Broussard followed Gatlin up the steps and down the hall to the elevator. When it arrived, it contained a young couple, facing front, both wearing an impish look of exaggerated innocence. Her blouse was rumpled and partially pulled out of her skirt. They hurried past without speaking. As the elevator doors shut behind Broussard and Gatlin, they heard the couple laugh.

"You ever been that goofy?" Gatlin asked.

"Sure. And so have you."

Mixed with the lingering traces of the girl's perfume, Broussard detected the faint but unmistakable odor of decomposing flesh. Over the years, he'd become so sensitive to the smell, he could discern it at levels imperceptible to others. He was so good at it that twice he'd located bodies in nearby swamps by the odor in the bubbles they'd sent to the surface. And he could even differentiate decaying animals from humans. It was a gift.

On three, the elevator doors opened onto a blue-carpeted hallway with blue-striped wallpaper, and the odor grew stronger. Gatlin got off and turned right, his long strides making Broussard hurry to keep pace.

At the end of the corridor, a uniformed cop leaning against the wall with his arms folded saw them coming and spruced up.

"Where's the manager?" Gatlin asked when he got close enough.

"Went back to his apartment," the cop said.

He was young—younger, Broussard thought, than his thinning hair would indicate. And hopefully still untouched by the departmental corruption the *Picayune* had been detailing in articles almost daily for weeks.

"He asked us to keep the door shut," the cop added.

Gatlin nodded perfunctorily, a disgusted smirk on his face. The odor now was strong enough for anyone to smell.

Abruptly, the door opposite the one the cop was guarding flew open and a man in a gray suit and carrying a briefcase came out. He looked at Gatlin and Broussard, sniffed the air, and waved his hand in front of his nose. "Jesus . . . what . . ." Now he saw the cop. "Is that smell what I think it is?"

"We're kinda busy right now," Gatlin said, "so if you'd just go along to work, we'd appreciate it."

"You gonna be able to get rid of that smell? 'Cause if you can't . . ."

"Smell's ain't our department," Gatlin said. "Now shift your load."

He didn't get it.

"Move."

Giving Gatlin a sour look, the guy headed for the elevator.

"Sir . . ." Gatlin called after him.

The guy stopped and turned around. "Yeah?"

"Have a nice day." Looking at Broussard, the old detective added, "Memo last week said to remember we're ambassadors for the city. How'd I do?"

"I think you've made a new friend."

Gatlin lifted his tie to his nose, opened the door to the guarded apartment, and stood aside to let Broussard enter.

"You gonna need me in there?" the cop asked.

"No. But stay right out here," Gatlin replied.

The odor in the apartment gave the air a tangible consistency. But more striking was the blood—great gouts of it in overlapping fuzzy-edged sunbursts on the cream carpet.

Broussard knelt in a clean spot and pulled on a pair of rubber gloves from his bag. He pressed the edge of a nearby sunburst with the gloved fingers of his left hand and noted that the blood was totally dry and crusted, as he expected. So there was no need to worry about tracking it around on his shoes.

He stood up and looked at Gatlin, who was still breathing through his tie. "Where are we on pictures?"

"Already got a set. Jamison left just before you got here."

Broussard then turned his attention to an open closet door on the opposite side of the room, where numerous articles of clothing, many still on hangers, were scattered over the carpet. He moved in that direction and detected an increase in odor intensity. He now had a pretty good idea where the body was.

Reaching the clothing, he saw that most of it appeared to have been scattered after the carpet had been bloodied. But there was a tweed sport coat and a tan poplin jacket with blood spatter on the upper surface that seemed to be part of a continuous pattern extending onto the carpet.

He looked in the closet, and there was the corpse, sitting on the floor, its back against the left wall, ankles crossed, knees spread apart, arms dangling on each side, head drooped.

"It's Walter Baldwin, the guy who rents this apartment," Gatlin said, holding back. "Apartment manager says he was a salesman for Crescent City Bar and Restaurant Supplies."

Broussard made a cursory inspection of the body with his penlight, then came back into the room.

"What do you think?" Gatlin asked, his words muffled by his tie.

"I can't examine him in there in that position. We'll have to get him out. But first, I want to look around."

To the right was a kitchenette with a sit-down counter separating it from the living room. There was dried blood on the linoleum floor and in the sink. Crossing to the hallway beside the closet containing the corpse, Broussard followed a blood trail to the bathroom, where he found blood in that sink, as well as on the floor around the toilet and in the toilet.

From there, the blood led to the only bedroom. As Broussard appeared in the doorway, the CO_2 in his breath and the heat from his body roused Walter Baldwin's killer, the third time that morning it had gone on alert. The first was when Gatlin and the cop had come into the room; the second, when Jamison, the photographer, had entered. Both times, because of poor position, it had been unable to take advantage of their presence. But now it was better placed—poised on a leaf of the artificial fig next to the dresser, where it waited, body erect, front legs lifted.

Broussard moved into the room and the killer's photo detectors went wild. It hadn't fed in days.

Broussard studied the blood on the floor by the bed, then passed between the bed and the dresser. The killer raised its front legs a tiny bit higher, muscles tensing. But the object of its excitement didn't pass quite close enough.

On the other side of the bed, Broussard picked up a bloody pillow, stripped off the case, and folded it on the covers. "I want to take this with me." As he headed back to the doorway where Gatlin waited, he brushed against the artificial fig.

"Could all this blood have come from one person?" Gatlin asked.

"A little blood often looks like a lot of blood," Broussard replied. "But this *is* a lot."

"I couldn't check him very well, either, in that closet, but I didn't see any wounds."

"Right now, I'm thinkin' there aren't any."

"So what happened?"

"Let's get him out where we can see better."

They went back into the living room, where Broussard bagged the bloody pillowcase. Meanwhile, Gatlin slipped on a pair of rubber gloves from his pocket. He then leaned into the closet, grabbed the corpse by the ankles, and pulled him into the room.

"Hope all this exertion isn't too much for you," he said to Broussard, letting the legs drop. "God, I hate this part of the job." Being a good Catholic, he crossed himself for saying the word *God.*

The corpse was clothed in an open-necked white dress shirt and slacks, both crusted with dried blood. And the body was quite swollen, so that its half-closed lids were stretched to tenuously thin membranes over the protruding eyes. Between the lips they could see the tongue, turgid and alien. The skin of the face was marbled with green and purple. Between buttons, the shirt gaped over the distended chest and abdomen. One bloated hand lay palm up, the other palm down. Noting on the latter an unusual discoloration in addition to the marbling, Broussard knelt for a closer look.

"What do you see?"

"Extravasated blood under the skin."

"Extravasated?"

"Leaked . . . from a vessel."

"Which means what?"

The things Broussard had seen in the last few minutes existed in his mind encased in a gossamer bubble that shifted and glinted with iridescent hues. Floating nearby was the bubble containing the autopsy results of Jack Doe. The two bubbles touched and bounced gently in opposite directions, but remained close enough to each other that they could easily touch again, perhaps with different results.

"I'm not sure what it means yet," Broussard said. He shifted his attention to the corpse's face and noticed a few blisters where the epidermis was beginning to slough, a postmortem event. Rigor had long ago departed, so there was no resistance as he turned the head toward him and then away as he checked in and behind the ears for wounds. Finding none, he inspected the clothing for evidence of bullet or knife tears and again found none. He lifted the corpse's right arm and looked at Gatlin. "Grab his wrist and help me turn him over. And get a good grip, or you might pull his skin off."

Reluctantly, Gatlin did as he instructed, and together they got the body onto its stomach, which, Gatlin noted with disgust, caused an evil-looking fluid to issue from its nose and mouth.

After inspecting the back of the corpse's head and neck and his clothing, Broussard struggled to his feet, breathing heavily. "I can't be a hundred percent sure until I get him in the morgue, but nobody'll be more surprised than me if I find any evidence this was caused by external trauma." He made a sweeping gesture at the carpet. "All this blood came from his stomach—vomited up. For example, over here." He led Gatlin to an asymmetric sunburst. "This blood spattered so much because it came fast from a source at least four feet high. These two oval areas where there's no blood are where he was standin', so the spatter hit him instead of the carpet. There's so much blood because he didn't die right away. This went on for quite a while. In the later stages, I also think he was bleedin' from his rectum. If it wasn't for that blood under his skin, I'd suspect a massive ulcer or ruptured varicose veins in his esophagus."

"Could he have been poisoned?"

"Rat poison comes to mind."

"Is that likely? Rat poison is generally only available in solid bait form. You can't lace a drink with it or hide it in food very easily. And this doesn't look like a suicide."

"The main ingredient in rat poison's also available medically as a blood thinner."

"Are we talking horse or zebra?" He was referring to the adage that if you hear hoofbeats, you should be looking for horses, not zebras.

Reflection on the question reminded Broussard that the anticoagulant they were discussing probably wouldn't produce the kind of sudden catastrophic events that had apparently happened here, but it would cause symptoms that developed so slowly there'd be adequate warning something was wrong. He therefore said, "Zebra."

"Why didn't he call for help? The phone's working."

"He was probably disoriented."

"Why'd he get in the closet?"

"I dunno. But he was still vomitin' blood when he cleared out those clothes."

"Because of the blood on the sport coat and the jacket?"

"Yeah."

"Can we get outta here?"

In the hall, they pulled off their rubber gloves and put them in a plastic bag Broussard provided.

"How long you figure he's been dead?" Gatlin asked.

"Hard to say. From the temperature in the closet . . . four or five days."

"That squares with an appointment book I found in his briefcase. It lists all his calls for the month, and there are check marks by each address until one o'clock last Tuesday. The apartment manager also says his car hasn't moved from the lot since then. That's six days. If he was sick in there for a day or two before he died, we're in your time frame. That reminds me, I found some bloody Kleenex in his car. Want a look?"

"Not necessary."

Gatlin sucked his teeth. "When I die, I hope there are some people who care enough about me to miss me before somebody starts complaining about the odor."

"Seems like little enough to ask. There's nothin' more I can do here."

"You go on, then. I'll call the wagon and we'll hold the scene until you finish with him. And just for the hell of it, when the odor clears, I'm gonna look around for that zebra."

As Broussard went down the apartment steps, he reflected on how he could go for months without encountering any real problems in either his work or his personal life, because both were under control. His accumulated forensic experience and knowledge made for few surprises at the autopsy table, and his lack of family meant no miscarriages, no relatives to bail out of jail, and no kids on drugs. As for finding his body, unless he was on vacation when it happened, Charlie Franks, the deputy ME, or one of the secretaries would realize something was wrong when he didn't show up for work. So that was pretty much covered, too.

But once in a while, despite his best efforts, problems cropped up, and contrary to the laws of probability, they tended to cluster. Take, for example, Jack Doe. That case comes in on Thursday and now, four days later, another very odd one he didn't understand. But of course, he hadn't done the autopsy yet or given Toxicology their shot.

As he approached the T-Bird and cast an admiring eye over it, he saw something drooping behind the front bumper. Kneeling for a closer look, two things happened simultaneously: He saw a twig caught in the car's undercarriage and the seat of his pants gave way.

Face flushing, he pulled the twig loose and stood up, then walked around to the driver's side of the car and opened the door to shield him from anyone watching. He probed the rip and his fingers found only air where there should have been fabric.

Problems in clusters—that's the way it worked.

Sliding into the little car, he wondered what was going to happen next.

6

Broussard drove home and went directly to the bedroom, where he changed pants. He folded the ripped pair and put them in the dresser drawer with his Ralph Lauren pajamas so he'd see them every morning and be reminded that they needed to be dropped off for repairs.

Rat poison was certainly a zebra. Even so, he decided to get a definite answer to that possibility before he started the autopsy. To do that, he called the office and had Guy Minoux paged.

"Guy, this is Andy. There's a partially decomposed body comin' in any minute. . . . Yeah, I wish he'd been found sooner, too. His name is Baldwin. I'd like you to get your fluids and send 'em over to Toxicology for a routine drug screen and also ask 'em to check specifically for warfarin. . . ." He spelled out the main ingredient in rat poison, then added two other anticoagulants, coumarin and heparin, spelling those as well. "I don't need the routine screen right away, but I'd like the others stat. The vessels and heart are probably gonna be so full of gas you won't get anything from 'em, so take a sample of chest fluid. That'll contain blood that leaked from the decomposin' lungs."

Guy protested that he already knew all those things and Broussard apologized before hanging up.

It was too late now to make the dish he'd planned for breakfast, so he decided to stop by Grandma O's, even though she wasn't open yet, and see if she'd be willing to whip him up some eggs Oustellette.

When he arrived at her restaurant, there were no lights on, but shading his eyes and looking inside, he saw Grandma O on a ladder, dusting the stuffed pelican on a shelf over the bar. He rapped on the glass and got her attention. A minute later, she turned the key in the lock and opened the door.

"Did you purposely wait until Ah got up on dat ladder before you knocked or do you jus' naturally have bad timin'?"

"Naturally bad timin'."

She grinned, showing the gold star inlay in her front tooth. "Well, Ah won't hol' it against you. Come on. . . ."

She stepped aside, but her black taffeta dress stuck out so far, he couldn't help but brush it as he went in.

"Lemme guess," she said. ". . . You got called out early an' didn' have no time to eat."

"Can't keep anything from you."

"Dis ain't exactly da firs' time dis has happened. How 'bout some eggs Oustellette, debris, a nice loaf of French bread an' applesauce, an' a hot cup of chicory coffee?"

"I'm in your hands."

"You go on to your table and Ah'll get started."

"His" table was the biggest one in the place, in the rear, by the kitchen doors. No matter how busy the restaurant was, that table was always reserved for him and sat there empty and waiting. He'd told her not to do that, but she wouldn't listen.

The kitchen doors banged open and Grandma O appeared carrying a big round tray. "You start on dis," she said, setting out before him a plate, some silverware, a steaming cup of coffee, and a basket containing a sectioned loaf of crusty French bread and a little dish of applesauce, "an' dose eggs'll be jus' a few minutes."

Broussard picked up one of the bread slices, broke the crust so he could roll it out, and slathered it with applesauce. Then, he put the bread on his plate, slid his chair back, and slinked to the kitchen doors, hoping to see through the little window in them just what it was she put in those eggs.

Rising to his full height, he looked through the window and into the kitchen, where he saw off to the left the big restaurant range but no Grandma O. Suddenly, a flyswatter smacked the glass, making him jerk backward in alarm. One of the doors opened and there she was.

"Ah had a hunch it was 'bout time for you to try an' steal mah recipe again."

"I don't know what came over me," Broussard said. "Everything went black and when I woke up I was lookin' in the window."

"You keep tryin' to get mah recipe, things'll go black for good," she said, waving the flyswatter at him. "Ah tol' you Ah'd give it to you on your eightieth birthday."

"Suppose I don't live that long?"

"You keep doin' what you were doin' an' you won't. Now, siddown."

Chuckling, Broussard went back to his table. They'd been playing this game off and on for years and it was still fun.

While Broussard waited for his eggs, across the river, in his dresser, Walter Baldwin's killer emerged from Broussard's torn pants and began to explore. It moved across the right lapel of his pale blue pajamas and paused on the label, its body covering the *R* in Ralph Lauren. Hungry and thirsty, it could do nothing about the former, but the latter was no problem. From a gland in a protrusible mouth part, it secreted a tiny salt crystal that quickly absorbed water from the air. Drawing the salt droplet into its mouth, its thirst was satisfied. Turning, it moved toward the rear of the dresser and up the back panel into the dresser carcass, looking for a way out.

GRANDMA O PUT BROUSSARD'S eggs and debris in front of him, then sat down herself with a cup of coffee.

"You ever fin' out who dat fella was dat had his attack in here las' week?"

"Not yet, but Kit worked on it over the weekend. Maybe she came up with somethin'."

Grandma O's dark eyes clouded. "Ah got a bad feelin' 'bout dat man. If she didn't learn anything yet, you should tell her to give up."

"Be better if we could turn the body over to his relatives. . . ."

"Ah don' think so. In fact, Ah'm feelin' uneasy right now."

Broussard stopped eating and looked at her with concern. "What do you mean? Upset stomach? Have you got a fever? Did you get that gamma globulin shot?"

"Not dat kinda uneasy. . . . Worried . . . about Kit. You know how she is . . . pushin' and pushin' sometimes 'till she gets in over her head."

"I know."

Broussard had been trained in one of the best forensic pathology programs in the country. And he read constantly to keep his knowledge up-to-date. In all that professional reading, it was cause and effect. This kind of bullet causes this kind of wound, unless it ricochets. . . . A wound from a double-edged knife has two crisp edges. . . . Uninflated alveoli in the lungs of a newborn fished from a bayou means the child had never taken a breath—therefore, no homicide.

But being born and bred in bayou country, where everybody knows not everything can be measured and weighed, he appreciated the value of a hunch. He played them himself, usually to good advantage. And when it came to hunches, Grandma O had a surprisingly good record, too, so he generally listened when she had one, although it wasn't always easy to understand what her hunches meant.

"An' Ah'm worried 'bout you, too," she said.

"Why me?"

She shook her head and stared at her coffee. "Ah don' know. But Ah think dere's trouble comin'."

"I ripped the seat out of my pants this mornin'. Maybe that's what you're sensin'."

"Dat's not it."

Broussard dressed another piece of bread with applesauce. "You never answered me about that shot."

"Ah don' get sick, so it's not necessary."

Knowing it was no use to argue with her once her mind was made up, he let the subject drop. He tried then to move the conversation into a more upbeat area while he finished his breakfast, but she was hard to move.

As he left, she gave him a parting instruction. "City boy . . . you watch out for da small things."

In this he needed no instruction, for he had always believed that it's not the big thing that pushes you over the cliff, but the untied shoelace.

Broussard's first act upon reaching his office was to call Toxicology. As expected, they'd found no warfarin in Baldwin, no coumarin, and only physiological levels of heparin, a substance the body normally produces.

He turned next to the bloody pillowcase he'd brought from Baldwin's apartment. He cut a piece from the stain, slipped it into a test tube with some distilled water, and shook it gently. After several minutes of this, he put a sample of the liquid from the tube on a glass slide, coverslipped it, and placed the slide on the stage of his microscope.

Taking off his glasses and letting them dangle against his chest by the lanyard at the temples, he looked into the eyepieces and touched up the focus, sharpening the blurred strands dominating the field into fibers from the pillowcase. Amid the fibers, he saw many distorted red cells and a few white cells. He also saw many large patches of cells attached to one another—epithelial cells, from the look of them.

Interesting . . . Whatever had afflicted Walter Baldwin had apparently caused the lining of his digestive tract to slough.

Entering the autopsy room a few minutes later, the first things he sensed were the odor and the sound of the exhaust fans laboring on their highest setting. Needing only masks and eye protection to complete their attire, Guy and Natalie were dressed out and waiting, standing as far from the bloated corpse of Walter Baldwin as the relatively small room allowed.

"We get time and half for this one, right?" Guy said.

"We can do that," Broussard replied, reaching into the box of booties. "But we'll have to start keepin' track of things like those two hours you took off Friday to meet your plumber."

"Good point," Guy said. "I vote for continuation of the old policy. Natalie, what do you think?"

"Old policy," Natalie said with less than her usual energy.

Natalie had short, curly hair the shade of the tan leather reading chair in Broussard's study and fair skin, so her tortoiseshell glasses always made her look a little on the pale side, but with enough color in her cheeks to seem in robust health. Today, as Broussard slipped his plastic apron over his head, he noticed that her color seemed a bit off, tending toward the yellow range. Thinking she was probably just trying out a new makeup, he said nothing.

After tying on her mask and donning her eye shield, Natalie moved to the stereo and stopped at the CD rack. "I'd like some Strauss today."

Guy turned and looked at her, wide-eyed. Broussard paused in his attempt to tie the knot of his apron strings.

This was a major departure from long-standing autopsy protocol. Broussard chose the music. Everyone knew that.

Puzzled, Broussard looked at Natalie, who was already selecting the Strauss disc. He rarely chose Strauss and from time to time had thought he should remove that disc from the stereo. Waltzes and polkas were just too frenetic for careful work.

As the lilting strains of "Thunder and Lightning" filled the room, Guy glanced at Broussard in horror.

"Yes," Broussard said, "Strauss today." And Guy relaxed.

Broussard picked up the Polaroid camera and checked it for film. Empty, and there was none on the counter where it should be.

He glanced again at Natalie, who'd joined Guy at the table bearing Walter Baldwin's body. It was her responsibility to make sure each autopsy began with film in the camera and several packs nearby on the counter. This was the first time she'd dropped the ball. He noticed that her eyes were focused on a distant point while her head bobbed slightly in time to the music.

He pulled the drawer with the extra film farther out than was necessary, hoping the noise would call her attention to her failure. But she didn't seem to notice. Not wishing to criticize her in front of Guy, he made a mental note to speak to her later about it.

He moved to the body, glanced approvingly at the red grease pencil circles around the punctures where fluids had been drawn, and took a facial shot that wouldn't rank as one of the victim's better pictures. He then began a careful inspection of the body, which, though they were difficult to see, exhibited a large number of ecchymoses that he noted on his superficial-exam forms. Wishing to document them photographically, he again picked up the camera.

"Guy, hold this hand up for me so I can get a picture of the skin on the back, will you? Natalie, I'll need a marker."

Guy came around the table, lifted the arm, and turned the hand to an appropriate angle. Natalie hadn't moved. "Natalie . . . a marker, please."

She came back from wherever her mind had been and reached into the pocket of her smock, then into the other pocket. Not finding the roll of ruler tape there, either, she began to search the countertops. Finding it finally, she went over to where the two men were waiting.

"Natalie, is anything wrong?" Broussard asked.

"No . . . Just a little headache," she said, peeling a small ruler from the roll of tape. "Where did you want this?"

Broussard showed her and she stuck it onto the corpse's skin.

They photographed several more ecchymoses, then turned the body so Broussard could examine the back. A few minutes later, after noting the last of the ecchymoses there, Broussard asked Natalie to bring him the camera.

As Broussard made his final entry on the superficial-exam form, there was a crash from Natalie's direction. Looking up from his clipboard, Broussard saw that she'd dropped the camera. Above her mask, her eyes were filled with confusion. Though the room wasn't particularly warm, there was a film of perspiration on her forehead.

"I don't know what happened," she said. "I had it in my hand and then I didn't."

She bent at the waist and closed her eyes. "Jesus, do I feel lousy." When she stood up a moment later, there was a red stain on the upper part of her mask.

"Natalie," Guy said, pointing. "I think your nose is bleeding."

As Broussard watched this unfold, the bubble enclosing the autopsy results of Jack Doe came bouncing over his mental horizon. "Natalie, I want you to leave now, get out of that autopsy gear, and go up to see Dr. Seymour in Internal Medicine . . . suite seven twenty-seven. I'll let him know you're comin'. Guy . . . go with her."

Natalie raised a hand in protest. "That's okay . . . I can manage myself."

"I'd prefer he go with you."

"No," she said ferociously. "I don't want help."

The two men watched her walk slowly to the dressing alcove, where she stripped off her gear and headed for the door, holding a clean mask to her nose. Before she reached the door, Guy sprinted ahead of her and pulled it open. She shambled through without thanking him.

Broussard went to the phone and punched Seymour's number into the plastic sheet covering the phone's buttons.

"Mornin', this is Dr. Broussard. One of my assistants is ill and I'd like for Dr. Seymour to examine her soon as possible. Could that be right now? . . . Good. She'll be there in just a few minutes. Tell him I appreciate the special attention."

Broussard hung up and looked at Guy, who was picking the camera off the floor.

"I sure hope she's gonna be okay," Guy said.

"Me, too."

Broussard went to the stereo and exchanged the Strauss CD for Mozart. Trying to put his concern for Natalie aside, he returned to Baldwin's body.

Guy showed him a developing picture he'd just taken of the counter. "Camera seems all right."

He handed it over and Broussard took the shots he'd wanted before Natalie had become ill.

Because of the time that had elapsed before the body had been found, the blood and the organs were surely so overgrown with bacteria they would be useless for most of the tests routinely done to determine if he'd picked up an unusual bug. There was, therefore, no need to draw more blood.

"Ready to move him?" Guy asked.

"Yeah."

Guy wheeled the table with the body into the adjoining alcove and lined it up with the autopsy platform. Together, they slid the body over. Guy then made the first two slanting scalpel cuts. As he opened the abdomen with the third, the foul smell in the room grew far worse. Acknowledging that with a war whoop, Guy began reflecting the chest flaps, his scalpel snicking away the restraining connective tissue.

Broussard turned his attention to sharpening his long knife and arranging his sample containers, aware that most of the organs would be so putrid, they wouldn't be worth sectioning. Hearing Guy's scalpel slice through the rib cartilages, he walked to the body, eager to get his first look inside.

Guy removed the breast plate and put it on the cadaver's legs.

The first thing Broussard noticed was how much fluid there was in the chest, far more than he'd anticipated. The lungs were black, as expected, but in places he could see purple, which meant . . . He pressed on one lung and found that beneath the sponginess produced by decomposition gases, there was an underlying firmness.

"Okay for me to take the chest organs?" Guy asked.

"Go ahead."

While Guy bent to his work, Broussard parted the abdominal slit and peered into the peritoneal cavity, where he saw a large amount of dark bloody fluid.

In short order, Guy delivered the chest organs into a stainless pan and carried them to the sink. With his suspicions aroused, Broussard transferred the organs into the sink rather than onto the cutting board. When he cut the tip off the left lung, dark bloody fluid poured out.

The bleeding was far more extensive then he'd imagined. In addition to his gastrointestinal tract and skin, this man had bled into his lungs and most likely into and out of most of his other organs.

Over the next few minutes as he worked on the thoracic and then the abdominal contents, Broussard found further support for that view. As would have occurred in most bodies in such a state of decomposition, they found that the brain had turned to soup.

While Broussard watched Guy clean out the cranial cavity, Jack Doe's bubble bounced into his field of conjecture and collided with the bubble containing all he'd learned about Walter Baldwin's death. This time, the two bubbles came to rest side by side, pulsing and shimmering, separated by the narrowest of spaces. From the neglected periphery, another, smaller bubble wafted into the picture and settled onto the two large bubbles, straddling them.

Ecchymoses.

Broussard shivered, feeling as though someone had poured a beaker of cold formalin down the back of his shirt. He went to the body on the table, leaned down, and peered at the roof of its mouth through the gaping angle of its lower jaw. The epithelium of the palate had sloughed in places, but he could still see that it was dotted with small hemorrhages.

Where there had been three bubbles, there was now only one.

Natalie . . .

He hurried to the phone. Seymour should be told what he'd found. The phone rang and rang, until he was considering going up there in person. But then the voice he'd spoken to earlier came on the line.

"This is Dr. Broussard. I need to talk to Dr. Seymour about my assistant."

"We were just about to call you regarding that Dr. Broussard. Dr. Seymour has an appointment at Tulane in about fifteen minutes. So if your assistant doesn't get here soon . . ."

"She's not there?"

"We haven't seen her."

"I'll check on it."

Heart pounding, he dropped the receiver and crossed the room, moving as fast as Guy had ever seen him go. He threw the door open and charged into the hallway, where he stepped into a pool of black blood.

7

In the light from the row of wire-caged bulbs overhead, Broussard saw bloody footprints leading to a second pool glistening darkly in front of the door to the room where the morgue assistants had their desks. Beyond that, the floor was clean.

Broussard could remember only a few times in his life when he'd been gripped by the kind of fear he now felt for Natalie. He took a big step to get out of the pool at his feet and rushed to the next one, where he circled around it and pushed the heavy green door to the assistants' room open.

There were four desks in the room, all facing forward, two on the left, two on the right. No one was at any of them. He glanced at the floor and saw it was not bloodied.

So where was she?

Natalie's desk was the one in the rear, to his left. She liked that one because the wall space behind it gave her room to display the winter scenes she'd collected from old calendars. Having grown up in New Orleans, she'd rarely seen snow and was infatuated with it.

Maybe she'd gone home. . . .

He couldn't remember her number, but Margaret, the senior secretary in his office, would have it. He stepped to the wall phone and punched in the number for the office.

"Medical examiner . . ."

Before he could answer, he heard a sound from the direction of Natalie's desk. He noticed now that her chair was pushed carelessly to the side.

He hung up and moved slowly down the aisle. Reaching Natalie's chair, he pulled it out of his way and peered under her desk. There, knees pulled to her chest, was Natalie, her clothes soaked with black blood.

"STOP RIGHT THERE. WHEN I say stop, I mean stop. Hand your end to him. . . . No. You stand right where you are. I don't want you tracking blood out of here."

Ruth Lamm, the hospital's infection-control officer, stood only a hair over five feet tall, and in her protective gear, she looked like a kid playing doctor. But tiny as she was, she left no doubt who was in charge.

"Careful."

The stretcher bearing Natalie D'Souza was passed from the two masked, gowned, and gloved men who'd brought her into the hall to the three similarly dressed men waiting well clear of the blood on the hall floor.

"You know where you're going?" Lamm asked in an accusatory tone.

"Tuberculosis isolation ward, twelfth floor," one of the men answered.

"That's right. They're waiting for you. And when you're finished, all your protective gear goes in a biohazard container. That's ready up there, too. And don't just take any elevator—use the one we've set aside."

The three men moved off down the hall.

"And your gear"—she gestured to the other two men—"goes in here." She rapped the biohazard box beside her with her fist.

Then her voice suddenly became more gentle. "Think of it like a dance," she said as they undid the straps to their booties. "You never let your bare shoes touch a part of the floor where your booties have been. Lovely, Mr. Carter. . . ."

The other man was having trouble getting his off. "It's those shoes, Mr. Marcus. You really should get another pair—one without such flared soles."

The change in her manner was so striking Broussard wondered if her Prozac had just kicked in.

The two men stepped up to the box and deposited their shoe covers.

"Now, the first pair of gloves. . . ."

The hall echoed with the snap and ripple of rubber, and four gloves were added to the container.

"Garments now. . . . No, Mr. Marcus, not your mask," she said sharply, destroying Broussard's Prozac theory, "your garment."

Following the other man's lead, Mr. Marcus simply tore his way out of his smock and stuffed it in the biohazard box.

"Next . . . gloves, and then your mask and head protection. Good. Thank you, gentlemen. You may go back to your other duties."

The two men headed for the elevators, talking in low tones, most likely about Ruth Lamm.

She turned to Broussard. "You said she cut herself . . . working on a body that showed the early stages of whatever she's got?"

About all Broussard could see of her face was sharp gray eyes behind a pair of silver-framed glasses, things that made him think of bullets. "I don't think there's any doubt that's the cause of her illness."

"Where's that body now?"

"In our refrigerator."

"You're through with it?"

"Yes."

"I'd like it double-bagged."

"We'll do that."

"Where are his—it's a he?"

"It *was.*"

"Where are his organs?"

"Parts of most of 'em are fixed in formalin. The rest have been incinerated." Broussard found that he did not like being questioned this way. The morgue was his territory . . . his responsibility. She was merely a visitor. So it was with more than a little reluctance he said, "There's another case on the table right now. An advanced one that's pretty well decomposed."

"Are you finished with him?"

"Yes. We'll double-bag his remains, too."

"Will you be sending any fluids from that body upstairs for analysis?"

"Toxicology already analyzed some. But that's all we're gonna do on him. We also sent samples from the first case to Toxicology, as well as to the Blood Bank and to Laboratory Medicine, where I'm sure they were relayed to Immunology, Micro, and Virology."

"Were any of those samples labeled as hazardous?"

"We didn't know then what we know now."

Clearly, she was displeased with his answer. "I'll have to talk with everyone who worked on those samples. Have them examined, warn them. I guess they didn't identify any organisms."

"I sure would have told you if they had."

"Any idea how the two victims you autopsied acquired the disease?"

He shook his head, far more unhappy over having no answers to her questions than he was at her asking them.

"Knowing the mode of transmission would be a big help," she said. "If it requires exchange of bodily fluids or some other type of intimate contact, we'll be a hell of a lot better off than if the causative agent can be transmitted through the air by a cough or a sneeze. When did your assistant cut herself?"

"Last Thursday."

She held up her gloved fist and ticked off the days by extending her fingers one at a time. "Friday, Saturday, Sunday, Monday . . . it has an incubation period of only three or four days when the organism is passed by direct contact. If it can also be transmitted through the air, the incubation period could be longer." She looked at Guy, who had been standing quietly behind Broussard, still dressed in his autopsy gear. "Did you work on either of the two cases we've been talking about?"

Loyal to Broussard and sensing his unreceptive attitude to her questioning, he glanced at Broussard for guidance. Broussard nodded.

"I worked on both of them."

"How are you feeling?"

"I'm upset over what's happened to Natalie, but I'm not physically ill."

"Pay close attention to your health. If you feel the least bit nauseous or start to run a fever—anything at all—get yourself up to Internal Medicine." She looked at Broussard. "Anyone else work on those cases?"

"No."

She gestured at Broussard's plastic apron. "That's not the way you dress to do an autopsy, is it?"

He drew himself up to his full five foot ten, pleased that it enabled him to tower over his inquisitor. "It is."

"No one else dresses that way?"

"I'm the exception," he said somewhat icily.

"Well, you're asking for trouble."

"I've been doin' my job a good many years dressed like this."

"And when you first began, there was no such thing as AIDS, at least not in this country. I'm telling you that AIDS is just the warning salvo in a war that's soon to erupt between us and the microbes of this planet. So you might want to rethink your position. I've got to get upstairs. I'll be sending a decontamination team down here to clean the hall and that room. I'd also like them to do the room where you performed the autopsies on the two cases. Which one was it?"

"End of the hall."

"And you'll see that those areas are kept off-limits to your people until that's done?"

"We'll take care of the two bodies; then we'll clear out."

"And you'll put your protective clothing in this box?"

"We have our own box. How long before your decon team will be here?"

"Within the hour." The little tyrant turned and walked swiftly toward the elevators.

"What a pistol," Guy said under his breath.

"Interestin' woman,"

Broussard and Guy went back to the autopsy room and hung a red infectious hazard toe tag on Baldwin's body, then put him in two heavy-duty zippered plastic bags. They wiped the outer bag with bleach and stuck several biohazard stickers on it. After they'd put him on a tray in the big refrigerator, they pulled Jack Doe out in his single bag and brought him up to the new standards. When they finished, Broussard instructed Guy to take a few hours off while the decon team cleaned things up.

Riding up to his office, Broussard thought about the hemorrhages in Jack Doe's cerebrum. Suppose that, given time, the focus of those hemorrhages had spread over the rest of the cortex, destroying higher centers and knocking out rational thought. That could explain why Walter Baldwin had made no call for help. And what if the deeper, limbic system, where the origins of instinctive behavior likely reside, was spared. Where do animals go to recover when they're hurt? Their dens. It's instinctive. Walter Baldwin in his closet . . . Natalie under her desk. Speculative to be sure, but intriguing.

Reaching his desk, he went directly to the phone and called Grandma O. When told what had happened, she was adamant that she wasn't sick and wouldn't be getting sick. Despite her feelings on this, he suggested that for her customer's safety, she take a little vacation and turn the running of the place over to her cook until things settled down. Her response was enthusiastically negative. But in the end, she agreed, an accomplishment he ranked as one of the most impressive of his career.

A call to Homicide produced the news that Gatlin was out, but the detective who answered the phone agreed to locate him by radio and tell him to call Broussard immediately. While waiting, Broussard called Charlie Franks, the deputy ME, to his office and brought him up-to-date. He reminded Broussard that the rescue team that worked on Jack Doe could also be at risk, and Broussard immediately called the appropriate office and told them of the problem.

Gatlin reported in just as Franks left, and Broussard briefed him as well, asking him to check on the cop and the apartment manager from the Baldwin case and to arrange to keep Baldwin's apartment and car locked up until somebody came around to disinfect them.

He was looking up the number of the city's Health Department when the phone rang.

"Broussard."

"Andy, Dick Mullen . . ."

"Dick, I was just about to call you."

"Ruth Lamm, the infectious-disease officer over there, says you had a strange couple of cases come through the morgue and that one of your assistants was infected from cutting herself doing the autopsy on one of them."

"That's right. It's a hemorrhagic disease that seems to precipitate DIC. It starts with a headache, mental confusion, and probably a fever. The victim starts to feel nauseous and may get a nosebleed shortly before they begin to vomit blood. They may also experience a loss of touch and position sense in their hands, so they drop things. Anyone else seein' this devil?"

"Yours is the first report. But we'll be sending out alerts to all hospitals and all physicians in the city. And I'll relay what you've told me up to the state level. Lamm says there's no data on possible airborne transmission . . ."

"We have very little data period. But there is an apartment that needs decontamination—the place where we found one of the victims. There's blood all over it. And you should also do his car."

"Where's that?"

Broussard gave him the address.

"We'll get on it right away. Can you give me a list of names of anyone you know of who had physical contact with either of the bodies or was in that apartment or car?"

"I've already alerted everybody I could think of."

"I'd still like the names."

In running down his list, Broussard realized he'd forgotten about Kit earlier and he added her name now.

"Okay, thanks," Mullen said. "I'll be in touch. Let me know if anything else breaks."

When the line was clear, Broussard called Kit to let her know what was going on.

Her phone rang three times and he heard a click, followed by a recorded message saying she was away from her desk. He punched in the number for the main office. "Margaret, is Kit in there?"

"I'm sorry, no."

"Have you seen her this mornin'?"

"Not so far."

"Did she say anything about what her schedule was gonna be today?"

"I wish I could be more help, but she didn't."

"Okay, thanks."

As he hung up, he was tweaked by an ugly thought that he dismissed as quickly as it had arrived. Probably, she'd just stepped into the ladies' room or gone downstairs for a Coke. Just to satisfy himself, he got out of his chair, went into the hall, and walked down to Kit's office, which was around the corner from his.

Turning that corner and seeing no light through the frosted window in her door, his pulse quickened and the same ugly thought he'd had a moment ago returned, bulkier and less willing to be ignored.

He hurried back to his own office and called Kit's home. There, too, he got the answering machine.

It wasn't like Kit to be late without notifying anyone, and she always filed a rough itinerary with Margaret on those days she had people to interview. This wasn't good.

He called Charlie Franks and asked him to keep an eye on Ruth Lamm's decon team when they arrived, then told Margaret he was going out for about an hour.

Reaching the street, he saw that the sky was overcast, and his nostrils filled with the sweet earthy scent of rain on the way. He'd been parking at the same lot for over twenty years and they knew to keep his car unblocked and ready to go at any time. But the guy who greeted him upon his arrival was new.

"Yo, where is it?" he asked. He was wearing jeans, a tan army jacket, and a black watch cap with moth holes in it.

"Up there," Broussard replied, pointing to one of those elevator racks that allow parking lots to stack one car over another. Not only was his car on the rack; the guy would have to move at least four other cars to get it out.

"Whoa, that's gonna take a few minutes," the guy said.

"For future reference, I'm the medical examiner and my car needs to be available to me at all times."

"Medical examiner . . ." The guy worked on it for a few seconds, then said, "What is that, somebody who gives doctors tests to see if they know everything they should?"

"When I've got more time, I'll explain it to you. Right now, I need my car."

"No problemo."

While he hustled away to free Broussard's caged T-Bird, a light rain began to fall, and Broussard stepped into the little attendant's guardhouse to stay dry.

Inside, a chipped green stool sat in front of a gray Formica counter, worn through in the center. Playing cards were spread across the counter in a game of solitaire. On the wall was a nude pinup photographed in gynecologic detail. It was nice for a change to see an unclothed body without any wounds on it. He leaned out to check on the attendant's progress and saw him backing the first blocking car out of its space. Broussard dealt with this unexpected delay by telling himself his concern for Kit was a gross overreaction and that there was a trivial explanation for her . . . He was thinking about it as a disappearance, but at this point it didn't even merit that designation.

He checked again and saw the attendant duck his head and get into the second car blocking access to the rack. The rain was now coming harder, its drops slapping loudly onto the blacktop. He looked up at the gray origin of the deluge and wished he had a raincoat or an umbrella.

Through the rain sounds, from the direction of the rack, he heard an engine turning over and over, and he hoped the attendant wouldn't flood it.

Of course Kit was all right.

The rain and the cramped guardhouse, along with the frustrating sound of an engine that just wouldn't catch, made him feel trapped. Trying to get his mind off it, he let his eyes again roam the guardhouse. On a narrow shelf holding a thermos and an open package of chocolate cookies, he saw a limp copy of *Bendigo Shafter,* a Louis L'Amour novel he'd never been able to find. He picked it up and turned to the first page.

"Okay, there she is. . . ."

Startled, Broussard looked in the direction of the voice and there was his idling T-Bird, the wipers click-slipping across the windshield.

The attendant was hugging the exterior wall of the guardhouse, trying to get under the slight roof overhang. Broussard looked back at the book in his hand and was shocked to see that he'd read ten pages.

He dug in his wallet and pulled out a five. Holding up the book and the money, he said, "I'll give you this for the book."

"Okay with me. It ain't even got any dirty parts in it."

It took twenty minutes to get to Kit's house, a trip prolonged by the rain, which at times layered onto the windshield so thickly, he could barely see the street.

He parked in front of her gates and rolled the window down. With alarm, he saw that Kit's car was in the parking alcove. If she was home, why hadn't she answered the phone?

Maybe she'd been out when he'd called and had just come home. . . .

Too worried to wait for a lull in the rain, he threw the door open and hustled to the gates, where the parking alcove's overhang was not deep enough to protect his backside. Through the raindrops on his glasses, he saw that Kit's car was dry. Unwilling to accept the mounting evidence something was terribly wrong, he reasoned that she could have been out and come home *before* the rain began.

He went to the pedestrian gate by the mail drop and found it locked. Above the mail drop was a brass doorbell and an intercom. He pressed the bell hard, silently urging her to answer.

But the intercom remained silent.

Illogically, he began pumping the button, but it did no good.

The sky rumbled and the image he'd been pushing aside broke through: Kit, sitting dazed in a pool of her own blood, the gore caking on her clothes.

He had to get inside.

He went back to the car and sped away, the tires slipping on the wet pavement.

"JUS' A FEW SECONDS more," Bubba Oustellette said, bending over the lock to Kit's pedestrian gate.

It was still raining, but Bubba had brought a huge orange umbrella, which Broussard held over both of them. But the rain pelting the sidewalk still spattered onto their pants. Suddenly, the gate was open.

Bubba picked up his toolbox and went inside, followed by Broussard, who had to close the umbrella before he could get through the gate.

"You know, Ah saw her Saturday an' she looked fine," Bubba said.

"That's actually a long time ago," Broussard said. The doorway from the parking alcove onto the courtyard was large enough that Broussard could reopen the umbrella before they both stepped again into the rain.

The entry to Kit's house was recessed and there was a small balcony over it, so that when they reached the front door, the umbrella became unnecessary. It took Bubba less than a minute to get the door open. Broussard rushed past him.

Bubba's tinkering with the lock had turned on all the inside lights, and in their welcoming brilliance, Broussard's eyes raked the interior, concentrating mostly on the floor, looking for blood. But everything appeared perfectly in order.

"Kit. Are you here?" Broussard called out. "It's Andy and Bubba."

No answer.

"Dere's an alarm system dat's gonna call da police in about twenty seconds," Bubba said. "But she showed me how to shut it off when Ah was helpin' her move in." He went to a control panel set into the wall above a small table by the door and punched in some numbers. Meanwhile, Broussard began searching the house.

"Kit. It's Andy. Are you here?"

Ten minutes later, they'd been all through the place, including the closets and the attic. They'd found Lucky in the backyard, but no Kit.

"You said dis disease causes you to vomit blood?" Bubba asked.

Broussard nodded.

"We didn't fin' any blood, so you think she's okay?"

"Not necessarily. This thing comes on you quickly and it makes you seek a safe, snug place, like a closet or the space under a desk . . ."

"So, if she was out for a walk an' got sick, she'd hide?"

"The latest victim we found vomited blood for quite a while before he sought out a closet. But Natalie, the morgue assistant who caught it from cuttin' herself during an autopsy, looked for a place right after the vomitin' started. So, the time varies with different people."

"Andy . . . we gotta fin' dat girl."

8

"**Teddy, this is Andy** Broussard. Is Kit there in Bayou Coteau with you?"

Across Broussard's desk, Phil Gatlin sat on the edge of his chair, listening to the call on speaker phone, hoping, as Broussard did, that the answer was yes.

"No, she isn't," Teddy said, the worry obvious in his voice. "Why'd you think that?"

Gatlin slumped in his chair.

"When did you last see her?"

"Six o'clock this morning. When I left to come home. What's—"

"How did she seem?"

"Same as always. . . ."

"No headache or nausea or a nosebleed?"

"No. What's going on?"

Broussard hesitated, trying to decide how to handle this. Did he want to minimize the situation or lay it flatly out there. Deciding that Teddy deserved the truth, he said, "We've got a problem here. Did Kit tell you about the man and the roses?"

"The one who died at Grandma O's?"

"That's him."

"Yeah, she did. We spent Saturday morning down at the docks, showing his picture, but didn't find anyone who recognized him. We thought we had a good lead on one of the ships in port, but the captain wouldn't give us access to the crew. We talked to the longshoremen who were unloading the ship, then gave up. What's the problem?"

"From the autopsy, it appeared that fellow might have been in the early stages of a bleedin' disease. One of my assistants cut herself while workin' on him and is now very ill, almost certainly with the same disease. There's no proof the disease can be transmitted through the air, but it's possible that people who came in contact with the man could have picked up the causative organism. And Kit didn't show up for work today. . . ."

"Oh my God. Has anyone gone over to her house?"

"Bubba and I did. Her car is there, but she isn't. This disease causes the victims to vomit blood, but there's no blood anywhere in her house. So that's a good sign."

"Then where is she?"

"That's our concern."

"Maybe she got sick out on the street somewhere."

"That's a possibility."

"What's being done about it?"

"We wanted to check with you before doin' anything . . . hopin' she was there. Phil Gatlin is sittin' right here in my office. When I hang up, we're gonna mount a search. We've got her home and office Rolodex files and we'll start by callin' every local name in 'em, unless you can give us some leads."

"Wait a minute," Teddy said. "I just remembered something. She mentioned that when she talked to her parents and asked them about this guy, they told her they had no idea who he was. But she doesn't think they were telling the truth. I wonder if she flew home to confront them?"

"Do you have their phone number?"

"I'm sure I do. I'll call them and get back to you."

"Let me know somethin' right away. If they're not home, we're gonna start our search."

The next few minutes crept by incredibly slowly, with no conversation as the two men waited for Teddy's call. The silence and the tension brought back memories of the parlor in Broussard's grandmother's house, where he'd been raised after his parents died. Its heavy drapes and plush carpet had acted as great sound insulators, so the room was self-contained, as though it existed unconnected to the outside world. He'd often go in and pull the big sliding doors closed and just sit there, listening to the grandfather clock marking off each passing second. Over twelve feet tall, the clock was made of oak whose stain had turned almost black from a hundred years of sitting in a room warmed in winter by a coal fire. The maker had carved the oak heavily with vines and clusters of grapes, sheaves of wheat and stalks of corn, foxes and pheasants and hunting dogs. His grandmother had given him a home and love, but on those days when he'd felt so alone and afraid of the ease with which life could be turned upside down, listening to the ticking of the big old reliable clock had helped him. And now, waiting for Teddy's call, he could hear it again, telling him everything was going to be fine. Unfortunately, he was no longer young enough to be comforted by a clock.

They sat silently watching the phone, as though it were a criminal whose nerves they were testing. Finally, it rang, and Broussard clapped his pudgy hand on the receiver. "Broussard."

"It's Teddy. No luck."

With that hope snuffed, Broussard and Gatlin tried to calm their emotions and focus only on what had to be done next. "What about her friends?" Broussard asked. "Any names we should check out first?"

Teddy recited half a dozen women's names and, at Gatlin's prompting, added their places of employment for the two he knew.

Gatlin jotted the information in his little notebook and said, "What was she wearing when you last saw her?"

"White pants with pockets cut straight across the top instead of angled, a blue-and-white horizontally striped pullover blouse with a boat neck, white sneakers, and a white cap with red capital letters on it—*AMAE . . . P . . . MA*, I think. It's Russian, the name of the ship whose chief mate gave her the cap when we were on the docks. And the cap has a little gold anchor on it that I bought her."

"Doesn't sound like she was dressed for work," Gatlin said.

"She was going to walk Lucky, then change. Andy, was Lucky there when you went to her house?"

"Yeah," Broussard said. "Bubba's got him. Don't worry, we'll find her."

"But in what condition? How bad is this thing?"

"It can be very bad."

"Lethal?"

"We know of one case where it was."

"If she does have it, how long before she . . ."

The evidence suggested that after vomiting, Walter Baldwin had lived at most only forty-eight hours. Turning from his path of complete disclosure, Broussard said, "We've got time. I'll let you know soon as we learn anything."

He hung up and looked at Gatlin. "How do we handle this?"

"I'll ask some people from Missing Persons to work on those files and the names Teddy gave us. But the fact her car is there suggests she's somewhere within walking distance of her house. It could be she got sick and someone took her in."

Broussard shook his head. "They might have taken her in for a little while, but once she started hemorrhagin', they'd surely get her to a hospital."

"We'll check on that. But I also think we ought to canvass the immediate neighborhood . . . see if anybody knows anything. I'll round up as many men as I can and send them door-to-door. I'll need a picture of her."

"You can probably get the one on her hospital ID from security."

"Is it any good?"

"It's actually not bad."

"They must have screwed up somewhere."

"What are our chances? We've probably got only forty-eight hours."

Gatlin sucked his teeth. "No way to know. We'll just have to get after it and see."

"Anything I can do?"

"Think positive."

When the door had shut behind Gatlin, Broussard's thoughts turned to Natalie and he headed for the TB isolation ward.

Upon reaching the first floor, he was joined on the elevator by an old man in baggy clothes and a Dallas Cowboys cap. With the old fellow was a slim young woman in jeans and a red jersey pullover, a four-year-old boy on one hand, a similar-aged girl on the other. Broussard guessed that they were here to visit the old man's wife or the young woman's husband. Either way, their lives had taken an unfortunate turn.

They were all forced to the back of the elevator by additional passengers—a couple of workmen with OTIS lettered above their pockets, a fellow with a clear plastic tube running from above the zipper on his jacket into his nose, a couple of nurses in purple scrubs, and an old woman oddly attired in a tailored blue suit and a red knit stocking hat. Whatever was in the black plastic garbage bag she carried was obviously heavy.

Broussard could name at least five serial killers whose careers would have been extremely short had the cops who pulled them over for minor traffic violations after their first kill looked in the garbage bag on the backseat. And more than once, a killer's handiwork had come to the morgue in such a bag. He was, therefore, probably more curious than anyone else on the elevator about that bag. But his interest was fleeting and his thoughts quickly returned to Natalie and Kit.

The TB ward was part of the Pulmonary Unit. When he arrived, the unit was structured chaos—phones ringing, people in every variety of hospital garb spilling in every direction, wheeling patients down the hall, pulling charts from the lazy Susan on the big round table behind the counter separating the nurses' station from the hall, sorting papers, checking reports on computers.

He stepped up to the counter, next to a balding, white-coated doctor he didn't recognize, and looked down at the black girl working the phone. She punched a button, switching the phone to intercom. "Team two call the desk . . . team two . . ." Switching to another line, she said, "Ma'am, I have no idea where that doctor is." And back to intercom: "Betty Jones, one-seven-nine-three . . . Betty Jones."

A woman in a beige suit came to the counter; she was carrying two green-backed charts. She gave the doctor next to Broussard one of them, cautioning him that, "He's not there. He's gone down for a bronchoscopy."

"Okay, thanks."

She looked at Broussard. Her name tag said she was the unit coordinator.

"I'm Dr. Broussard, the medical examiner. You have one of my assistants up here—Natalie D'Souza. I was wonderin' how she's doin'."

"I'll get the head nurse and you can talk to her about it." She picked up the phone and punched the intercom button. "Virginia Gardner, please come to the desk."

Two minutes later, a surprisingly young woman, who appeared to enjoy food as much as Broussard, presented herself. "Virginia, this doctor is inquiring about Natalie D'Souza. I don't seem to have her chart."

"Dr. Seymour has it." She looked at Broussard with brown eyes that had a slightly panicky look in them, and he suspected she'd only recently been given the responsibility of head nurse. "And you are Dr. . . ."

"Broussard. Natalie works for me. If Seymour is on the floor, I'd like to talk to him."

"Certainly. He's down here." Watching to see that he was following, she moved off in the direction from which she'd come.

The isolation ward was at the end of the hall. When they reached Natalie's room, there were two white-coated men conferring quietly in front of it. The one facing him and holding a chart was a slim, long-faced fellow wearing a thick brown Charlie Chaplin mustache and oversized pink-framed glasses: David Seymour.

"Dr. Seymour, this is Dr. Broussard. He'd like to talk to you about patient D'Souza."

Seymour smiled and extended his hand. "Hello, Andy."

As they exchanged a handshake, the other man turned, and Broussard saw that it was one of the few people in the city he'd cross the street to avoid.

"Andy, I think you know Mark Blackledge, chairman of Tropical Medicine at Tulane. . . ."

Blackledge nodded but offered no hand.

A broad shock of brown hair hung down almost to his eyebrows and on top his hair was quite disheveled, a look that could have been explained by the stiff breeze now drying the streets, except Broussard had never seen him groomed any better. He was not particularly heavy, but his face always showed a certain slackness, suggesting he'd recently dropped about thirty pounds. He had hard narrow eyes that reminded Broussard of the window slits in an armored car, and there were tight little bags under them. His pointed nose was thin like his lips, but his chin was round and fleshy. Under his unbuttoned lab coat, he was wearing a fuchsia sport shirt open at the neck, and no undershirt, so you could see chest hair. The total effect, especially when he gave that sly little grin now on his face, made you want to see if you still had your wallet.

They'd once been friends, and Broussard wasn't sure what had happened to change that. However, he knew *when* it had happened. Back before there was such a thing as the impaired-physician program, Blackledge was an alcoholic, and it had gotten to the point where the dean at Tulane wanted to fire him. But Broussard had intervened, convincing the dean to give him a leave of absence instead to get his problem under control, which he did. Since then, he'd become such an effective teacher and scientist he'd been made department head.

The trouble began immediately upon his return from his leave. He started making snide remarks about practically anything Broussard said at the local medical society meetings and did the same thing at social gatherings, where they seemed inevitably to cross paths. Broussard would comment on the high quality of the offerings in the current opera season; Blackledge would say it was third-rate and wonder aloud if Broussard had a tin ear. Broussard would decry the destruction of the Louisiana coastal marshes by the oil industry; Blackledge would sneeringly call him a Greenpeace fanatic who cared more for birds than people. And there were always nasty remarks about Broussard's weight. Once, when an ME trainee had mixed up some records and caused a minor but widely publicized problem for the police, Blackledge had written a scathing letter to the *Times-Picayune*, criticizing the ME's office for shoddy procedures.

It was all quite inexplicable, and eventually Broussard had given up on him. Now they shared a mutual dislike of each other. But with all that, Broussard's distress at seeing him had more to do with Blackledge's medical specialty and what it would mean to Natalie than it did with his personality.

"Hello, Andy." Blackledge looked him up and down, then turned to Seymour. "Wouldn't you think a physician would know the dangers of carrying all that weight?"

Clearly, Seymour didn't know what to say.

"Don't worry yourself, David," Broussard said. "Mark has decided to make a career out of boorish behavior."

"Look," Seymour said. "I don't know what you two have going, but could we forget it for now and get our attention on what's important here . . . the patient in that room?"

"Of course. You're right," Broussard said.

Blackledge said nothing.

"We haven't had time to do much lab work, but I know her blood chemistry and her clotting cascade are shot to hell and we're doing what we can to control that. I never thought I'd hope a patient had typhoid, but I'd rather she had that than most of the other possibilities. It'll take awhile for the cultures to come back, but she doesn't have a coated tongue or rose spots, so I think typhoid is out. I believe we can also rule out leptospirosis or an amoebic disease. Unfortunately, that leaves us with—"

"Viral hemorrhagic fevers," Broussard said grimly. Because most of these diseases are unknown in this country, Broussard was not alone in never having seen such a patient in his training days and probably wouldn't have seen one even had he chosen any other specialty than forensics. But he'd read enough to know that if Natalie had a viral hemorrhagic fever, she was in terrible trouble.

Seymour said, "That's why I asked Mark in. Nobody in the country knows more about those things than he does."

Broussard noticed that in response to Seymour's compliment, Blackledge subtly struck a pose he thought might look good on a coin. Then he looked at Broussard. "Was anyone with her before she became obviously ill?" he asked.

"I was."

"How'd she act? Did she say how she felt?"

Broussard related what had taken place in the morgue, including Natalie's odd behavior before she began to feel sick and her nosebleed began. While Broussard talked, Seymour added that information to her chart. Because it was largely conjecture, Broussard did not mention his speculations about the apparent susceptibility of the cortex and the resistance of the limbic system to the causal agent.

"I don't know exactly what she's got," Blackledge said. "But I've seen enough of these fevers to believe it's almost certainly a tropical virus, most likely a slight variation on one we've already cataloged. Unfortunately, none of them has a cure. Depending on the virus, ribavirin *sometimes* ameliorates the seriousness if it's given early in the disease, but when it's advanced, as in that girl's case in there, all you can do is deal with her physiological imbalances and hope she can fight it off. I understand she was infected from working on a cadaver in the morgue and that you now have two bodies that came in with it?"

"That's right."

"The girl's fate is out of our hands. The people we can really help are the other inhabitants of this city. We've got to know what the virus is. If we knew that, we'd have some idea of the way it's spread. And we've got to know soon." He looked at Broussard. "Brief me on the other two victims."

He listened carefully, then said, "Is there any information linking them with each other?"

"None."

"It sounds like Baldwin may be our index case. It's possible he infected the other one. Or they may both have become infected from a host that isn't sick."

"An animal?" Seymour said.

"Possibly."

"The police have an address book listin' all the calls Baldwin made before he got sick," Broussard offered.

"That's going to be important. I want that book."

"Isn't that somethin' that should go to the state's epidemiologists?"

"Those salaried little hepatitis chasers?" Blackledge sneered. "They're not mentally equipped to deal with this."

"Maybe they wouldn't agree."

"They already have. I'm the state's consultant for tropical fevers."

"Then I'll make a call and get you the book."

"Are you going to bring in the CDC?" Seymour asked.

Blackledge shot him a cold look. "Hell no. What do I need them for? I trained the people they'd send." Then to Broussard: "You've got slides on the two cases?"

"Only on the John Doe. There hasn't been time to process Baldwin's tissues, but his organs were so deteriorated, they're not likely to be of any use."

"What sort of pathology did you see in the John Doe?"

"The most significant was early stages of disseminated intravascular coagulation."

Blackledge's lips curled down at the corners and he shook his head. "I doubt that. In most of these hemorrhagic fevers, DIC isn't generally a feature."

"It may not *generally* be a feature," Broussard said. "But it was there."

"I'd like to see the slides."

Broussard hesitated, wavering between telling Blackledge that he knew DIC when he saw it or letting him take a look for himself. Finally, realizing how sweet it would be to hear him admit that DIC *was* present, he said, "You can see 'em."

"Good." He turned to Seymour. "I'll need a blood sample from the patient in there, double-tubed, with the outside of both tubes thoroughly wiped with bleach."

Seymour reached into the pocket of his lab coat. "Already done."

Blackledge put the tube in his pocket and looked at Broussard. "Okay, let's stop by your office and get those slides."

"We're not gonna *get* 'em. You're lookin' at 'em in my office and leavin' 'em there."

"Aren't we territorial?" Blackledge said. "As you wish."

Broussard looked at Seymour. "I'd like to see Natalie before we go."

"She's barely conscious," Seymour said. "And she won't know you're there. So, for your own safety, why not just look through the glass in the inside door. Otherwise, you'll need to gear up."

"I don't have time to waste," Blackledge said testily. "I've got to get this sample to my lab."

Broussard persisted. "Just a peek then."

The TB ward consisted of a series of double rooms with negative pressure, where all the airflow was directed from the hall into a staging room, then into the patient's room and out through a filtered exhaust.

Broussard went into the staging room, which, except for a sink and an isolation cart holding protective clothing, was bare. Above the inner doors, a red light that would come on if the pressure in the room rose too high remained off. He stepped to the windowed doors and saw Natalie in her bed—her face covered by an oxygen mask, monitors and machines for company, clear plastic tubing publicly trafficking in matters that should be private.

"Oh Natalie . . ." He sighed. He felt so damned responsible for what had happened. Saddened, he turned and went back into the hall, where he said to Seymour, "Have you notified her family?"

"Her mother's on the way."

"The slides . . ." Blackledge sniped.

"I'm ready."

The first word either of them spoke after leaving the Pulmonary Unit was when Blackledge saw Broussard's office.

"My God, man, how do you find anything in this mess?" he said, gesturing to the piles of reprints and journals.

"I manage," Broussard said. "The slides are over there on that tray."

Blackledge went to the microscope, sat down, and picked up a slide, which he put on the stage of the scope.

Broussard pulled another rolling chair around to where he could watch Blackledge's face while he examined the slide, but he saw no reaction.

Blackledge put that slide back on the tray and chose another.

Still no reaction.

He briefly studied three more slides, then stood up. "I've got to get this blood to the lab."

His unwillingness to discuss what he'd seen through the scope was an unceremonious sort of victory, but it was enough.

"I can't wait for that address book. You get it and I'll call and tell you where to bring it."

"I'll get it," Broussard said, "but don't count on me takin' it to you."

Blackledge looked incredulous. "Are we having a peck-order snit? That's one of your employees upstairs fighting for her life. As her superior, it was within your power to insist that anyone doing any dissection wear chain-metal gloves. Had you done that, she'd still be healthy. So I'd think you'd be more concerned with helping to get control of this disease than staking out turf."

It was a low but effective blow. "I'll get the book and then we'll see," Broussard said. "How long before you'll have results on the blood?"

"Twenty-four hours, maybe more . . . certainly no less."

9

When Blackledge was out the door, Broussard called Homicide and left a message for Gatlin to check in. He then got out a catalog, looked up chain-metal autopsy gloves in the index, and turned to the correct page. He carried the catalog into the main office, where Margaret, the senior secretary, turned from her computer screen.

"Any word on Natalie?" she asked.

"Things don't look good, but we've got to keep hopin'." He put the open catalog on her desk. "Would you order a pair of these gloves for each of our morgue assistants and for Charlie . . . and get 'em here as fast as you can?"

"What about you?"

"I don't need any."

The phone on Margaret's desk rang. "Medical examiner."

She looked at Broussard. "It's Lieutenant Gatlin."

"I'll take it in my office."

"Phillip . . . Andy. I just spoke with the person who'll be workin' the epidemiological angle on this disease and he wanted me to get that call book you found in Walter Baldwin's briefcase. Can you drop it by?"

"I expect he's in a big hurry."

“Anytime today will do. What do you hear from the hospitals?”

“She’s not in any of them.”

“I don’t know if that’s good news or bad.”

“It’s the best I can do for now. I’ll get the book to you later.”

As he hung up, there was a knock on the door and Charlie Franks came in.

“They’re finished cleaning up downstairs and we’ve got two fresh bodies to do, both gunshot victims, both clearly homicides, but apparently unrelated. Can you take one of them?”

“I’ll do both,” Broussard said.

“No need for that.”

“I’ve ordered chain-metal autopsy gloves for everybody. Until they come in, I’m the only one who’s gonna be doin’ any cuttin’.”

“Andy . . . you’re overreacting.”

“Probably so. But I’m also responsible for all of you. And I can’t take any chances.”

Franks shrugged. “You’re the one who has to do the extra work. If you change your mind, I’m available. How’s Natalie?”

“No good. They think we’re dealin’ with a tropical hemorrhagic fever virus.”

Franks’s face twisted in anguish.

“Yeah, I know. Mark Blackledge took some of her blood to see if he can identify the virus, but whatever it is, there’s no cure.”

“Any word on Kit?”

“She’s not in any of the hospitals.”

Franks looked at the floor. “Boy is this week off to a bad start.”

While Franks was on his way out, Broussard’s stomach rumbled and he checked his watch: 12:30—lunchtime.

Even for a food lover like Broussard, enjoyment of a meal requires the proper state of mind. The way this day had unfolded, his couldn’t have been less receptive. Still, the body must be served, so he bought a limp tuna-salad sandwich, an apple, and a can of orange juice from one of the hospital's mechanical canteens and ate in his office.

Performance of the actual autopsy by one person was not difficult, but turning the body front to back and moving it from the stainless gurney onto the autopsy table by yourself was tough. Therefore, he waited for Guy to get back from lunch before he started.

Three hours later, as Broussard was finishing with the second body, he took a call on the morgue phone from his secretary.

"Dr. Broussard, there are some people up here to see you."

"Who are they? I don't have any appointments scheduled for this afternoon."

"Teddy LaBiche and Dr. Franklyn's parents."

KIT'S PARENTS INSISTED THAT Broussard call them by their first names, Beverly and Howard. Beverly was a handsome woman—long dark hair with gray streaks in it, Kit's intelligent brown eyes, a fine nose, and a sensitive mouth. Dressed in a navy blue suit with white piping, she sat quietly in a chair in front of Broussard's desk, her hands resting on the purse in her lap—a proud private woman who didn't share her emotions with strangers.

More open about *his* feelings, Howard Franklyn paced. He was tall, trim, and square-jawed, with short sandy hair and a neatly trimmed brown mustache that went well with his tweedy brown suit. They looked like a prosperous and responsible couple, like the parents in TV sitcoms from the fifties.

Dressed as he always was, Teddy sat on the edge of the long table that held Broussard's microscope.

"Wish I could tell you more," Broussard said, coming to the end of what had been a distressingly short briefing.

"It isn't very damn much, is it?" Howard said indignantly.

Beverly gave him a cool look. "Swearing won't help."

"Sorry. I'm just . . . not good at handling unexpected adversity, and it makes me angry when it happens. I'm a banker . . . or I *was* before I retired. Made my living avoiding surprise reversals. And I don't let it happen in my personal life, either. So . . . this is hard for me."

Broussard nodded. "I understand."

"Kit talks about you a great deal," Beverly said. "About your ability to assess a situation correctly with very little to go on. What do you believe happened to her? Is she sick, do you think?"

"We don't have enough information to draw any conclusions. Actually, she hasn't been missin' all that long. It could mean nothin'. Maybe a friend of hers had some sort of emergency and needed her help."

"Why isn't her car missing, too?" Teddy asked.

"Whoever needed her help could have come by and picked her up."

"Why do that?" Teddy asked.

"Maybe the emergency wasn't at her friend's house. It was somewhere else and it was easier to drive Kit there. She could show up at any time, completely healthy and unharmed."

"Do you really believe that?" Howard Franklyn asked hopefully.

Broussard hesitated. No, he *didn't* believe it. Teddy had last seen Kit at 6:00 A.M., so if such an emergency had arisen, Kit would have realized she'd likely be late for work and would have called and left a message on the office answering machine. He glanced at Teddy and saw that he didn't believe it, either. "All I'm sayin' is, it's too soon to accept the worst."

There was a knock at the hallway door.

It was Phil Gatlin.

"Sorry to interrupt," he said, seeing everyone else there. "Andy, I brought that appointment book you wanted. Hey, Teddy . . . guess I know why you're here."

He crossed the room and handed the book across Broussard's desk.

Broussard introduced Gatlin to the Franklyns and they all shook hands.

"Is there any news?" Beverly asked Gatlin.

"Not yet. We've got men talking to her neighbors and people calling all the local numbers in her home and office Rolodex files. There are a couple of her friends we haven't been able to contact yet, but we'll probably reach them when they get home this evening. And every cop in the city has been alerted to the problem and given her description."

Howard made a slow rolling motion with his hand. "And . . ."

"Right now, that's all we can do. Where are you folks staying?"

"We haven't given it any thought," Howard said.

"You might as well stay at Kit's place," Teddy said. "I've got the key." Then he looked at Broussard. "Or is that a bad idea? I mean, is it safe?"

"There's no evidence Kit's even sick. And the house is extremely clean. So it would probably be okay. But why not play it ultracareful and stay elsewhere?"

"Where?" Beverly asked.

"This is a pretty popular time with tourists, but I'll find us all something," Teddy said.

"If you'll tell me where you end up, I'll let you know if anything happens," Gatlin said. He produced a card and gave it to Teddy.

Beverly got up, thanked Gatlin and Broussard for their time, and she, Howard, and Teddy gathered at the door, where Beverly turned and said, "This man who sent Kit flowers—the one who died—has he been identified?"

Broussard shook his head. "Not yet."

"Where are his . . . remains?"

"Downstairs. It doesn't look promisin' right now, but I still have hopes we'll turn up a relative so he can have a decent funeral."

"And if he stays unidentified?"

"A pauper's grave."

"With a headstone that says what?"

"No stone, just a little marker and number that won't last a year."

"I see."

She turned and the little group filed out.

Gatlin stood looking at the door, sucking his teeth in thought. Then he turned to Broussard. "That was odd . . ."

"What . . . Beverly's interest in the guy who died?"

"Yeah."

Broussard's phone rang. He picked it up and was told a small plane with five people on board had gone down in the sparsely populated eastern part of the parish and apparently there were no survivors. Could anything *more* possibly happen today? he thought.

Learning what had happened, Gatlin left so Broussard could deal with it. Before the door had shut behind the old detective, Broussard had Charlie Franks on the line.

"Charlie, grab your bag and meet me at the elevator. We got a plane crash."

Knowing he'd probably go home directly from the crash site when they finished, Broussard put Walter Baldwin's call book in his own bag and stuck his head into the main office. "Margaret, Charlie and I are gonna be at the scene of a plane crash near the space center. Call Mark Blackledge's office at Tulane and tell him I've got the book he wanted but I'll be tied up for several hours. If he wants to talk, he should call me later at home."

THE PLANE HAD EXPLODED on impact and the only parts of it still recognizable were the tail and the two engines. The rest was scattered like confetti over an area the size of four football fields, where it lay among the dirt cones pushed up by burrowing crayfish, which were already claiming the smaller pieces of the five victims. The gathering and matching of body parts was a garish, tiring endeavor and when Broussard and Franks were finished, they each felt amid the devastation around them a guilt-ridden tug of pleasure.

Upon arriving home, Broussard went to his study and checked for messages, his cat, Princess, trotting along behind him. Thankfully, the light on his machine glowed steadily.

Exhausted, he dropped into his leather reading chair and Princess jumped into his lap. Too tired to pet her, he let his hand rest on her neck, barely massaging it with one finger. He closed his eyes. But all that did was bring back the worst parts of his day and remind him he needed to check on Natalie. He shifted position to reach for the phone and Princess yowled in displeasure.

His call to the Pulmonary Unit went unanswered for so long he finally hung up in disgust. He sat for a few more minutes, managing to muster enough strength to add another finger to Princess's massage. Then he began to think of those quail eggs he hadn't had time to use. My God, was that only this morning? It seemed like days ago.

Heartened by the thought of what he could do with those eggs, he carried Princess to the kitchen and started laying out ingredients, all the problems he'd encountered in the last sixteen hours making the distant consequences of all the cholesterol he seemed to be eating lately of little significance.

Later, comforted by a full stomach, his blood warmed by two glasses of Chevalier-Montrachet, he changed into his pajamas, stretched out on the bed, and picked up the story of Bendigo Shafter where he'd left it.

After only ten pages, the book grew heavy in his hand and he put it aside and turned off the light.

Walter Baldwin's killer had probed the interior of the dresser for an hour after Broussard had left home following his misfortune with his trousers. In that time, it had not found its way to freedom. With no stimulus, it had grown quiescent and ceased its search. But tonight, when Broussard had opened the dresser to get his pajamas, the carbon dioxide in his breath had roused the little murderer and it had resumed its wanderings.

This time, it eventually found its way down the rear of the dresser's interior, to a place where a screw securing the back had loosened, allowing an eighth of an inch gap to develop.

And then it was free.

The carbon dioxide was stronger now and though the room had grown warmer during the night, it sensed a focal heat source nearby. Turning toward the bed, it scurried across the carpet.

In the bed, Broussard slept heavily, too tired to dream.

The tiny killer reached the carved legs of the bed and began to climb. At the intersection of the foot with the side rail, it ran along the rail to the dust ruffle and again began to climb.

A ballooned edge of the flannel sheet loomed in its path, but legs that could climb polished wood found this no obstacle, and it moved onto the flannel.

Upward . . .

Then, horizontally, hanging upside down as it traversed an overhang . . .

Around the lip of the overhang . . .

Along a slanting valley and up its edge to the corrugated surface of Broussard's lightweight green blanket.

A vertical ascent . . .

Then, the summit achieved . . .

Its simple nervous system tingling, legs flitting quietly over the blanket, death ran for Broussard's right hand.

10

Finally realizing that it had grown too warm for a blanket, Broussard sat up and threw it toward the foot of the bed in two motions, unknowingly catching the little murderer in a double fold. For hours thereafter, the killer tacked back and forth across the fold's short dimension, tethered by the heat from Broussard's feet below, so it made no progress toward escape.

At 3:00 A.M., the phone rang.

With effort, Broussard found the receiver and mumbled his name.

"Detective Evans here, NOPD Homicide. We've got a body lying in the gutter on Burgundy Street between Frenchmen and Touro. . . ." Suddenly, Broussard was wide awake. Burgundy . . . that was just a few blocks from Kit's place. "Is it a female?"

"No . . . a male, and he looks to have been strangled."

"He have a wallet?"

"No."

"Anything strike you as unusual about the case?"

"Well, he's wet, but that's because a street sweeper sprayed him."

To Broussard, this sounded like a common robbery-homicide. "No need for me there. Get him transported and I'll look at him in the mornin'."

Less than a minute after hanging up, Broussard was again asleep.

There was only one day of the week when Broussard made the bed before leaving the house, and that was Friday, the day the maid came. This being Tuesday, Walter Baldwin's killer was left folded in the blanket.

Upon arriving at the hospital, Broussard went directly to the Pulmonary Unit and headed for Natalie's room without speaking to anyone at the nurses' station.

Reaching the isolation ward, he went into Natalie's staging room and looked through the glass. Her bed was empty.

Heart pounding, he went back into the hall and stopped a pretty young nurse. "The patient in that room . . . is she out for a procedure?"

"What's her name?"

"D'Souza . . . Natalie D'Souza."

Her eyes clouded and Broussard's vision tunneled until he saw only her face. Heart in his throat, he waited for an answer.

"I believe she passed away."

"You believe," Broussard said sharply. "That's somethin' you say only if you know it for certain."

Anxiety flashed in the girl's eyes and she backed up a step. "I'll check at the desk. . . ."

Broussard followed her back to the nurses' station, where the girl beckoned the unit coordinator to the counter. "This man is inquiring about the patient in twelve twelve . . . D'Souza."

The unit coordinator looked at Broussard and her eyes went soft. "Yes, Dr. Broussard. . . . I'm sorry to have to tell you that Natalie went during the night."

"Went—" what a quaint way to put it, as if she might be back.

Working with death every day does nothing to harden you against the loss of someone close to you, and when you feel responsible for that death, it's much worse. When Broussard reached his office, he felt so tired, he wanted to lie down, but two of the seats on his sofa had journals stacked on them and he didn't have the energy to move them. He went instead to his desk chair, dropped into it, and rocked back.

Fingers laced over his belly, he sat staring at the door to the hall, picturing the last time Natalie had come through it. He sat that way for several minutes, trying to find the strength to face the day. Gradually, his concern for Kit washed over Natalie's death, temporarily muting its clarity.

He thought about calling Gatlin and checking on Kit, but surely he'd have called if there was news. Lord, if she was dead, too . . .

There was a knock on the door and Charlie Franks came in.

"Morning," Franks said. "Have you checked on Natalie?"

Broussard nodded. "She didn't make it."

"I know. I just called up there."

They both fell silent, neither of them knowing what to say about Natalie's death, neither wanting to trivialize it by changing the subject.

"She was one of the best techs I ever worked with," Franks said finally.

"One of the best," Broussard echoed.

Another gap appeared in the conversation, eventually flushing the rat gnawing at Broussard's conscience into the open. "If I'd ordered chain-metal gloves for everybody when they first came out, she'd still be alive."

"And if I'd scheduled her to work with me that morning instead of with you, she'd still be alive," Franks said. "If she'd been more careful, she'd still be alive. If that guy had died in Plaquemines instead of here, she'd still be alive. And if—"

Broussard lifted a limp hand. "I get the picture."

"Sometimes bad things just happen. Not because of oversight or carelessness, or bad judgment. Events occasionally simply converge to produce disasters. And to think you were responsible for Natalie's death is a pompous piece of horseshit."

Despite his troubles, Broussard managed a tepid smile. "Don't think I've ever heard you swear before."

"I suppose you'll want the blame for that, too."

Franks was as worried about Kit as Broussard was, but he quelled the impulse to bring that into the discussion, for fear it would cause the little tapestry of encouragement he'd woven around Broussard's sagging spirits to unravel. Figuring that more than anything else Broussard needed work to occupy his mind, Franks said, "I see we got a homicide downstairs along with the bodies from the crash. How do you want to divide the effort?"

Broussard did indeed feel a little better, but he still wasn't about to let Franks work on any body that might be carrying disease. The plane that crashed was coming from Jackson, Mississippi, so all those aboard should be safe to work on. "How about you take crash victims number one, two, and three. I'll do the rest."

Franks shook his head. "Not going to let me near that homicide, huh?"

"Not without metal gloves."

AT THE TOP OF the steps leading to Spanish Plaza, Phil Gatlin nearly collided with a guy in drag walking a pair of matching dalmatians. After they'd sorted out their respective routes, Gatlin watched the three of them depart, marveling at the sight. No sir, you just don't see that many matching dalmatians.

He then headed for the plaza fountain and the entrance to the Riverwalk, a linear mall that appropriately enough stretched along the river.

Inside, he took the stairs to the Hilton's Vieux Carre annex, picked his way through a herd of AARP members on their way to the casino, and stepped up to the annex elevators, vowing that when *he* retired he wouldn't travel in packs and he sure as hell wouldn't wear one of those kangaroo pouches in public.

He took the elevator to the third floor and found room 3019. This is going to be interesting, he thought, rapping on the door.

His knock was answered by Beverly Franklyn, wearing a clingy white blouse with wide lapels and pleated white pants with a two-tone brown belt, pearl earrings peeking from beneath her perfectly arranged hair. The woman had taste, no doubt about it. Over her shoulder, he saw that Howard Franklyn looked pretty spiffy, too, in a loose cream-colored pullover with flaps over the pockets, olive pants, and brown loafers.

Beverly wasted no time on small talk. "Have you found her?" she asked, obviously afraid of the answer.

"Do you mind if we don't do this in the hall?" Gatlin said.

"I'm sorry." She retreated into the room, allowing Gatlin to step inside and shut the door.

"Have you found her?" Beverly said again.

"No, but I can tell you she's not missing because she's sick."

"How do you know that?"

"We finally got in touch with her maid, who told us that when she arrived yesterday morning at eight o'clock, Kit was gone and the place was a wreck. She got it cleaned up and left before Dr. Broussard got there, which is why we didn't know about it then."

"And it never occurred to her to report that to anybody?" Howard asked.

"She just cleans houses, an' she don't meddle in other folks' affairs."

"When you say the house was a wreck . . . you mean like there was a struggle?" Beverly asked.

"More like someone looking for something."

"For what?" Howard asked.

"I've no idea. But I think whoever it was now has your daughter."

"I need a cigarette," Beverly said, going for her purse on the dresser.

"Are they holding her for ransom?" Howard asked.

For a nicely dressed guy, he could sure come up with some dopey questions. "We'll only know that if they ask for one."

Beverly came back holding a long cigarette with a filter tip between her fingers. She took a quick, nervous pull on it and turned her head to exhale the smoke. "Kit's been after me for years to quit," she said. "But I just don't have the willpower. Let's sit down."

She waved him to one of the chairs at a circular table in front of a broad window whose view of the river was blocked by a big sign on the building. She took the chair opposite him and pulled a nearby ashtray closer. Howard sat on the bed, which looked as though it hadn't been slept in. Neither had the other. Nor were there any clothes strewn around the room. Neat people.

"What do we do now?" Howard asked.

"Do you have an answering machine on your home phone?"

"Yes."

"Can you access it from here?"

"Of course . . . I should call and see if the kidnappers have contacted us."

He got up and went to the nightstand between the beds, where he punched in his home number. After a short pause, he added three more numbers, listened, and then hung up. "There's been no call."

"Somebody picking up your mail?"

"A neighbor, but there couldn't be anything there yet. Yesterday's mail came before we left and"—he looked at his watch—"today's won't come for another—"

"Remember, it's an hour later there," Gatlin cautioned.

Howard nodded. "It'll be there in another two hours."

"When it arrives, you should call and see what's in it. I'm gonna get the phone company to forward all your home phone calls here and I'll send somebody by to put a tape recorder on the phone."

"What do we do if they call?" Howard asked.

"Just listen and act cooperative. We'll come up with a plan when we hear what they have to say. We've contacted the issuers of Kit's credit cards and they're gonna flag her accounts, so if anybody tries to use them, they'll be spotted."

"I'd like to offer a reward for information about her," Howard said. "Do you have Crime Stoppers here?"

"We've got it, but I'd advise you to hold off on that."

"Why?"

"They hear there's a reward, they're gonna know that every snitch in town'll be on their trail. If they're still in the area, that could spook them into running and taking Kit with them. Then it all gets harder. Or they might panic and harm her. Cut us some time on this and let us see what we can do."

Howard nodded.

"That brings me to a question for you, Mrs. Franklyn," Gatlin said.

"What's that?"

"There's no doubt in my mind that Kit's disappearance is related to this fellow who arranged to meet her at Grandma O's restaurant . . . the guy in the morgue. . . . There's also no doubt in my mind you know who he is."

Beverly tried to look innocent, but better actors than she was hadn't been able to fool Gatlin.

"What makes you think that?"

"When we were all talking yesterday, you were too interested in him."

"I was simply showing concern for an unfortunate fellow human being."

"Uh-uh. You know him."

"This is outrageous."

"Look, if you want to see your daughter again, you're gonna have to talk to me."

Beverly looked at the floor for a while, then at Howard.

Sensing she was on the verge of tipping, Gatlin pushed her a little more. "If I knew who he was, it might help me locate her."

"It won't help," Beverly said. She stared at Gatlin for a couple of seconds, then caved. "He's my brother, Jack. But I haven't had contact with him in nearly fifteen years."

"Why'd you tell Kit you didn't know him?"

"He ran off with my parents' life savings, leaving them penniless. After that, I wanted nothing to do with him. When Kit asked us about him and I learned he was dead, I thought the simplest thing was to deny I knew him. But when we got to Dr. Broussard's office, I couldn't forget he was family."

"He sounds to me like a guy capable of kidnapping his sister's daughter for money."

"I'm sure you're wrong," Beverly said.

"Maybe so, but it needs to be pursued. Do you know the names of any of his friends?"

"It's been too long."

"No idea what city he lived in?"

"Not recently. Years ago, I got a couple of letters from him postmarked in Yuba City, California."

Gatlin entered this in his little notebook. "What was your brother's last name?"

"Hamilton."

"Any other brothers or sisters?"

"No."

"Wouldn't happen to know his Social Security number, would you?"

"It's all I can do to remember mine."

"Mind if I use the phone?"

Howard got up and moved away from the table between the beds.

Gatlin went to the phone and got the number for the Royal Sonesta from the operator. There was no answer in Teddy's room, so he left his name and office number with the desk clerk. Before leaving, he gave his card to Howard. "If you see Teddy, ask him to call me. And it might be a good idea for one of you to stay close to the phone here."

BROUSSARD FINISHED WITH HIS two plane crash victims a little after noon and returned to his office, still thinking about Gatlin's phone call. Kit kidnapped . . . possibly in a plot hatched by her mother's brother.

It was bizarre. And if true, Kit was in double jeopardy. Too many times when kidnap victims were found, it became clear they'd been murdered shortly after being taken. And Beverly's brother had been in the early stages of a disease that had already killed at least two others, so there was a good chance that whoever was holding Kit might also be infected and contagious. It just kept getting worse. . . .

His eyes fell on Walter Baldwin's call book on his desk, where he'd put it that morning when he'd come in. There had been no messages from Blackledge and he considered calling him about the book, but the man already knew he had it, so the ball was in Blackledge's court.

Still feeling guilty over Natalie's death, and believing he didn't deserve a decent lunch, he walked over to Canal Street and had the blue plate special at a five-and-dime, where he sat on a stool at the counter, next to a scruffy old man in a tattered army jacket who was nursing a cup of coffee and a doughnut. Finally, after he caught the guy staring at his plate for the third time, he bought one for him.

On the way back to his office, as the door was about to close on the hospital elevator, Nick Lawson, crime reporter for the *Times-Picayune*, got on.

"Hey, Dr. B. You're just the guy I was looking for."

"Obviously, you're havin' a better day than I am," Broussard said, pressing the button for his floor.

"I heard that Kit's missing, but I don't have any details. So I thought I'd check with you."

"Because you and I are so close?"

"You're not still upset over my story on the body mix-up in the morgue, are you?"

"Upset? No. Eager to grant your every wish . . . no again." The elevator stopped and the door opened. "Nice talkin' to you."

"I'm not asking this as a reporter," Lawson said, pursuing Broussard down the hall, "but as Kit's friend. I'm worried about her. And you wouldn't just be helping me. You'd be helping her."

Broussard unlocked his office door and turned to Lawson. "Helping Kit how?"

"I have a lot of contacts in this city. Most of them the kind of people you wouldn't open your door to, but they hear things and they'll talk to me. I need guidance, though. So how about it . . . for Kit's sake."

Broussard mulled this over. "Anything I say will be off the record?"

"I promise."

"What's your promise worth?"

"Off the record means I don't write about anything you tell me . . . ever, unless you say I can."

"Come on in."

Not completely comfortable about it, Broussard reluctantly told Lawson all that had happened. Afterward, sitting alone in his office, Broussard hoped he wouldn't have reason to regret his candor.

There still had been no message from Blackledge, so Broussard moved on to his next order of business, the strangulation victim.

He called downstairs, alerted Guy that he was coming, and headed for the elevator.

When he got to the morgue, Guy was putting the victim's clothing in a brown paper bag.

That morning when they'd worked on the crash victims, they'd done so without music, Broussard intentionally disrupting the routine as a tribute to Natalie. But everything had become so chaotic, he now longed for the old routines and some stability in the events around him. "I'd like some Mozart this afternoon. Disc four."

Guy went to the stereo and Broussard stepped over to the box of booties.

As he finished tying the first one over his mesh shoes, Violin Concerto no. 3 began, coming out of the dual speakers with such richness, he could almost touch it, feel it caressing his skin, filling the empty places in his heart, giving him hope. He donned his plastic apron, pulled on two pairs of gloves and a mask, and went to do battle with the other side of man's nature.

The body was that of a poorly nourished male between thirty and forty years old, with his mouth gaping in silent protest. Around his neck was a discolored band of skin an inch wide that bore no textural imprint, making Broussard suspect he'd been strangled with a belt.

The pressure of the ligature on the corpse's neck had produced petechiae, small hemorrhages in the whites of the eyes and the skin over the upper cheeks, so that he looked freckled. Broussard had lately become a palatal-mucosa connoisseur, looking at it on every cadaver at the earliest convenience. When the mouth was closed, that meant waiting until the cut along the lower jaw had been made and the tongue pulled down. In this case, there was no need to wait.

He got a dental mirror and a penlight from a nearby drawer and inserted the mirror into the corpse's mouth. Trying to keep the penlight from obstructing his view, he played its beam into the small, dark cave.

A scant second later, he woofed quietly, as though he'd been struck in the belly.

The palate was covered with red spots.

11

"What is it?" Guy asked as Broussard straightened up and looked off into space.

"He has palatal petechiae, like the body Natalie was workin' on when she cut herself."

Guy backed away. "So this one is infectious, too?"

It was a question Broussard couldn't answer. "Too soon to tell. It's not common to find petechiae on the palate in a strangulation, but it's not unknown."

"Maybe you shouldn't work on him."

"He may not be infected. And even if he is, you and I were both in the same room with Natalie's case and the one after that and we're fine, so unless I cut myself and some of his fluids get into the cut, there's no danger. And I'm not gonna cut myself."

Remembering that the detective who'd called about the case the night before said the victim had no ID, he checked the tips of the fingers to see if Homicide had already printed him. Finding inky evidence they had, he set about obtaining a set of dental X-rays.

When that was accomplished, he continued his external examination, finding nothing further of note until he got to the right hand, which was missing the tip of the index finger. He also recorded the presence of an appendectomy scar and an old wound on the lateral aspect of his right calf, which still looked as though something had taken a divot out of it. The calluses on his feet were extremely heavy and hard, suggesting he'd had some long-term occupational exposure to arsenic.

After turning the corpse facedown, Broussard noted on its back a mole with irregular edges and variable coloration that, had the man still been alive, would have called for a biopsy.

They turned him faceup again and Guy was made to stand well away from the body while Broussard carefully took blood, urine, and vitreous samples. All these were double-test-tubed and marked as biohazards. Then it was time to look inside.

Guy wheeled the gurney over to the autopsy table and together they lifted the body onto it.

In a strangulation case, it's important to document damage to the structures of the neck. This is best done in a dry dissection field. To accomplish this, Guy placed a wooden block under the corpse's shoulders so that when the brain and the organs in the thoracic and abdominal cavities were removed, the blood would drain away from the neck.

"Okay, thanks," Broussard said. "Now get outta here."

"You be careful," Guy said. "I kinda like working with you."

As Guy left, Broussard found himself wishing he'd told Natalie that when he'd had the chance.

Eager to get a look at organs that rarely if ever showed petechiae in a strangulation case, Broussard did not begin dissection at the chest, but went directly to the abdomen, opening it with a single decisive scalpel stroke from breastbone to pubic bone. Parting the incision, the first organ he saw was the liver.

Through his mask, he woofed again, for it was decorated with tiny pinpoint hemorrhages.

Ninety minutes later, with the autopsy completed, Broussard turned his mind to the consequences of what he'd found. A third case . . . and once again no identification on the body. No way to know where he'd come from, who he'd been with, and how he'd contracted the disease.

Concerned that they might find no match for the prints and knowing that even if they did, it wouldn't necessarily be very helpful, he decided to search for answers to those questions in the victim's clothing.

After changing gloves, he put a piece of plastic-backed absorbent paper on the gurney and spread the damp clothing out on the paper.

There wasn't much—a camouflage-colored T-shirt with a single pocket, a pair of black jeans with the seat worn thin and the legs turned up several times at the cuffs, brown socks with the elastic shot, and a pair of all-purpose black shoes with a dressy style but with padding sewn into the uppers so you could also run comfortably in them.

The label in the T-shirt was too faded to read, but the jeans had been made by Wrangler, not that it helped. Any lettering that had once been inside the shoes was gone.

Remembering the clues he'd found on the bottoms of the shoes belonging to Beverly's brother, he turned this pair over for a look, but he saw only smooth, unremarkable rubber, most likely washed clean by the street sweeper that had sprayed him.

He picked up the jeans and unfolded the left cuff, finding for his trouble only some damp lint. As he was unfolding the other cuff, something in it made a crinkling sound. It proved to be a crushed piece of tan cellophane.

Tan . . .

A color he'd seen before.

With fingers suddenly rendered stiff and clumsy, he unfolded the cellophane and drew a sharp breath.

The name was the same. . . .

Maybe it was just a coincidence. He couldn't be the only one who did that. . . .

He searched the smaller lettering on the cellophane. There . . . that should help him decide.

Not wanting to remove any of the victim's artifacts from the morgue, he memorized what he'd found and put the clothing back in the bag. He put a biohazard sticker on the bag and two on the corpse, then quickly shed his autopsy gear and hurried to the elevator.

Reaching his office, he dashed to his desk, pulled out the middle drawer, and shoved his hand inside. He came out with one of the cellophane-wrapped lemon balls he regularly bought for Kit from a confectioner in Paris. The cellophane he'd found in the pants downstairs had once held the same candy.

He'd never seen them available anywhere in this country, but if *he* could buy them through the mail, so could others. He found the lot number on the candy from his desk. . . .

It was the same as the one downstairs.

There was a chance he was wrong, but he knew he wasn't. The man on the table in the morgue had been involved in Kit's disappearance.

THAT'S LONG ENOUGH, TEDDY LaBiche thought angrily, throwing his legs over the side of his bed in the Royal Sonesta. Kit's father had told him about Gatlin's belief Kit might have been kidnapped, and he'd called Gatlin as requested. The guy who'd answered had said he'd contact Gatlin and have him return the call as soon as possible. That was ten minutes ago, and he wasn't waiting any longer.

A minute later, he stepped out of the hotel's front door and into the usual throng of tourists ranging down Bourbon Street. His destination was about fourteen blocks away, but there was no point in taking the truck . . . easier to go on foot.

He headed downriver, walking as briskly as the crowd would allow, ignoring a guy swallowing a four-foot red balloon, and, a few yards later, barely glancing at a magician standing in the street, marking off a circle around his props with water from a squeeze bottle. "Come on, folks, step up to the circle. We're not allowed to block the sidewalks."

At St. Louis Street, he turned toward the river and walked down to Royal, where the antique trade drew a somewhat smaller crowd. He had no real plan, just anger and the belief that the *Schrader,* the ship whose captain had been so uncooperative when he and Kit were down at the docks on Saturday, had something to do with her disappearance. All through the weekend, he'd had the feeling she wasn't through with that ship. If she'd returned to it Monday morning and become too aggressive . . . There his imagination stalled, because he had no idea why the captain would want to hide the fact the guy Kit was asking about had been on the *Schrader*—if indeed he had been on it.

He stayed on Royal until he reached Esplanade ten minutes later and turned toward the docks.

Another ten minutes brought him to the dock warehouse, which was much busier than when he and Kit had been there on Saturday, the forklifts now creating an obstacle course that gave him an uneasy feeling as he walked the central roadway between stacks of grain and cotton. Over his concern about being run down from behind, he began to think about what he was going to do. And he soon realized that if he met much resistance, he'd be thwarted.

Then, remembering the tiny pistol he always carried so he'd never be caught in one of his alligator pits unarmed, he felt better about his chances.

If necessary, he'd force them to show him every inch of the ship. The fact he'd never bothered to get a permit to carry the gun was of no consequence.

He arrived at the big door where the *Amaepma* still blocked the view of anything else and he went out onto the docks. He continued downriver until he cleared the stern of the *Amaepma,* then froze in disbelief.

The spot where the *Schrader* had been tied up on Saturday was now occupied by a different ship.

His concern for Kit blinded him to the simple truth that his trip down here was based purely on conjecture, and he became convinced that had the ship still been there, he'd have found her. But it was totally out of his hands now. The police would have to enlist the Coast Guard to run the ship down.

Hurrying back the way he'd come, he kept his eyes open for anyone using or carrying a cell phone, but he saw none. Reaching the point where he'd entered the warehouse, he went down the steps and across the crushed gravel and the railway tracks to N. Peters Street, where he paused to think.

Suppose he did find a phone? Who was he going to call—Gatlin? He hadn't been in earlier and might not be there now. Then what—stand around next to a pay phone or hang out in a grocery store for God knows how long?

When he was here Saturday with Kit, they'd walked down to the French Market and had seen three NOPD patrol cars, as if the area was some kind of cop hangout. And those cars would have radios that could probably contact Gatlin wherever he was. So that's the direction he went, arriving at the flea market section a few minutes later.

Saturday, the cops had been in the street that runs along the right side of the market. From where he was standing, the view of the street was obscured by hundreds of people and dozens of temporary flea market stalls with dolls and kites, straw hats, Chinese lanterns, and lacquered alligator heads hanging from their superstructures.

He plunged into the crowd, sidestepped his way along a display of sunglasses in a long white plastic display case, edged past a tarot reading table, a display of fossils, and a stall selling voodoo dolls, and then he was in the street, which was congested with vans and old pickup trucks loaded with produce . . . but no patrol cars.

Damn.

Hoping to find one, he crossed the street, stepped up on the sidewalk, and headed toward Jackson Square, passing on the way empty storefronts, produce wholesalers, and a lot of shabby endeavors whose purpose was not apparent.

At Ursulines Street, a plywood construction barricade around the next section of the French Market forced him to go right on Ursulines and continue his search down Decatur. Decatur was no Rodeo Drive, but at least it was lined with stores and shops that had real doors instead of chain-link gates and see-through windows instead of glass thick with paint.

But for all the improvement, it didn't produce a patrol car.

He was still looking for one when a guy carrying a brown paper sack stepped out of a grocery and came his way. He was wearing a red-and-green-checked short-sleeved shirt, olive slacks, and black Boston Celtics sneakers. He was clean-shaven and young—maybe mid-twenties—an ordinary guy who'd never have drawn Teddy's attention had he not been wearing a white cap with AMAEPMA across the front in red letters.

Teddy was aware that the cap the chief mate from the AMAEPMA had given Kit could not be the only one in the world and this fellow might even be from that ship. But as the two men passed each other, Teddy saw a small gold anchor on the cap.

12

Teddy kept walking in the same direction he'd been going, but at a slower pace and with a glance backward every few seconds. When the fellow in the cap was half a block away, Teddy stepped into the doorway of a Vietnamese restaurant and watched to see where he'd go.

At Ursulines, the guy turned toward the French Market and Teddy felt a stab of fear, realizing if he got in that crowd, he could just disappear. As the guy passed out of view behind the construction barricade, Teddy darted across the street and sprinted along the barricade after him.

At the corner, he pulled up and cautiously leaned around the barricade for a quick look. That same instant, a big mustard-colored camper turned onto Ursulines from Decatur and stopped behind two cars held up by some pedestrians crossing at the next intersection, so now his view was totally blocked.

Heart pounding in his ears, Teddy started around the rear of the camper, and for some fool reason the damn thing started moving in reverse, forcing him back to the barricade. Cursing under his breath in Cajun French, he ran along the camper and got a look at the sidewalk on the other side.

Empty.

He darted between the camper and the car ahead, leapt onto the sidewalk, and edged one eye around the corner of the intersecting street. Ten yards away, the guy in Kit's cap opened a chain-link gate and went through it.

Arriving there himself, Teddy saw the gate was set in a wall of chain link that sealed off an open storefront. He couldn't see what lay beyond the chain link because there was a paint-spattered tarpaulin hanging against it on the inside.

What to do?

He glanced down the street, but there were still no cop cars around.

The guy was in there now. Leave to get help and who knows where he'd be when it arrived.

Teddy's hand went to his chrome .22 pistol. Carefully, he lifted the gate latch, praying the gate wouldn't squeak on its hinges.

But it did.

He froze, then carefully let go of the gate so it wouldn't announce him again.

Anxiously, he looked behind him, toward the temporary plywood wall separating him from the produce market in the open-air building on the other side. He briefly considered running over there and looking for a bottle of olive oil, but to do that, he'd have to go around to the entrance on Ursulines, which meant he'd lose sight of the gate.

Pocketing the pistol, he went to an old Chevy nearby and popped the hood. It took about two seconds to find the dipstick, which he pulled and carried back to the gate. There, he stripped the clinging oil from the lower half onto one hinge and the rest onto the other. Wiping his fingers on his jeans, he went back to the car, replaced the dipstick, and lowered the hood.

This time, the gate barely whispered as it opened. Pistol in his right hand, Teddy moved forward, put his left hand through a slit in the tarp, and pulled the flap back.

In the small amount of light that crept into the building from the top of the tarp and came like dirty dishwater from a large passageway in the rear, Teddy saw that the place was a bare, bombed-out shell with piles of bricks and shattered pieces of lumber scattered over a cement floor. Watching his feet so he wouldn't kick anything, he moved toward the passageway in back.

When he reached it, he found himself at the mouth of an oval-roofed brick tunnel about fifteen feet high and thirty feet long that ended in an obviously sunlit space. Unaware that he was breathing through his mouth, he moved down the tunnel. At its end, he hugged the brick and stole a look at what lay beyond.

It was a courtyard containing an overgrown rose garden and a large but shabby house trailer. The thought of going for help surfaced again, but the possibility Kit was in that trailer shelved it.

The question now was how to approach the trailer. It was a problem he didn't have to solve, for his head suddenly exploded in a supernova of white noise.

THERE . . . THERE WAS SOMETHING he hadn't seen before. Between Broussard's gloved fingers, amid the strangulation victim's spread pubic hairs, was a raised welt with a central punctum . . . a bite of some sort. He hadn't noticed that the first time around. It wouldn't help lead him to Kit, but if he'd missed one thing, he could have missed another that *would* help.

He bent again and continued his minute scrutiny of the body, determined to find that lead.

But he discovered nothing, so when the phone rang twenty minutes later, his frustration was evident in his voice.

"Broussard."

"Hey, whatever troubles you're having, I'm not the cause," Blackledge said. "You got that book?"

"Did you receive my message?"

"Now I say yes and then you respond with something acid. Is that the plan? Never mind. I don't have time for these games. Yesterday, we inoculated some tissue cultures with samples of D'Souza's blood. . ."

"She died last night."

"I didn't know. . . I'm sorry. It won't help her, but I think we're close to knowing the causative organism. This morning, those cultures I mentioned had cellular inclusions in them and we began processing them for indirect immuno-fluorescence, using antibodies against every known hemorrhagic fever virus. Those results should be ready in about forty-five minutes. If you like, you can watch them come in on our closed-circuit TV. And you could drop off that call book."

Broussard hesitated. He wanted Blackledge to come to him for the book, but he also wanted very much to see the killer who'd taken Natalie, and perhaps by confronting it, find some respite from the guilt burning in his belly.

But there was Kit to consider. . . . He looked across the room at the eviscerated body of the strangulation victim, who had yet to give up the secret to Kit's whereabouts. He needed to keep looking. But he was tired now and his mind felt heavy and slow.

"You coming or not?" Blackledge asked tersely.

"Where are you?"

"Across the river."

Broussard had heard that Blackledge operated a lab on the West Bank in an old remodeled army ammunition bunker located in a sparsely populated area appropriate for work on hot viruses. But he didn't know exactly where it was. "I'll need directions."

Before leaving, he called Gatlin, who surprisingly was at his desk.

"Phillip . . . Andy. I got another body here showin' early stages of hemorrhagic fever. He was strangled sometime last night not far from Kit's house. And I found a lemon-ball wrapper tucked in his pants cuff, from the same French maker as those I buy for Kit, with the same lot number as my last shipment."

"I'm interested. We know who he is?"

"No. The detective handlin' it said there was no wallet on the body, and he got no match when he ran the victim's prints. I've been over the body twice lookin' for somethin' to tell me where he's been, but so far, nothin'. It didn't help that he was sprayed by a street-sweepin' vehicle."

"You don't know where Teddy LaBiche is, do you? He called me earlier, but when I got back to him, there was no answer at his hotel, and the Franklyns haven't seen him all day."

Broussard shook his head. "Can't help you. Somethin' I said made you think of that?"

"There's obviously a relationship between this disease we're seeing and Kit's disappearance. When we called Teddy in Bayou Coteau yesterday, he said something about going down to the docks with her and thinking they'd found a lead to the ID of the guy who died at Grandma O's. But the captain of some ship wouldn't let them talk to the crew. I want to know the name of that ship."

"If I hear from him, I'll get it for you."

"Who in Homicide is working the strangulation?"

"Evans."

"I'll get with him and make sure those prints have been properly run. Call me right away if you come up with anything."

"I sure wasn't gonna keep it to myself."

Broussard was soon headed across the Mississippi River in his turquoise T-Bird. Reaching the other side, he took General de Gaulle Drive and followed it over the Intracoastal Waterway all the way to its end, where he turned onto Highway 406. Shortly thereafter, he saw the sign Blackledge had told him to watch for, pointing to a road on his left: TULANE CENTER FOR VIRAL STUDIES, 2 MILES.

He turned the steering wheel against the buttons on his shirt and sent the T-Bird onto the side road. The area certainly couldn't be described as *heavily* populated, but it did contain an elementary school and a baseball diamond, things he never expected to see this close to the lab. About a mile from where he'd left 406, the Mississippi River levee suddenly loomed before him. On the levee was another sign, directing him left again, to an open gate and down a road that for a time ran through a grassy stretch where an amazing number of armadillos nosed the turf. Their presence made him reflect on what odd creatures they were, the only animal known to contract leprosy and one that when pregnant always bore identical quadruplets. He wondered if they also got tropical hemorrhagic fevers.

The grass gave way to marsh and a verdant carpet of sharp-leafed arrowhead lilies that were being plied by two egrets and a night heron, so intent on what lay in the water around the lilies, they ignored the car. One of the egrets stabbed at the water and came up with a crayfish that he expertly downed, tail-first.

The marsh disappeared into swamp, made darkly sinister by legions of skinny black gum and tupelo that closed ranks against the sun. But where the swamp was cleft by asphalt, the sun was given opportunity, and it clothed the trees in wild roses and yellow jasmine. Broussard rolled his window down and breathed the jasmine scent deep into his lungs; then, picturing viruses from the lab riding that fragrance, he quickly closed it.

A short time after he'd entered it, the swamp suddenly yawned, the blacktop widened, and he was there.

The lab was in a sprawling gray cement structure built like a Quonset hut, its long silhouette clandestinely hugging the ground.

Five cars, a pickup, and a van occupied half the available spaces arranged vertically in front of the lab. Broussard pulled into one designated for visitors, picked Walter Baldwin's call book off the passenger seat, and left the T-Bird.

He didn't go in immediately, but paused to assess the place.

There was a strip of well-tended grass along the roadside here as well as around and, presumably, behind the lab, creating a civilized oasis. But where the grass ended, the swamp waited, pressing in on the little clearing, seemingly waiting to reclaim it.

Removed as it was from the bustle of the city, one could reasonably expect it to be quiet, but it was spring and the frogs were in full throat. Adding to their green din was a loud mechanical hum from behind the lab.

There was a big vent above the glass doors at the entrance, and as Broussard went in, he saw a veritable moth museum plastered against its gridwork, apparently pulled to it and held there by the lab's constant need for fresh air.

Inside, in a carpeted, windowless alcove, he found a gray-haired lady behind a chrome and black-metal desk backed by a row of black file cabinets. On the wall above the files hung a large photo display of geometric shapes with fuzzy protrusions all over them. The largest photo around which all the others were arranged looked like a child's concept of an alien—a diamond-shaped head, a stick body, and six filamentous feet. Broussard recognized this as some sort of bacteriophage, a virus that preys upon bacteria. He could not call the names of the other viruses shown.

"Would you be Dr. Broussard?" the gray-haired lady asked kindly.

Broussard admitted his identity and she directed him through the double doors behind him to the first door on the left.

He entered a short hallway and knocked on a dark mahogany door with Mark Blackledge's name and all his degrees displayed on a brass plaque.

From inside, he heard a booming, somewhat exasperated voice, say, "Come on."

Blackledge was seated at the largest French *bureau plat* Broussard had ever seen, inlaid with tooled red leather, gleaming ormolu figures mounted on its delicate legs. And it wasn't a reproduction. The man might be a bore, but he had excellent taste in furniture.

He waved Broussard into a gilt-trimmed French chair of pickled wood and resumed the phone call Broussard had interrupted.

"I don't care if he is your best man—that hood is not drawing correctly. . ."

From his chair, Broussard briefly admired the Boulle ebony cabinet intricately inlaid with brass and red tortoiseshell sitting a few feet to Blackledge's left, then shifted his attention to a pair of matching two-tiered George III mahogany bookcases on the adjacent wall. Opposite the bookcases and against the other wall was a huge French bombe commode under an oil painting depicting an Amsterdam canal scene, the latter almost certainly done by Bartholomeus Van Hove. Van Hove was not a major star, but the painting was certainly a quality work worthy of the other furnishings. Three other items were totally out of keeping with the rest of the decor. But they were so interesting Broussard left his chair for a closer look.

One of those items was a black Moorish hat rack exhibiting three heavy scroll-carved brackets under a thick shelf that rested at each end on the back of a crouching, beaked gargoyle. On the shelf, held upright by a wire stand, was an African mask made of wood, but with a green patina that almost gave it the appearance of metal. It had a wide mouth full of sharp teeth and a wild head of flyaway hair made of some kind of dried grass woven into a mat where it rested on the skull.

"For years that was worn by a member of the Ekpo secret society of the Ibibio tribe in Nigeria," Blackledge said, joining Broussard. "It was primarily used to exorcise demons at the yam harvest. They gave it to me in appreciation for my help in stopping an outbreak of *chikungunya.* This one"—he pointed to an adjacent dark brown mask shaped like a light-bulb; it was hairless and bore very simple features; a smooth band ran from the top of the head to the nose, but the rest was heavily grooved with parallel white lines—"is a Kif-webe mask from the Bena Mpassa tribe," Blackledge continued. "Appropriately, the tribal priest wore this one in ceremonies to drive plague from the village. It was given to me for saving them from a particularly nasty strain of dengue hemorrhagic fever."

"And how did you save 'em?" Broussard asked.

"By showing them that the mosquito vector was living in discarded water-filled tin cans in the village dump."

Seemingly from nowhere, a bodiless voice said, "Dr. Blackledge, I'm about to look at those slides. . . ."

Blackledge returned to his desk and pressed an intercom button. "Give us a few minutes to get set up."

He turned the Boulle cabinet so that it faced directly forward and opened the doors, revealing a TV and a VCR. He flicked on the TV and looked at Broussard.

"Pull a couple of those chairs over in front of the screen, will you?"

Broussard put the call book he'd been carrying on Blackledge's desk and arranged the chairs. Behind the desk, a bank of drapes hung from floor to ceiling all along the back wall. Blackledge touched another button and the drapes opened. Behind them were two wide glass windows through which two laboratories could be seen.

On the right, a figure in a yellow space suit with an oxygen line plugged into the wall sat at a tissue-culture hood, pipetting a red liquid into a stack of petrie dishes. In the other, a technician dressed only in a blue lab coat was adjusting the settings on a microscope fitted with a TV camera.

"The lab on the right is a level-four containment facility," Blackledge said. "On the left, it's an ordinary lab. You'd be surprised how diligent your help is when they know you can see them anytime you wish. There's a decontamination chamber in the wall separating the two labs to allow things to be passed from the hot side to the cold."

"And the fellow at the microscope is working with slides from cultures exposed to D'Souza's blood?"

"That's right."

"Why isn't he doin' that in the hot lab?"

"The slides have all been treated with gamma radiation, so they're now harmless." He leaned toward the intercom. "All right, we're ready."

The tech at the scope put a slide on it, bent his head to the eyepieces, and fiddled with the stage controls. On the TV screen, blurred ghostly images slipped by at a nauseating pace. Then the movement stopped and the image cleared, showing a field of translucent pancakes dotted with granules—the typical appearance of cells viewed with phase contrast.

"Those are green-monkey kidney cells," Blackledge said, sitting in the chair beside Broussard. In his hand was a sheet of paper Broussard guessed was a list of the slides in the order they were about to be examined.

"And you think these cells are infected?"

"We wouldn't be sitting here if they weren't."

"How can you tell? They look healthy to me."

"That's why I'm in charge and you're not."

The tech at the scope pressed a foot pedal and the lab was plunged into darkness.

"This first slide was treated with antibodies to the yellow fever virus. If we get a positive, it'll show up as green dots."

In the lab, a narrow beam of bright green light flashed on at the scope as the tech pulled the filter blocking the UV light source. But the TV screen remained black.

"One down," Blackledge said, marking off the first entry on his sheet of paper.

The tech in the lab turned on the overhead lights so he could change slides.

"This next one is Lassa," Blackledge said.

The lab lights went off and the green light came on. Still the TV screen remained black.

The third slide had been tested for Machupo, and again the screen remained black.

One by one, Blackledge called the roll of the most dangerous organisms on earth. . . .

"Junin."

A black screen.

"Ebola."

A black screen.

"Marburg."

Black.

"Kyasanur Forest disease."

Black.

"Hanta."

Black.

"Dengue hemorrhagic fever."

Black.

The lights in the lab came on again.

"We could be in trouble," Blackledge said. "There's only one left. If it's negative, we're dealing with something entirely new."

The lab lights went out and the green beam flicked on. On the TV screen, the black universe lit up with dazzling green stars.

"Gotcha, you bastard," Blackledge said, leaping out of his chair. "It's CCHF," he said, looking at Broussard. "Congo Crimean hemorrhagic fever. We got very lucky. The symptoms your technician had and the DIC on those slides you showed me—that's not classic CCHF. So we're probably dealing with a slightly altered form. Fortunately, it still has many of the same antigens as the parent strain. Now we know what we're looking for."

He went behind the desk and leaned into the intercom. "Good job, Dan." He pressed the button for the drapes and they slid shut.

"So what *are* we lookin' for?" Broussard said.

"Follow me and I'll show you."

Blackledge led Broussard to a door between the two mahogany bookcases. On the other side was another laboratory. He beckoned Broussard to an aquarium half-filled with sand and topped with a screen cover. "Wait there."

He crossed the room to a bank of cages and came back with a hairless, pink-skinned newborn mouse. "Watch this."

He lifted the screen and put the mouse in the aquarium, where it lay squirming and kicking on the sand. They watched the mouse for perhaps twenty seconds, during which nothing happened.

Broussard looked questioningly at Blackledge, who held up a cautioning finger.

"Don't be in such a hurry."

Suddenly, the sand began to boil and it came alive with wiggling legs thrusting upward. Soon, the sand was carpeted with tiny creatures that skittered toward the little mouse. In an astonishingly short time, the mouse was completely covered with them, until not one millimeter of pink skin could be seen.

"Ticks," Blackledge said. "They'll feed until he's exsanguinated."

Broussard turned away in disgust.

"Oh, come on," Blackledge said. "You've seen worse things than that."

"But none that I caused."

"It's a natural part of life—predators and prey. Get over it."

As disgusted as Broussard was, he now knew what had made the small reddish nodule on Beverly's brother and the obvious bite mark on the strangulation victim.

"Of course, these are soft ticks," Blackledge said. "We're probably looking for a hard tick, most likely Hyalomma. The virus is in their saliva. When they bite, there's a transfer."

"The heart attack case with early symptoms had a bite mark on his calf," Broussard said. "This mornin' we got in a strangulation victim with early stages of the same disease as the others and he had a bite mark in his pubic area."

"Why haven't I heard about bites before this?"

"Before today, I'd seen only one and I didn't know what it meant."

"Well, now you do."

Blackledge went to a refrigerator and removed a transparent plastic vial whose top was sealed with gauze held on with a rubber band. He took it over to where Broussard was standing and held it up. Inside, near the bottom, was a large dark spot. He lifted the vial to his lips and exhaled into it. Immediately, the blob burst apart as tiny flyspecks scattered in all directions.

"Seed ticks," Blackledge said. "Responding to heat and carbon dioxide. They've got receptors for both on their front legs. When they sense either one, they know there's prey nearby and they go after it. They can also detect ammonia and hydrogen sulfide, so they could find a cow by its piss and its farts even if it was ice-cold and holding its breath."

He put the vial back in the fridge.

"Even in the driest of climates, they never want for water, because they secrete a hygroscopic salt on their mouth parts and drink the water it draws. If there's no food available, they're very patient. There's a cave in Africa where ticks have been known to lie dormant in the sand for twenty years, and then, when an animal wanders in, they come up out of the sand just like in the aquarium and feed. When a female becomes infected with something like CCHF, she passes the virus to all of her offspring, which, in the case of the species we're most likely dealing with, can lay upward of fifteen thousand eggs."

"Obviously, these ticks are found naturally in the Crimea and Africa . . ." Broussard said.

"Obviously."

"We found an African coin in the pocket of the victim who died of a heart attack. Maybe he and the strangulation case were bitten in Africa and flew here before the disease progressed very far, which would mean there aren't any African ticks in the city."

"I don't have a grasp of the chronology of events, so I can't address that yet. Let's reconstruct things over here."

Eyes shining with excitement, Blackledge went to a calendar hanging on the wall and picked up a lab marker. "John Doe died when?"

At the moment, there seemed no point in telling him they now knew that victim's name, so Broussard simply said, "Last Thursday."

Blackledge entered this in the appropriate square on the calendar. "And Baldwin was found . . ."

"Yesterday, but he'd been dead four or five days and had been in the terminal stages another two before he died."

"Which would mean he likely became seriously ill the previous Monday or Tuesday." He entered it as Monday. "D'Souza cut herself the day John Doe died?"

Broussard nodded and Blackledge entered that data.

"And she became seriously ill yesterday." He added that, briefly studied what he'd done, and turned back to Broussard. "It's certainly not true that the incubation period will be the same for all routes of infection, and it will likely vary somewhat in different individuals infected by the same route, but let's use D'Souza's four days as the average time between exposure and advanced symptoms. That would place Baldwin's exposure around the sixteenth." He entered that and boxed it. "Now, John Doe was in the early stages, so let's say he was exposed two days earlier, which would be the twenty-first." He put that on the calendar and boxed it. "Did you find a bite mark on Baldwin?"

"No, but his skin was so decomposed, there could have been one I didn't see. The bites I found were on both the others."

"Let's put the strangulation on here. Died . . ."

"Late last night, early stages about like John Doe."

Blackledge wrote the exposure date for the strangulation victim as the twenty-fifth. "And he had a bite?"

"Like I said."

"Baldwin was exposed five days before John Doe was and nine days before the strangulation received his. So *they* couldn't have passed it to *him* in any way. The timing is such that theoretically, Baldwin could have passed it to John Doe, but that guy had a bite mark to account for his exposure. There are just three ways Baldwin could have acquired the disease—from another person, from being bitten in Africa, or being bitten here. Where's that book?"

"On your desk. I'll get it."

Broussard returned with his nose in the book. "On the fifteenth, sixteenth, and seventeenth, he made calls all day around the city."

"So much for being bitten in Africa. It also tells us that if he was infected from someone else, it had to be someone nearby. But there've been no other cases reported in the entire state. I checked."

"Maybe there were others but they weren't severe enough to draw any attention."

"We know of four cases so far, two in which the disease was the cause of death and two . . ."

"That looked like they were gonna be bad," Broussard admitted.

"Even a fifty percent fatality rate suggests that any case would be severe," Blackledge said. "Then, too, where are all the cases the salesman could have infected if it can be transmitted person to person? There should have been some fatalities from that by now. But there's been nothing else. No . . . we've got ticks in the city—most likely that have come in on some animals."

"Any particular kind?"

"They'll parasitize almost anything."

"So if the hosts come from a dealer who trades in animals from a lot of countries . . ."

"It wouldn't have to be an animal indigenous to the Crimea or Africa," Blackledge said quickly, seemingly not wanting Broussard to score *any* points in the conversation.

Broussard chalked it down as just another flaw in Blackledge's character, forgetting all the times he'd done the same thing himself to Phil Gatlin. "Could those antibodies you analyzed the infected cells with also be used to treat the disease?"

"Possibly, if I had more of them. All I've got is enough for testing."

"Let's get some more."

"We can't. They came from a fellow in Zaire who nearly died from the disease. Two months after he gave us the blood we used to extract the antibodies, he fell out of a tree and broke his neck."

"There must be other people there carryin' 'em."

"I'm sure there are. But it's such a chaotic country—there are no records to tell us who they might be, and even if you knew who they were, you couldn't find them. Hope you didn't have any plans for tonight."

"Why?"

"We'll be busy tracking the source of those ticks." Seeing Broussard's surprised expression, he added, "Surely you're coming along."

Having never given this any thought, Broussard had no answer ready. At first, it seemed like an easy call. This was Blackledge's responsibility, not his, and the sooner they parted company, the better. But then his frustration at not being able to affect in any way the events raging around him and the fact this disease was at the core of Kit's disappearance caused him to say, "Of course I'm comin'."

13

Teddy's eyes flickered, then opened wide in surprise.

"Thank God," Kit whispered. "I thought you might never wake up." Kit had just been through the worst day and a half in her life and now, because of her, Teddy was in the same situation. She hated that and herself for finding comfort in his presence.

They were lying face-to-face on a bed in the trailer, hands bound behind them with twine, ankles tied, as well. Not realizing the situation, Teddy tried to change position.

"I can't move."

"Your hands and feet are tied," Kit said. "Mine, too."

"What's going on? I feel like I've got a bowling ball on the back of my head."

"They hit you with something and you're cut."

"Who hit me?"

"Roy . . . I don't know his last name. From what they said when they brought you in, I gather you followed his brother Larry in from the street and Roy followed *you*. I'm sorry you got involved in this."

"Where are we?"

"A trailer in some courtyard, but I don't know where. When they brought me in, I was blindfolded."

"I came in from French Market Place. How'd they get you in here without anyone seeing what was going on?"

"They dressed me in a big hat and coat that hid my blindfold and the fact my hands were tied."

"Anyone else in the trailer?"

"Not at the moment."

"I guess the door to the room is locked."

"And the trailer, too."

"Let me try and untie you."

They rolled in opposite directions and Kit wiggled toward the foot of the bed so Teddy's fingers could reach the knot at her wrists.

"Can you do it?" she asked.

"I'm trying, but the knots are really tight. What's this all about?"

"I don't really know. When I came back from walking Lucky yesterday morning, three men jumped me in front of my house, took me inside, and began questioning me about some money Jack, the heart-attack victim, supposedly gave me. I told them the only things he gave me were three roses and that he said only one word to me before he died. But they didn't believe me."

"Why'd they think he gave you money?"

"They won't say. They took me to an ATM and forced me to get a balance statement to see if I'd made any big deposits recently. When they saw how little was in my accounts, they emptied them and took me back home and tore the place apart. Now they're trying to starve me into telling them where it is."

"Bastards," Teddy muttered, continuing to pick at the twine knots.

"I heard Roy yelling at Larry for being so stupid as to wear my cap out on the street. Does anyone else know we're here?"

"No."

Kit closed her eyes and moaned. "I was afraid of that."

"You say there are three of them?"

"It started with three, but Roy killed the one called Burras—right in front of me. It was horrible. But it may help us. You know that big bowl of lemon drops from Andy that's in my pantry? . . . Well, Burras found them and took a handful. When we got back here, he put them on the kitchen counter and had been sucking on them constantly."

"Come this way a little. . . ."

Kit turned. "Are you getting it?"

"Not so far. What about Burras?"

"He was a horny little shit, like Larry. Both of them had been taking turns coming in here and running their hands over me until Roy stopped them. . . ."

"We get out of here, I'm gonna be running my hands over *Larry*."

"So Burras came in here, sat down on the bed, unwrapped a lemon ball, and offered it to me. I refused, but he kept trying to put it in my mouth. Then, Roy came up behind him and, without saying anything, strangled him with a belt and left the body lying next to me while Larry went for the panel truck they drive. I heard Roy tell Larry that Burras stole part of some shipment they're guarding and Larry should take that as a lesson."

"Damn, these knots are tight."

"While I was alone with the body, I managed to tuck the wrapper from the lemon ball in the cuff of Burras's pants, hoping they'd dispose of the body in the city limits and it'd end up in the morgue, where Andy would find it. They weren't gone long, so I'm hoping for the best. I have been missed, haven't I?"

"That's how I came to be here. At first, Andy thought you were sick with the same disease Jack had."

"What do you mean, heart trouble?"

"Jack had a disease that makes you hemorrhage to death. One of Andy's assistants cut herself during Jack's autopsy and she's sick with it."

"Natalie? Is that who it was?"

"I don't know her name. Roll away from me a little. . . . Good. What if Andy does find the wrapper? How's that gonna help him find *us?*"

"Occasionally, they both leave for about thirty minutes, and when they come back, they have something glittery on their shoes. After a few hours, it seems to wear off; then when they go to that place again, it's back. They must have gone there just before Roy strangled Burras, because when I was left alone with his body, I saw a lot of it on *his* shoes. I'm hoping Andy can figure out what it is and can track them to wherever they're picking it up."

"Those aren't odds *I'd* put any money on."

Kit had been trying to stay optimistic and not give in to despair. Teddy's criticism of the one thing she'd been able to do to help herself was more than she could take. "Well, it's the best I could do. And if it seems far-fetched, you come up with something better."

"Sorry, you're right. If I'd been in your place and was smart enough to think of it, I'd have done the same thing."

There was a sound from the front of the trailer—a key in the lock.

"They're back," Kit hissed.

A door opened out of sight and the trailer vibrated under the kidnapper's footsteps. A metallic scratching came from the other side of the bedroom door and it slid open.

"He's awake," Larry yelled over his shoulder.

In one hand, he held an ugly revolver; in the other, a pocketknife.

"I got a score to settle with both of you for getting me in Dutch with Roy over that cap," Larry whispered. "So have no doubts, when this is over, I'll feel better about it. Maybe I'll take a down payment now."

He advanced on Teddy with the knife and slid the tip into Teddy's left nostril. "I saw this once in a movie with Jack Nicholson and I've been wanting to try it ever since."

"No . . . please don't hurt him," Kit pleaded.

What Larry was about to do was made doubly horrible and almost surreal by the fact there was not one hint of evil in his face—no glint in his eye, no bared teeth—just a good-looking, well-groomed kid you'd think probably made a small fortune mowing lawns when he was in high school and invested it all in Walmart stock.

"What's the holdup in there?" Roy yelled from the front of the trailer.

"Nothing. We're coming."

Larry pulled the blade from Teddy's nostril and bent toward Teddy's feet, where he cut the twine binding them.

"We'll get together another time," he said, as if they were all great friends. "Now, Roy wants to see you."

He cut the twine at Kit's ankles and stepped back into the adjoining bathroom. "Go see Roy."

Teddy started out first, then hesitantly stepped back and allowed Kit to precede him. She had trouble herself deciding which was the better choice—first to see Roy or having Larry directly behind her.

Roy was sitting on the living room sofa, one leg crossed over the other, both hands cradling a small bottle of apple juice perched on his knee. He was wearing faded black denim jeans, a similarly colored denim shirt, and heavy work shoes that laced around metal studs.

From the first moment Kit had seen him, he'd reminded her of an android. Mostly, it was his eyes—the palest color of blue, with tiny pupils that never changed diameter—eyes with no feeling, a mannequin's eyes, worked by machinery located in two faint lumps halfway up his high forehead. And he had thin, colorless mannequin lips that looked as cold as plaster.

"Kit, you sit there." Roy nodded to a ratty armchair by the door.

Kit glanced back at Teddy. "He needs to see a doctor about that cut on his head."

"Sit down."

Since it was pointless to resist, Kit sat.

"And Mr. LaBiche—is that how it's pronounced?"

His pronunciation was flawless, but Teddy said nothing, his black eyes blazing.

"I see. Well, that's too formal, anyway. Let's just make it Ted. Larry, put Ted in that chair. . . ." Roy gestured to a metal folding chair someone had painted white so it would blend with some obviously crappy decor.

Larry led Teddy to the chair and pushed him into it.

"Kit, you know what we want, yet have refused to help us. As I have great respect for women, I've resisted Larry's suggestions as to how we might convince you to cooperate. Instead, I've chosen to deny you food or water. That, of course, is a slow method, and now I believe providence has sent us another. . . ." He looked at Teddy. "That would be you, Ted." He turned back to Kit. "Incidentally, I think you two are doing the right thing by determining if you're sexually compatible before you take such a major step as marriage. Very wise . . . I didn't always think so, but I've seen so many marriages break up over that one thing, I've changed my views. It's one of the reasons I left the ministry. Larry, get two towels from the bathroom."

Roy dropped his right hand to the sofa and picked up Teddy's pistol, which was resting beside him.

Larry returned shortly, carrying two faded green towels with tattered edges.

"Put one on Kit's lap," Roy said.

Larry began to drape one of the towels over Kit's thighs.

"Better fold it a couple of times," Roy said.

Larry adjusted the towel and replaced it in her lap.

"Now put the other over Ted's left shoulder."

Larry did that and waited for further orders.

Kit's heart was thudding in her temples and the drought in her parched mouth deepened, for she knew what Roy had in mind.

"Kit, where is the money Jack gave you? Larry, if she doesn't answer in five seconds, cut Ted's left ear off and put it in her lap."

Kit was certain this was no idle threat, but there *was* no money. How could she give them money that didn't exist? "It's coming by mail," she heard herself say. "Jack said to start looking for it on . . ." Her mind grappled with the days of the week, trying to remember what day it was. "On Wednesday." No. She should have said Friday to buy more time. Stupid, stupid, stupid.

Roy waved his hand at Larry and focused those android eyes on her. "Why did he mail it? And why the delay?"

"He didn't say. We actually didn't have much time to talk."

"Jack died last Thursday. So if he did mail it to you, he'd have had to do it that day or earlier. Why did he think it would be six days before it arrived?"

"Could it be that he perceived the postal service as poorly run and inefficient?" Kit said.

Roy lapsed into thought and he sat for a few seconds absolutely still, as though his batteries had given out. Finally, emerging from this glacial state, he abruptly said, "I'm going to clarify my position, then give you a chance to modify what you've said. If you tell us where the money is, we'll hold you until our business in the city is finished; then we'll depart, leaving both of you unharmed and with the means to free yourselves after we've had sufficient time to be safely away. On the other hand, if you're lying about the money, which will become apparent if it doesn't arrive by Saturday, we'll kill you. Now, do you want to change anything about the story you've told me?"

When it came to spotting a liar, Kit was a professional—but even an amateur would have realized Roy was lying. Kit had seen him strangle Burras. There was no way he was going to let them go. She and Teddy were dead regardless of what she said. "The money is in the mail, like I said."

"When is it delivered each day?"

"Between nine and nine-thirty."

"How do you know that?" Larry said. "Aren't you usually at work by then?"

"When I take an occasional day off or when I'm on vacation, that's when it comes."

Roy once again lapsed into a voltage deficit while everybody else waited for his next pronouncement. When it came, it was the first welcome thing he'd said.

"Larry, go out and get us four orders of gumbo, some good French bread, and four large drafts."

"I'd prefer iced tea," Kit said.

Roy turned to Teddy. "And what would you prefer?"

"That you not do me any favors."

"Of course. I understand. Larry, make that three gumbos, two drafts, and an iced tea. Before you go, put Ted away and retie his feet."

Larry picked up a ball of twine from the kitchen counter, cut off a hefty length, then ushered Teddy back into the bedroom.

"Kit, so far, how would you rate Ted's behavior in this situation?" Roy said. "Personally, I think he's doing well. He followed Larry in here from the street knowing there had to be risk, he's been defiant, he's refused food, he's managed to convey quite clearly how much he dislikes me, and he showed no reaction over the possibility he might lose an ear. But then, he knew you wouldn't allow that, so I guess we'll have to withhold those points.

"Has he disappointed you in any way? What I mean is, would you think him more manly if he had jumped to his feet and charged at me? Or made some other aggressive, albeit futile, move?"

For the first time, Kit saw a trace of a person behind Roy's eyes. And what she saw convinced her he wasn't taunting her. He was simply curious.

"Being a man isn't defined by taking foolish risks," she said. "Real men create things. They go to work every day even if they don't feel like it. They pay their bills with honestly earned money and keep the promises they make. They subjugate some of their desires to benefit others. When things are good, they share with those who are struggling. When they're bad, they work harder. Real men don't take the easy way."

Roy looked penetratingly at her. "You're not being honest even with yourself. There's a part of you that wanted to see Ted turn the tables on us. And the fact he didn't even try disturbs you, makes you wonder if he's who you thought he was. Admit it."

Anger is a destructive emotion. When you're angry, you can't think, and Kit was sure that if she was going to find a way out of this, it wasn't anger that would show her the way. But it had been difficult. The discomfort of having her arms pulled behind her for hours at a time made her angry. Her hunger made her angry, and her thirst. But she had conquered those. Now Roy's comments concerning her feelings about Teddy sent her anger index off the board, partly because it was a subject that was none of Roy's business, partly because there was merit in what he said.

"Oh, I should have told you earlier," Roy said. "For every day the money isn't in the mail, there'll be a penalty."

14

Barbaric, Broussard thought as they drove. There had been bits of cork in his wine and a pinch too much paprika in the stuffed zucchini. Blackledge had a lot to learn about choosing a restaurant. His car, though, was quite nice, a Mercedes with plush leather seats and a smooth ride—still, it was no T-Bird.

They had disagreed over the best way to proceed. Broussard had told Blackledge about Kit's disappearance and his belief that two of the CCHF victims were clearly involved. He told him about the diatoms and sludge on the shoes of the man they'd known as Jack Doe and about Teddy's comment that he and Kit thought they had a lead to Jack's identity through a ship at the docks. He'd finished by pointing out that a ship would be the ideal way to smuggle in exotic animals.

Blackledge had reminded Broussard that animals could also be transported in a lot of other ways. He'd held Baldwin's call book in Broussard's face and recited the epidemiologist's credo: When backtracking a contagious disease, victim contacts are the gold standard. And since he was the epidemiologist, that's the way they were going.

They were still on the West Bank, looking for Chester Good's, the first call in Baldwin's book for the fifteenth, the earliest date he could have been exposed.

"There it is," Blackledge said, wheeling the Mercedes into the parking lot of a place built to look like an old-time western saloon.

In the window, a red neon lariat surrounded the saloon's motto, also in red neon: CHESTER GOOD'S—A GOOD PLACE TO BE.

Most of the vehicles already in the lot were pickups, with a fair number advertising NRA sympathies on their bumpers. Blackledge parked between two of them and Broussard followed him inside to a dimly lit hall that smelled of beer and leather.

On the jukebox, an adenoidal male with a voice resembling a hound dog answering the call of an ambulance was expressing the fact he had died and, as a result, "stopped loving you today." A rather predictable consequence of his death, Broussard thought.

The walls were hung with Indian rugs, skulls of hoofed animals, and sepia-tinted photos of cowboys with outrageous amounts of facial hair. Broussard thought the leather odor was from the bar stools, which were fashioned in the shape of saddles, but when he approached the bar, he saw they were plastic. Because the saloon reminded Broussard of his beloved Louis L'Amour novels, he couldn't help but like the place, even going so far as to climb onto one of the saddles.

"Howdy gents," the middle-aged barkeep said, stepping over to them. He was wearing an apron over a striped shirt with a black garter for an armband. "What can Ah can get you? We got plenty drink here . . . all kinds."

The western illusion wavered a bit under the weight of the barkeep's heavy Cajun accent.

An attractive blonde in cowgirl dress suddenly appeared at Blackledge's elbow. "Hi there, city slicker, want to ride the pony?"

"Not today, miss, but my friend might."

The girl vamped over to Broussard and rested her hand on his shoulder. "My, but you're a big one," she said. "I've always liked men with healthy appetites. It makes a girl feel so . . . appreciated."

She moved her hand to the back of Broussard's neck, which by now had become about as red as his face. "Maybe you'd like to see the pony before you decide," she purred.

"It's temptin' miss, but I been tryin' to cut down on sweets."

"Well, if you change your mind, I'll be around."

"Very gallant," Blackledge said. "But you mixed your metaphors."

"They weren't metaphors; they were euphemisms," Broussard replied.

Blackledge turned to the barkeep. "We're from the Health Department. . . ."

"We got no problems dere," the barkeep said. "We got a good score las' time."

"It's not about that. Do you know a salesman named Walter Baldwin?"

"Not dat Ah can recall."

"Crescent City Bar and Restaurant Supplies—his call book says he was in here about two weeks ago."

"We get a lotta salesmen."

"This one is dead, from a disease he probably contracted from a tick bite, and we're here to see if this is where he was bitten or where he picked up the tick. Has anyone connected with this place recently acquired an unusual animal as a pet?"

"Ah don' know dat much about da help."

"Have there been any animals of any kind on the premises in the last month?"

"Not while Ah been here, but we open long hours. Maybe da other bartender knows somethin'. Ah could call an' ask."

"We'd appreciate it. Before you do that, have any of the employees been seriously ill lately?"

"One of da cleanup ladies got a hysteriaectomy."

"That's all?"

"She talk like it was enough."

"Go ahead and make your call, and ask the other bartender about sick employees, too."

"Soon's Ah get dis cowboy down here a refill."

"Suppose the tick that bit Baldwin came in on a customer's pants," Broussard said.

"That'd make our job harder."

"So what we're doin' won't necessarily produce results."

"That's what makes it so much fun."

The barkeep placed the call but got nothing useful. Over the next four hours, Broussard and Blackledge visited seven bars and ten restaurants, covering all of Baldwin's calls for the fifteenth. Blackledge then took Broussard back to the lab so he could pick up his T-Bird.

They kept the gate at the entrance to the lab access road locked at night, so Blackledge had to get out of the car, unlock it, drive through, get out again, and relock it, a surprisingly unsophisticated way of doing things for an operation that included a biosafety level-four lab.

The armadillo population in the grassy area was even larger at night, and in the marsh, the headlights caught a family of nutrias crossing the road. In the swamp, Blackledge swerved to avoid a snake that Broussard first thought was a piece of inner tube from a bicycle tire lying in the road.

When they reached the lab, Blackledge slid the Mercedes into the slot beside Broussard's car and said, "I'll pick you up at the corner of Tulane and La Salle at nine tomorrow morning. Don't be late."

"I still think we ought to check out the dock angle."

"Known contacts first," Blackledge said.

Broussard followed the Mercedes back to the gate, waited while Blackledge unlocked it, then followed him through and drove off, leaving him to relock it.

Twenty minutes later, when he pulled into his garage, Broussard was still thinking he shouldn't have wasted time barhopping with Blackledge—but should have spent that time going over the body and clothing of the strangulation victim again and again, until it yielded something. The thought that Gatlin might have found a match for the guy's prints sent him directly to the phone in his study, pursued by Princess, who thought she should come before prints.

Finding no messages, he dialed the office and entered the code to get any that might have been left for him there. He learned only that the chain-metal gloves had arrived. Then, suddenly, out of nowhere, he saw Natalie in his mind's eye, her mask stained with blood. Reminded of her death, he stood quietly by the phone, reviewing his role in what had happened to her.

Finally, feeling Princess pushing on his shins with her head, he picked her up and made amends for his inattention by taking her into the kitchen and giving her a dollop of cream in her Wedgwood bowl. While she drank it, he went to the bedroom, sat on the bed, and thought again about Natalie and then about Kit.

He was sitting close to the edge of the blanket he'd thrown back the previous night, and even though it was a good blanket, it transmitted a tiny amount of his body heat, more than enough to set off the sensors in the front legs of the tick folded inside.

Broussard sat for a minute or so, turning things over in his mind, until he felt the need to visit the bathroom. With him gone from the bed, there was no longer a focal heat source seeping through the blanket, so the still-activated tick inside was free to roam. It soon emerged from the end of the blanket fold and dropped to the floor.

Small as it was, the tick was ferrying in its thin blood and saliva thousands of life-forms so tiny and so primitive, they could barely be called alive—organisms incapable of thought, unable to move on their own from place to place, lacking even the capacity to experience the pleasures of replication, which in their twilight existence was their only function. Clothed in a few paltry proteins and containing a smudge of nucleic acid, they were among the most efficient assassins on earth, able to trick their way smoothly into the cells of competent hosts, hijack the machinery inside, and subvert it to the synthesis of their progeny, committing Paleozoic rape before they killed.

There was half an inch of clearance under the bathroom door that allowed the carbon dioxide in Broussard's breath and his body heat to make their way into the bedroom. The tick turned in that direction and scurried over the carpet.

It ran under the bathroom door and paused on the other side. Sensing its quarry immediately ahead, it quickly set off again at intercept speed. At the sink, Broussard finished drying his hands and started for the door. Aware of his advance, the tick paused again and lifted its front pair of legs to hook him. But with Broussard's next step, a sort of shuffle that adjusted his stride so he could hit the lights on the way out, the tick was flattened under his shoe and was spread over the tile floor.

In the bedroom, Broussard sat on the bed and took off his shoes. The cracks in the soles of his feet were not as severe as last year, but they still gave him a twinge as he briefly massaged and kneaded his tired toes. He then undressed and put his dirty clothing in the hamper by category—socks in the bag on the side, shirts in the rear compartment, pants in the middle, underwear in the front. He slipped into his pajamas and returned to the bathroom to brush his teeth. In doing so, he stepped squarely on the tick's still-wet remains.

15

A vehicle pulled to a stop in front of Kit. Roy yanked her forward. She heard a latch thrown and the sound of doors opening. Before they'd blindfolded her the morning of her abduction, she'd seen that they drove a white panel truck. It seemed likely this was the same vehicle. She couldn't tell because she was blindfolded again. This time, though, Roy had not hidden her blindfold with a big hat and her bound wrists with a coat, probably because the streets at this hour were deserted.

"Get in," Roy said, nudging her. "Then lie down."

Her feet were free, but her hands were still bound behind her, so she had to crawl into the truck without using them. She had no idea where they were going and couldn't ask, because Larry had stuffed a terry-cloth headband in her mouth and had sealed it in with a strip of duct tape.

At first, the headband had rested so near her throat, it gagged her, but she'd gradually used her throat muscles to work it forward a bit, so now it was merely an obnoxious fuzzy ball in her mouth, sucking up every bit of moisture.

"Hurry . . . get down," Roy urged.

She dropped onto her butt with a jolt that rattled her teeth, then went down on her side, her shoulder absorbing the force when she hit. Roy set about retying her feet. She was sure now it was the same truck, at least it bore the same repulsive tomcat odor.

She hadn't seen Teddy since Larry had taken him back to the bedroom. The rest of them had eaten in the front room and Roy had then read *The Old Man and the Sea* aloud to Larry and her for nearly three hours, during which his voice showed no effects of its prolonged use. When she'd suggested they watch the news, Roy had vetoed it, saying television was a corrupt medium.

At ten o'clock, Roy had declared that everyone should get some sleep, and Larry had retied her hands and feet. Instead of being returned to the bedroom with Teddy, she'd been assigned the sofa. Roy and Larry had taken the second bedroom.

With the discomfort of being all trussed up, the need to figure out some method of escape, and the hope that she'd hear something encouraging on the police scanner Larry had left on in their bedroom at night, she'd stayed awake for quite a while, then miraculously had dozed off. She'd been awakened by the feel of Larry's hand between her thighs.

He'd tried to stifle her scream with a hand over her mouth, but she'd bitten him. Then Roy had stormed into the room and thrown Larry off her. It was then that Roy told Larry to get the truck and bring it to the Decatur gate, which meant the trailer was accessible from either French Market Place or Decatur, for whatever that was worth.

"All right, go around the block while I get the other one," Roy said. "And don't run any lights or stop signs."

The rear doors slammed shut and the truck took off.

"I don't know why you made such a big deal about me touching you," Larry said over the sound of the police scanner, which he'd brought along. "It's not as though you've never been touched there before. What would it have hurt? I'd about decided it wasn't your fault about the cap, and then you had to do that. So don't count on me to take up for you later."

Phil Gatlin started his car and eased it away from the curb. He'd been sitting for over an hour on Burgundy Street between Touro and Frenchmen—the location where the strangulation victim had been found—watching for anyone whose routine might have brought them by this spot around the time the body was dumped. But the only people he'd seen were Sally Harmon, waitress at a nearby bar, and Carl Letcher, a zydeco musician who worked at Mulate's, over by the Convention Center. Both had already been interviewed by Jake Evans.

He dug in his shirt pocket for a Rolaids and vowed to cut back on his coffee consumption. It'd been a crummy day, during which he hadn't detected shit, having been unable even to figure out where the hell Teddy Labiche was. Teddy was still registered at the Royal Sonesta, but he hadn't answered the phone all evening, and when Gatlin had dropped over there around 11:00 P.M. and gotten the management to open his room, nothing appeared out of the ordinary, except he wasn't there. Considering the circumstances, it didn't seem as if he'd be having a night on the town. So where was he?

In his frustration, Gatlin wondered if maybe Teddy had gone to Kit's place and something had happened to him there. It was only a few blocks away and easy enough to check.

Larry turned another corner, drove for a minute or so, then cornered again. He quickly made one more turn, drove for perhaps half a minute, then stopped. The rear doors were quickly yanked open.

"Inside, Ted . . . and lie down. Watch out for Kit."

Teddy got in and arranged himself on the floor beside Kit. Roy retied Teddy's feet and closed the doors. A few seconds later, Kit heard Roy get into the passenger seat and buckle his seat belt.

"Hook up, Larry. You two in the back stay quiet or I'll quiet you for good."

There had to be a lot of reasons why Roy would haul them out this late, but the only one Kit could think of was that he'd decided to kill them now. She scooted close to Teddy and sought his fingers, which, unlike her own, were warm and dry. The thought of meekly accepting her death was so disgusting, she decided that the first time she heard a car next to them at a traffic light, she'd throw herself into the front seats and try to kick the window out.

But then Roy said, "I hope Jack just underestimated the postal service."

With this, Kit realized they weren't about to die, at least not yet. They were going to check her mail.

GATLIN SLIPPED HIS CAR into the only available space on the street and killed the engine. He helped himself to a pair of rubber gloves from the box on the seat beside him, shoved them into his pocket, and got out. He crossed the street and walked down to Kit's gate, where he pressed the button above the mail slot and waited to see if anyone would answer.

LARRY MADE A RIGHT on Ursulines, turning so sharply, Kit and Teddy slid in that direction. "Take it easy," Roy cautioned. "We're in no hurry." The heat from the truck's exhaust system had begun to warm the carpet, so that in back, the stench of tomcat was growing worse.

GETTING NO ANSWER, GATLIN picked the lock and let himself in, making sure the gate locked behind him. He walked through the parking alcove, entered the courtyard, and surveyed the house, which, except for some illuminated green plastic toadstools in the flower bed, was quiet and dark. Standing there, Gatlin was struck once again by the indifference of the physical world to violence. Kit had been forcefully abducted, perhaps even . . . He didn't want to admit it, but she might even have been murdered here, but the fireflies didn't care, the crickets didn't care, the jasmine still smelled the same, the bricks in the courtyard hadn't changed, and the toadstool lights still burned. Only people cared—and not very many of them. It just didn't seem right.

AT DAUPHINE STREET, LARRY turned left. They were now only a block from Kit's house.

"When you get there," Roy said, "drive slowly past her place, then take a right on Dumaine and stop just around the corner."

A few seconds later, as they passed Kit's home, Roy studied her gates and the parking alcove, looking for any signs of a stakeout. He also checked the cars lining the curb to make sure they weren't occupied. There was no reason for the cops to believe he'd come back here, but it was always best to anticipate trouble, even if it seemed unlikely.

GATLIN HEARD AN ENGINE out front and he wondered why the driver was moving so slowly. But then it went on by and he turned his attention back to the house. Now that he was here, it seemed even more unlikely Teddy was inside. And there was also the possibility the house was dangerously contaminated. Remembering how over the years some real long shots had paid big dividends, he slipped on the rubber gloves and picked the lock on the front door, causing the house to light up inside. He'd learned the code for shutting off the alarm system from Bubba when he'd toured the house earlier, so he had no trouble disarming it now. He then began a room-to-room search.

THE TRUCK ROUNDED THE corner, with Roy satisfied that they were in no danger. Even so, he wasn't about to put *himself* on the spot. He held Kit's key ring out to Larry. "The mail drop is just inside the small gate on the left. Grab whatever you find and do it fast. And be sure to lock the gate behind you."

"Which one is it?" Larry said, taking the keys.

"You'll have to try them and see. Stay in your seat until I come around."

Roy left the truck, circled to Larry's side, and got in the driver's seat when Larry got out. Larry then disappeared around the corner.

Roy turned the volume down on the scanner. He put the truck in reverse and backed up so he could look down Kit's street. Because of the parking alcove, he was not aware of the lights in Kit's house.

Hands in his pockets, Larry strolled to Kit's gate and began trying keys.

It wasn't the big brass key with the square head or the chrome-plated one or the short one, so it had to be . . . The key with the round shaft slid into the lock and levered the bolt back with liquid ease. The gate emitted a tiny friction squeal that echoed in the parking alcove as it opened, but there was no one to hear it, so what difference did it make?

Larry slipped through and went to the mail basket. Bending quickly, he emptied it and darted back onto the street. The echo of the gate closing behind him died away just as Gatlin finished his search and came out of the house.

Gatlin paused and cocked his head, his hand still around the front doorknob. Had he heard something? He listened hard, trying to filter out the boisterous cricket noise.

Deciding that the sound had been an illusion and remembering that the house lights were still on, he leaned inside and flicked off the master switch.

On the way out, he paused at the mail basket and looked in. Obviously, Kit didn't order much from catalogs. There'd been two mail deliveries since she'd disappeared yet the basket was empty. Two days of mail at his house would keep the fire in a woodstove burning for a week.

"THAT'S ALL THERE IS," Larry said, tossing three catalogs and a couple of sales circulars on the seat.

"Too bad," Roy replied, punching the gas.

DUMAINE WAS A ONE-WAY street away from the heart of the Quarter, so there was no reason for Gatlin to look to his right as he crossed it on his way back to Canal. Even had he done so, all he would have seen would have been Roy's taillights, so far away they would have resembled synchronous twin fireflies.

TEDDY HAD BEEN IN the back bedroom when Roy had said there'd be a penalty for every day the money wasn't in the mail, so he didn't have that to worry about. It was foremost, though, in Kit's thoughts.

What kind of penalty? Surely he wouldn't apply any penalty to *this* trip. In the lie she'd told, the money wasn't even supposed to show up until tomorrow. She continued to worry about this until she realized they'd been driving long enough to be back at the trailer. They drove about ten minutes more, then stopped.

Roy got out and opened the rear doors. Because of the tomcat odor, Kit had been breathing shallowly. Now, provided with some fresh air, she took a deep breath.

"Ted, you're going to perform a little service for me," Roy said. "And I want you to understand the ground rules before we begin. I'm going to free you. . ."

Kit's heart leapt with the words.

"Then you're going to walk over to the ATM about fifteen feet from where we're parked and withdraw the maximum daily limit from your checking account and, if you can get it, the same amount from savings. Then you'll give me the money and the receipts and we'll return to the truck. If you attempt to communicate in any way with the TV camera that records those transactions, I'll signal my brother and he'll kill Kit. If you attack me, he'll kill her. If you run, he'll kill her. Do you understand these rules?"

Kit felt Roy climb into the truck. There was the sound of tape being pulled free and then Teddy's voice hoarse and cracked. . .

"Yeah, you sorry. . ."

He said something in French that Kit couldn't interpret.

"I understand," Teddy said. "But you remember this. I've only got two bad habits. I eat too much red meat and I never forget who my enemies are. Guess which habit involves you."

"Very eloquent," Roy said. "Next time I need a sermon punched up, I'll give you a call. Turn over so I can get to your hands."

Kit heard twine snapping as Roy cut Teddy's hands free. The truck jiggled as Roy climbed out. There was more snapping and Roy said, "Come on. We've been here too long already."

Kit felt Teddy get out. Then the doors closed and Kit was left alone with Larry.

"I'm kind of glad the money wasn't there tonight," Larry said. "I would have enjoyed getting my share and all, but if it arrives tomorrow, I'll still get it, but I'll also have enjoyed what's gonna happen later."

With the headband in her mouth and the tape over it, Kit couldn't ask him what he meant, but she was pretty certain he was referring to Roy's penalty.

Another couple of minutes passed, during which Larry said nothing and the only sound was the scanner. Then the rear doors opened and Roy said, "Kit, you ought to know that Ted had only two hundred dollars in his checking and a hundred and fifty in his savings. Between the two of you, you couldn't come up with enough cash to rent a nice one-bedroom apartment. You should consider dumping this man and finding someone who can provide for you."

"I guess you don't want to use *his* credit cards, either," Larry said.

"It could be just as dangerous with his cards as hers," Roy replied.

With Teddy again tied up and gagged, Larry drove back to where they'd started and Roy returned Teddy and Kit to the trailer by reversing the procedure he'd used to bring them out. Larry took the truck away to park it.

As before, Teddy was put in the trailer's rear bedroom. Kit was ordered into the armchair in the front room, where Roy retied her ankles and removed the tape and headband from her mouth.

Kit quickly discovered that her lower jaw was frozen open. Ignoring the pain it caused, she forced it closed. The lining of her throat felt exposed and raw. She ran her tongue over the dry scales curling from her lips, but there was no moisture to soften them. "What about Teddy?" she croaked, turning to look at Roy, who was standing in front of the fridge, with the door open. "Did you remove his gag, too?"

Roy took a small bottle of apple juice from the fridge and twisted off the cap. He came around in front of her and held it out. "Care for some? You must be thirsty."

"First, tell me about Teddy."

"You're too concerned about others," Roy said sharply. "Take care of yourself. Nobody else will."

"I'll drink when he's given the same opportunity."

Roy stared at her for a few seconds, then headed for the rear bedroom. He returned in a few minutes, shaking his head. "It's really quite amazing . . . this selfless behavior you two exhibit toward each other. He didn't want to drink until I told him if he didn't, you wouldn't, either." He held up the empty bottle. "You can see the results."

He got a fresh bottle from the fridge and opened it, then put the mouth of the bottle to Kit's lips and gently tilted it.

The juice was sharp and cold and was the closest thing to paradise Kit had ever experienced. It was so wonderful, she was able to suppress her resentment against being fed like an infant, and she emptied the bottle.

"Would you like your arms untied?" Roy asked. "Ted had his free while we went to the ATM, so you're entitled."

Kit had suffered so many abuses at their hands, it was hard to rank them: the headband in her mouth, having to ask permission to use the bathroom and knowing Larry was listening at the door, hunger, thirst, fear. . . But all those were episodic abuses. The agony of having her arms pulled behind her and the impossibility of finding a comfortable position sitting or lying was chronic. And it was true that Teddy had been freed for a few minutes.

"Yes, I'd like to be untied, but only for as long as Teddy was."

"Of course, fair play above all," Roy said, reaching in his pocket for his knife. "Stand up and turn around."

She did as he said and he cut her bonds.

"Sit."

Wincing at the pain in her shoulder joints as she moved her arms to their normal position, she returned to the chair while Roy got another bottle of juice from the fridge. Feeling time-deprived and forgetting that they'd taken her watch, Kit looked at her wrist.

"How does it feel to be free?" Roy asked, taking his juice to the sofa.

"I'm not free. If I was, I wouldn't be here."

"Sorry, my question was unclear. How does it feel to have your *hands* free?"

"What do you care?"

"I care a great deal. More than you know."

"I don't understand how someone like you could have ever been a minister," Kit said.

She wasn't sure he was going to reply, but after taking a sip from the bottle, he said, "Why, because I'm cold?"

"That's the least of it."

"I can be warm and fuzzy when it's necessary."

Kit doubted that.

"Then, too, I just took over the family business."

"Your father was a minister?"

He nodded. "A small church in—" Then, catching himself, he said, "Never mind. It's not important."

But it was important to Kit. If she ever got free and he escaped, knowing where that church was might help track him down. "What denomination were you?"

"Never mind about that."

"How does someone go from being a minister to . . ."

"This wretched excuse for a human you see before you?" Roy said.

"Your words, not mine."

"How does anybody get to any point in his life . . . accidents, genetics, luck. . . ."

"Of course, things you couldn't control. You're just a victim."

"And I'm passing it along."

"That must have been some church you ran."

"I was doing okay until somebody in my flock figured out it was Larry burglarizing their homes on Sunday mornings."

"With a few hints about floor plans from you?"

"Every young man needs guidance from time to time. We didn't target just anyone. Only those who never seemed to have problems . . . those who never came to me for counseling . . . the ones who kept all their feelings to themselves . . ." Realizing he'd slipped again, he changed the subject. "Let's not talk about me. You're more interesting. This is a bad situation, isn't it?"

"I've been in dicey spots before and I'm still here."

"That sounds very confident. But honestly, how do you see your chances?"

"Honestly? I'm surprised that's a word still in your vocabulary."

"There you go wanting to talk about me again." He crossed one leg over the other and balanced the juice bottle on his knee. "Seriously, how do you think this is all going to end?"

"You and Larry will be caught."

"How?"

Thinking of the candy wrapper she'd put in the third kidnapper's cuff and the glitter on his shoes, she said, "You've already made one big mistake."

The words were barely out of her mouth before she regretted having said them, because Roy's android eyes slowly shifted from her face to his raised shoe.

Damn.

She must have glanced at the shoe when she'd answered him.

Damn . . . Damn . . .

She was going to have to be more careful, much more careful.

She kept her attention on Roy's face, making sure she wore a blank expression. Finally, he stopped staring at his shoes and looked again at her, those pale bottomless eyes probing.

Was a blank expression the correct decision? Or was that an obvious admission he'd been on the right track when he'd caught her looking at his shoe? Should she start talking to defuse the situation, or would that merely confirm his suspicions? She was spared a decision by Larry's return.

"What are we doing now?" he asked, coming in and putting the police scanner on the kitchen counter.

"Shut that radio off and sit down," Roy ordered. He looked at Kit. "Time for that penalty I mentioned."

"That's not fair," Kit said. "The money isn't even due until tomorrow."

"Fair?" Roy said. "Does anything about all this strike you as fair? Now, what would be an appropriate penalty? It should be something with symbolic significance for both parties."

He thought about it briefly then reached in his pocket and fished out a half-dollar. He looked at one side, then the other. "Yes, this will do." He held the head side out toward Kit. "The word *Liberty* for you and Ted, and *In God We Trust* for Larry and me."

He flipped the half-dollar to Larry, who caught it with both hands.

"There's a small pot in the drawer by the stove," Roy said. "Put the coin in it, put the pot on the stove, and turn it to high."

"Oh, I see where you're going," Larry said, getting out of his chair. "Good one."

"The letters are in such low relief, there probably isn't much chance they'll transfer their pattern to skin," Roy said. "And even if they did, they'd be reversed, but I don't view those as important considerations. Do you, Kit?"

Over by the stove, Larry pulled a drawer open and rattled among the contents.

"You're despicable."

"The question now is, who should the penalty be levied against, you or Ted?"

Kit heard the coin drop into a pot. "This is pointless."

"What do you mean?" Roy said. "Why is there no point? I hope you're not about to tell me you made up the story about the money coming in the mail, because that would make me very upset and the penalty would have to be much more severe. That isn't what you mean, is it?"

"No. I meant it accomplishes nothing. You're exacting a penalty from us for an event we don't control."

"So it's not fair. We've already covered that."

"Don't do this," she pleaded.

"The issue isn't whether it will or won't be done, but, rather, to determine the recipient. I know what your vote is and I'm inclined to disagree with you, but I'll listen to argument."

Kit looked back at Larry. Still deluded by his appearance into believing he was basically a good person who'd been misled by Roy, she said, "Larry, don't help him. This is wrong. It's sadistic. People who do things like this aren't human. Imagine yourself in our position. We haven't done anything to harm you. Why hurt us? If you don't want to think of us, think of yourself. Help Roy and you cross a line that will take you to the lowest levels of human existence—to a black hole with no self-respect and no meaning."

Larry had been staring into the pot. He turned now to look at Kit, and she saw he was puzzled. "But it'll be fun," he said sincerely.

"I'm afraid Larry was born on the path you mentioned," Roy said. "Do you want to plead your case or not?"

"How am I gonna pick this thing up?" Larry said.

"There's a pair of pliers in the drawer by the sink," Roy said. Then to Kit: "Your argument . . . quickly."

"Teddy has nothing to do with this," she said. "He's only here by—"

"Accident?" Roy said. "See, it's like I told you earlier." He waved at the air. "Sorry, I interrupted."

"All right, by accident. The point is, you shouldn't even be considering him. This is all between you and me."

"Is that it?"

"I *don't* want him hurt."

"Your plea to Larry was much more convincing. I'm sorry. . . . Larry, when you're ready, take the coin into the bedroom and place it on Ted's—"

"Forehead," Larry said. "I want to do it on his forehead."

"The boy's a natural," Roy replied. "Not this time, Larry. This time . . . his back. You should probably take some twine in there now and secure him."

Larry grabbed the ball of twine they'd been using and left the room.

"What are you feeling?" Roy asked Kit. "Anger . . . guilt?"

"Loathing," Kit said, skewering him with her eyes.

"That's natural," Roy said. He finished his apple juice, got up, and crossed the room to put the empty bottle with the others on the counter.

Kit's eyes widened. In the spot where Roy had been sitting was Teddy's pistol. She thrust herself out of her chair, took one hop, and threw herself at the sofa. She bounced when she hit, but her hand closed on the pistol. Teddy had once showed her how to use it, so as she rolled onto her back and leveled the barrel at Roy's chest, the gun felt familiar in her hand.

16

Kit wanted to scream with relief that this nightmare was finally over, that she and Teddy were safe, that Roy and Larry could no longer harm them. But she quickly realized this was far from being resolved. There was still danger. Inside, she was trembling like crazy and she fought to keep it from showing.

Her gun hand began to waver and she raised the other hand and cradled it as Teddy had taught her. Her mind was racing. Larry was the wild card. Did he have his gun with him? If he did, he could threaten Teddy and it would be a standoff. She had to keep Roy from realizing that. Oh, God . . . there was only one way to be sure: Shoot Roy and then Larry when he came out to see what had happened.

"Larry . . ." Roy slowly called his brother's name, not taking his cold eyes from hers.

Did she have to? Maybe in a standoff, one of *them* would fold. Certainly not Roy, but Larry might. . . But if Roy told him not to . . . Oh, God . . . there was only one way to be sure. . .

Her finger tightened on the trigger and she steeled herself for the discharge. Roy could tell what was about to happen, but his expression never changed. She didn't want to see the bullet hit him, but she didn't dare look away. Oh, God . . .

The click of the hammer falling seemed to echo through the trailer, followed a fraction of a second later by . . . Larry's voice. "Be there in a minute."

The gun hadn't fired.

She pulled the trigger again, with the same result. Her eyes shifted focus from Roy to the back of the cylinder.

Empty . . . the damn thing was empty.

"A little test," Roy said, walking over and taking the gun from her, "to see what you're made of. You should be proud. You analyzed things correctly and had the courage to act. I can see I'm going to have to watch my step around you. Stand up."

"Drop dead."

"What do you want?" Larry said, joining them.

"Let's get her up."

Larry put the twine ball on the counter and Roy and Larry hauled her to her feet, Larry taking the opportunity to let his fingers stray to her right breast.

"Retie her hands."

That done, they pulled her to the upholstered chair and pushed her into it.

"I'm sure the coin is hot enough now," Roy said, taking his seat across from Kit on the sofa.

A moment later, Kit heard the coin slide along the bottom of the pot, followed by the clatter of the pliers as Larry went after the coin with them.

"How long should I leave it on him?" Larry asked.

"Until it's cool enough to touch," Roy replied. "And press it on with the pliers."

Larry headed for the back bedroom.

Kit's heart felt huge in her chest, its power too great for her fragile vessels. Every beat thundered in her ears and throbbed at her temples. Across from her, Roy was studying her like a child might watch an ant colony. And she finally understood. . . .

He was an emotion parasite that lived off the reactions and experiences of others because he was incapable of feeling anything himself. Well, she wouldn't allow it. He would not profit from his abuses.

Kit reined in her thoughts and wiped away all emotion until her eyes were as cold as his. She flaunted her defiance, staring at him, letting him look where he would, knowing he would find nothing to feed upon.

In this state, time ceased to exist for her, so that when Larry came back to the room and said, "He's done," she truly had no idea how long he'd been gone.

"Put her back there with him," Roy said. "And lock their door; then we're going for a walk."

If Roy was disappointed, he didn't show it.

Larry cut the twine at Kit's ankles and ushered her into the back bedroom, where Teddy lay on his side, his face toward the far wall. There was a long horizontal slit in Teddy's shirt and a vertical slit up each side, forming a flap that could be thrown upward onto his neck. Kit had come back from the emotionless place to which she'd fled and she wanted to weep at the thought of what lay under that flap. Whatever means Larry had used to hold Teddy while he burned him was not evident.

Larry pushed her onto the bed and retied her ankles.

Kit longed to hold Teddy in her arms and whisper things that would make him forget what Larry had done. But her arms were tied, and even if she could think of words that sweet, Larry was still watching.

"You heard what your brother said," she hissed. "Get out of here and leave us alone."

Larry left without reply and closed and locked the door. Kit held her tongue until she heard the front door open and close, then held it awhile longer until the murmur of their voices faded away.

"Oh, Teddy, I am so sorry to have caused this."

Teddy rolled toward her and his mouth twisted in pain as his back touched the mattress. He turned onto his side and looked into her eyes. "You didn't cause anything. It was those two mental cases. Did they hurt you?"

"No, but Roy burned *you* to see how *I'd* react. So I *am* responsible."

"That's nonsense. Besides, I'm all right."

"I told them you had nothing to do with all this and if it had to be done, it should be to me."

"That was a crazy thing to do. What if they'd listened?"

"Then you wouldn't be hurt."

"It's over and I'm fine."

"I would have stopped them if there'd been any way. Roy said it was a penalty for the money not being in the mail. But he also said there'd be a greater penalty if I changed my story."

"That doesn't make sense. The only reason to impose a penalty would be to get you to admit you lied about the money being in the mail and to force you to tell him where it really is. Why'd he do it?"

"He knows there's no money. I think he's known it from the moment I made up that story."

Behind the trailer, Roy sat quietly under the slightly open window, feeding on their conversation. At first, he'd believed Jack *had* given her the money. But even before the boyfriend arrived, he'd begun to doubt it. Then, when she'd come up with that utterly implausible story about it being in the mail—under the kind of duress that would have forced the truth out of her—he had indeed known. It would be another three days before the truck arrived from New York. And this was as good a way as any to pass the time.

His mind returned to Kit's comment that he'd already made a big mistake. What had she meant? He was sure she hadn't just been blowing smoke. And it had something to do with his shoes. So tomorrow, while Larry was getting the other stuff, he'd visit a shoe store. Then, tomorrow night, to be on the safe side, they'd move.

BROUSSARD HURRIED FROM THE hospital, irked that another examination of the strangulation case had turned up nothing that would help find Kit. He was also upset at the peculiar fact he'd awakened a full hour later than usual and as a result would feel out of synch the rest of the day. And he was in no mood to waste it by tagging along with Blackledge as his cheerleader.

He got to the rendezvous corner five minutes late. Three minutes later, Blackledge's Mercedes made a left from Tulane and stopped in front of him. Broussard stepped into the street, opened the door, and looked in.

"I told you to be punctual," Blackledge said. "I've had to go around the block twice waiting for you."

"I'm not goin' today."

Blackledge scowled. "Why not?"

"There was nothin' we did yesterday you couldn't have done by yourself."

"I want you with me."

"Sorry. I got better things to do."

He shut the door, retreated to the sidewalk, and started back to the hospital, the small glow of pleasure he felt at denying Blackledge something he wanted flaring brightly at the sound of the Mercedes's engine revving and its wheels squealing on the pavement.

Upon reaching his office, Broussard fished a lemon ball from the bowl on his desk, slipped it into his cheek, and reached for his appointment book to refresh his memory on the dates he'd need to know for the call he was about to make.

Baldwin had been exposed on the fifteenth, sixteenth, or seventeenth. He circled the seventeenth. And Teddy had said that he and Kit had found a lead down at the docks on . . . the twenty-fifth. He circled that date.

A minute later, he punched in the port of New Orleans marine information number and waited for an answer.

"Mornin', this is Dr. Broussard at the medical examiner's office. I'd like to talk to the person who keeps the records on ship arrivals and departures."

The voice on the line said he was the guy.

"Could you give me the names of all the ships that were in port between the seventeenth and the twenty-fifth of this month?"

"Arrived on the seventeenth and left on the twenty-fifth?"

"Not necessarily. In port on those dates."

"Don't get many that stay so long. Lemme check."

Broussard heard pages riffling; then the voice came back. "Only one fits those dates—the *Schrader.*"

The *Schrader* . . . Broussard straightened in his chair. The note Beverly's brother had in his wallet . . ."

"Course she left yesterday mornin'," the voice added.

He thanked the fellow for the information, broke the connection with his finger, and called Phil Gatlin, who, remarkably, was at his desk.

"I think I got a lead on Kit. Beverly's brother had a note in his wallet that mentioned the name Schrader. And Mark Blackledge has figured out the disease he had was carried by ticks that came into the city on some kind of exotic animals. When we were talkin' to Teddy after Kit first disappeared, he said they thought they'd found a lead down at the docks, but the captain wouldn't let 'em on the ship. Well, guess what ship was in port between the time Walter Baldwin was probably exposed to the disease and the day Kit and Teddy were on the docks?" Without waiting for Gatlin to answer, Broussard said, "That's right, the *Schrader*."

"Why didn't you mention the note before this?" Gatlin asked.

"With everything that's been happenin', it slipped my mind. And I didn't know what it meant until now."

"Teddy's disappeared, too."

"What?"

"He called me yesterday afternoon when I was out and left a message that he'd wait at his hotel for me to get back to him. When

I did, he didn't answer. And it looks like he wasn't in his room at all last night."

"How do you know that?"

"He wasn't in when I dropped by at eleven P.M., so I taped a hair to his door. It was still undisturbed when I looked this morning."

"Could he have spent the night at Kit's place for some reason?"

"I checked that."

"I wonder if they're both on the *Schrader*?"

"Is it still in port?"

"Left yesterday mornin'."

"Then to find out, we'll probably have to call out the Coast Guard."

"So do it."

"I'd like a little more evidence first."

"We could go to the docks and talk to the longshoremen who worked the *Schrader* and see if they know anything."

"Couldn't hurt. Did I hear you say *we* could go?"

The ME's office had hit one of those rare dry spells where there were no bodies waiting for autopsy. Also, because the chain-metal gloves had arrived, when the next case did come in, Charlie could handle it. "You drivin'?"

"I'll pick you up in twenty minutes in front of the hospital. You got mug shots of all three fever cases?"

"They're not pretty."

"Neither are we."

17

"Yeah, I seen this guy," the longshoreman said, looking at the morgue photo of Beverly's brother. "What kind a picture is this, anyway? He looks . . . dead."

The fellow had the thickest neck Broussard had ever seen. And his skin was as black as the Boulle cabinet in Blackledge's office.

"He *is* dead," Gatlin said. "When did you see him?"

"Week before last."

"How can you remember somebody from that long ago?"

The man's expression grew hostile. "I look to you like somebody who don't know what he saw?"

"Nothing personal. Sometimes even the smartest people make mistakes about things like that."

"Yeah . . . well, okay. We don't get too many people down here that don't fit in . . . like you two. I ain't gonna forget you, either."

"Where'd you see this fellow?"

"On a ship that brought in a shitload of aluminum. I don't mean like that flimsy aluminum foil—this was blocks of it, a foot thick, six feet wide, and about eight long. Dangerous damn stuff. One mistake with that crap and you'll look like this guy." He waved the picture in his hand, then turned it on edge. "And about this flat. Anyway, he came on board."

"You remember the name of this ship?"

"Sure, the *Schrader.*"

"How about the other pictures?"

The longshoreman shifted to the photo of the strangulation case. "No . . . never seen *him.*"

Then he moved on to the one of Baldwin. "Him, neither."

Reaching Kit's picture, he looked at Gatlin and said, "Nice lookin' woman."

"She was here last Saturday," Broussard said.

"I don't work on weekends—weekends, I wrestle. Maybe you heard a me . . . Mack Truck?"

"You're kidding," Gatlin said.

"It's a professional name."

"What about a slim guy in a straw hat, jeans, alligator boots?"

The guy shook his head. "He could a been here, though. Most of the time durin' the day, I ain't in a position to see who's on the docks."

"Was anything other than aluminum unloaded from the *Schrader*?" Broussard asked.

"Mostly aluminum, but also a half dozen empty containers."

"Containers?" Gatlin echoed.

"Truck trailers. It's done a lot. Shippin' line needs containers somewhere, one ship'll drop 'em off, and another'll pick 'em up. I gotta get back to work." He handed the pictures to Gatlin and put on his hard hat.

"Those trailers you mentioned . . . where are they?" Broussard asked.

The longshoreman pointed at the warehouse's downriver end.

"Let's take a look," Broussard said, moving off and motioning for Gatlin to follow.

A few minutes later, they arrived at the first trailer. Broussard walked around to the rear and threw the door latch, which wasn't locked. He opened the door and looked inside. It was empty. He opened the other door and inspected the floor as far as he could see without climbing in. Apparently satisfied, he closed the doors, latched them, and moved to the next one, where he did the same thing.

Gatlin had no idea what Broussard was doing, but having known him for so long and having seen him pull off some impressive stunts, he let him work unimpeded.

Broussard finished with the second trailer and moved to the third. Finally, as he inspected number six, he abruptly turned and began to look around the warehouse. Spotting a damaged pallet, he hurried to it, wrenched a piece of broken board free, and carried it back to the trailer.

Gatlin could keep still no longer. "What are you doing?"

Visually searching the trailer floor, the board poised above his right ear, Broussard did not reply. Methodically, his eyes swept the floor, back and forth. Suddenly, he saw what he was looking for and brought the board down quickly, end first. At the last second, he shifted the board's trajectory and pounded it against the floor. After raising the board and inspecting the floor under it, he turned to Gatlin.

"You got any crime-scene ribbon in the car?"

"Some in the trunk. What'd you kill?"

"A tick. And there're bird droppin's in this trailer and the second one. The *Schrader*'s been smugglin' birds."

Returning to the trailers with the ribbon, Gatlin tied one end to the latch on the first trailer in the row and Broussard tied the other to the latch on the last one. Gatlin then dropped Broussard back at the hospital and went off to contact the Coast Guard.

Broussard took the elevator to his office and alerted the Health Department to the danger posed by the trailers. Then, remembering something he'd seen next to Chester Good's saloon when he'd been there the previous night with Blackledge, he left the office and headed for his car.

THE WINDOWS OF THE Birds of a Feather pet store were filled with cages and signs advertising their specials. Inside, the place was a chirping asylum dominated by a large rainbow-hued parrot that announced Broussard's arrival. "New customer. Rawwwwk. New customer. Move your tail, Bob. New customer."

A man in the rear who was assembling a birdcage stand stopped work and came to the front. "Yessir, what can I do for you?"

The man's hair was dark brown but had odd white patches in it that at first made Broussard think it'd been spotted by bird droppings. "I'm Dr. Broussard, medical examiner for Orleans Parish, and I'm tryin' to gather some information on a man named Walter Baldwin."

The guy shook his head. "It's not a name I know."

Because his picture of Baldwin was so distorted by post-mortem decomposition, Broussard had decided not to lead with it. "He was a salesman for Crescent City Bar and Restaurant Supplies. Chester Good's was one of his customers."

The guy's face brightened. "A guy about six two, big ears, little quarter-moon scar under one eye?"

"That's him."

"Yeah, he's been in here three or four times in the last year. Seems to want a parrot but can't ever make the move. I've showed him some beauties, but he never buys. Could be the money. They're not cheap."

"Have you bought any birds in the last two weeks from anyone other than your usual sources?"

"I thought you were interested in this . . . Baldwin, was it?"

"Walter Baldwin's dead . . . from a disease he acquired after bein' bitten by a tick that appears to have come into the city on some . . ." Thinking that it might not be wise to use the word *smuggled*, Broussard instead said, ". . . exotic birds. So if you *have* bought any birds lately, they could be part of that shipment. And Baldwin could have picked up that tick here, which means you're in danger, too."

The guy's face turned five shades closer to the color of the spots in his hair and his eyes went to a big wrought-iron cage holding two gray parrots with white featherless faces and red tails.

"I bought those African Greys over there two weeks ago from a guy who said his wife wouldn't let him keep them anymore. And last time he was in, Baldwin helped me switch them from the cage they were in to that one. Jesus, it could be me that's dead."

"The seller of the birds give you a name and address and maybe a phone number?"

"Yeah, I've got it here somewhere."

He went behind the counter, picked up a shoe box, and began rummaging through it, pausing every few seconds to glance around him, presumably for ticks. Broussard found himself doing the same thing.

"Here it is." The guy handed Broussard a slip of paper.

"I need a phone."

The guy reached under the counter and brought one out. Broussard punched in the number and got a recorded message from the phone company. He tried again, with the same result.

"It's a bogus number," he said, hanging up. He fished the morgue photos from his shirt pocket and handed two of them to the guy. "Recognize either of these men?"

The picture of Beverly's brother rang no bells, but when he saw the strangulation victim, he said, "That's him." Some of his color had come back, but suddenly, it drained away again. "Oh, my God."

"What?"

"I bought four birds from that guy—those two and two that I sold right after they came in to a couple of women from Natchez. And I got a call yesterday from a guy who said he was the executor of the estate of the one who bought the birds and that she had died. He wanted me to buy the birds back."

"You got *his* phone number?"

He went to the shoe box and sifted all the way through it, with no luck. Brow knitted in concentration, he paused over the shoe box for a few seconds, then remembered. He found the number under the money in the cash register and handed the slip of paper on which it was written to Broussard, who inspected it and said, "What's his name . . . Harbison?"

The guy nodded and Broussard reached again for the phone.

This one was a real number—of a legal firm, judging from the name the secretary recited when she picked up. She didn't want to put him through at first, but when he told her it was an emergency, she did.

"Mr. Harbison, this is Dr. Broussard, medical examiner for Orleans Parish, Louisiana. I understand that a client of yours who recently died bought two African Grey parrots in New Orleans. What was the cause of her death?"

"The doctors didn't seem to know," Harbison said. "What's going on?"

"Did she vomit blood?"

"That was mentioned, yes."

Broussard got his client's name and the name of the hospital where she'd been treated, then said, "Mr. Harbison, there's good reason to believe your client was bitten by a tick carried on the birds she bought here. I'm gonna call the appropriate Mississippi authorities and inform 'em of the situation. In the meantime, whoever is keepin' those birds should leave the house immediately and not return until the authorities have determined it's safe."

"I understand. I'll see to it. How will I know what's happening?"

"I'll give your name and number to the appropriate people."

Broussard hung up and turned to the store owner. "You need to close up and get out of here. I'll call the Health Department and they'll take care of things from here on."

"Am I going to be held legally responsible for what happened to that woman?"

"I have no idea."

"What about my birds? Are they going to have to be destroyed?"

"Again, that's somethin' for others to decide. I hope not."

Broussard drove back downtown and returned to his office, where he found a message on his machine asking him to call Grandma O. He checked his watch: 12:05. If he called the two health departments now, he'd probably just hear that the people he needed to talk with were at lunch. This was too important to trust with anyone but Dick Mullen and his counterpart in Mississippi. He considered contacting Gatlin but realized he hadn't learned much, if anything, that Gatlin could use in his search for Kit and Teddy. Besides, the *Schrader* was the key. Best to wait and see what turns up there, he thought. With that decision made, he was free to call Grandma O.

She must have been sitting next to the phone, because she picked up before the first ring ended.

"Hi, this is Andy. What's up?"

"You fin' dat girl yet?"

"We got a solid lead this mornin', but it'll be awhile before we know."

"Ah hope she gonna be all right."

"We all do."

"How much longer am Ah gonna have to stay away from da restaurant? Ah've practically worn da linoleum on mah kitchen floor clear through Ah've washed it so many times. Mah furniture's polished, mah rugs are shampooed, an' Ah'll give you a bran'-new hoop net if you can fin' even a speck of dust over here."

"How many days has it been since you were exposed . . . five?"

"Six. Don' you be shortin' me on dat."

"Problem is, we haven't much experience with the disease, so we don't know how long the incubation period might be in folks exposed like you were. I'll be callin' the Health Department in a little while and I'll talk to 'em about you and see what they think. So, hang on, you're doin' a good thing."

"Yeah, well mah spies at da restaurant tell me you ain't been in since Ah lef'."

"It's been so hectic here the last two days, I've barely had time for lunch. But there's no reason why I can't head over there right now."

"Ah'm gonna call in ten minutes an' see if you're dere."

"I'd better get started, then."

Things were far from settled, but for an hour Broussard allowed himself the luxury of pretending it was a normal day. When he stepped out the restaurant's front door, though, reality came rushing back, bringing with it oppressive guilt for having seen to his own comfort while Kit was still missing, quite likely in the hands of people capable of murder. On the way back to his office, his meal, which at first had rested lightly in his belly, turned sodden.

He conveyed his messages to the two health departments and got the opinion from Dick Mullen that Grandma O should probably stay at home until the first of the week. He also contacted Blackledge's secretary and told her that if her boss checked in, he should know that the source of Walter Baldwin's infection had been found. She gave him the number of the lab across the river and he left the same message there. He then reluctantly called Grandma O and told her she'd have to stay home a few more days.

Though guilt continued to rest in a grimy layer on his perceptions, he was dimly able to see he hadn't wasted the morning. He'd beaten Blackledge at his own game and in the process had most likely saved some lives. And he'd generated information that might lead to Kit. But even this small glimpse of light was eclipsed by his secretary, Margaret, who came in with the news that Natalie's funeral service was to be held at the Chapel of the Roses on St. Philip the next day at 2:00 P.M. and that there would be no trip to the cemetery because the Health Department had ordered the body cremated.

After Margaret left, Broussard reflected on how the damnable virus that had claimed Natalie had taken even her family's right to mourn her as they pleased. It was as complete a defeat as he could imagine.

He arranged for flowers to be sent, then went down to the morgue to see how the day was shaping up, hoping there'd be plenty to do so he could keep from thinking about what the Coast Guard would find when they intercepted the *Schrader.*

Charlie Franks was just beginning the post on a man who had fatally shot his estranged wife in the parking lot of the Claiborne Winn-Dixie and then turned the gun on himself. It didn't require much persuasion to convince Franks that Broussard should do the post on the other member of the unfortunate pair. There was far more discussion, however, about why Franks wasn't wearing his metal gloves. Broussard was unyielding on this point, so when he left the suite, Franks was peeved, but he was also wearing his gloves.

Broussard was saddened to see how young the slain wife was. The tragedy of her death and the work he had to do to close out her life fully occupied his mind for the next few hours.

A little before 5:00 P.M., Phil Gatlin showed up in Broussard's office. The look on his face told the story.

"They didn't find 'em?" Broussard said.

Gatlin wiped his big mitt over his face, fuzzing his eyebrows. "No." He dropped his big frame into a chair and gripped the armrests as if it were a carnival ride about to take off. "But you were right about the ship. They did smuggle some birds into the city. One of the crew spilled the whole story. Two of the crew apparently died at sea of that same disease. The rest of the crew was afraid they were contagious, so they threw them overboard."

"But not the birds?"

"They didn't realize the birds and the disease were connected, so they kept them. They didn't report the deaths because they didn't want to generate any curiosity while the birds were still on board. The plan was that as soon as they got a couple of hundred miles into international waters, they were gonna report that they'd just lost the men overboard in an accident of some sort."

"Did they know anything about Kit and Teddy?"

"Apparently not."

"Who was their contact here?"

"From the description, it was Beverly's brother."

"Is that gonna produce anything?"

"Nothing I can see."

"I got some information, too, but don't get too excited about it. I found a pet store that bought four parrots from our strangulation victim."

Gatlin slid to the front of his chair. "That's good. Now we've got a direct connection between Beverly's brother and him."

"I'm afraid that's all we've got. The guy gave the pet store a fake phone number, and I'm sure the name he gave is phony, too."

"Which is . . ."

"C. F. Dumond."

Gatlin thought a moment then said, "Cafe Dumond?"

"I think so."

"I'll check it out."

"What if we're right about the name—are we at a dead end?"

"Maybe not. Before the *Schrader* hit port, they taped the birds' beaks shut and stuffed each bird in a short length of plastic pipe that they packed in crates labeled as sewing machine parts. Those crates were in the trailer when they were unloaded."

"Customs didn't look in them?"

"This ship line drops empty containers off here all the time. Customs used to check, mostly for drugs, but they've been clean for so long, they just quit checking. But there must have been a truck that hauled those crates away. It's too late today, but tomorrow morning I'll go down there again and ask around. Now, I'm gonna go check on C. F. Dumond."

At the door, he paused and stared for a moment at the frosted glass panel; then he turned. "You ever go two weekdays without mail at your house?"

"Not that I can recall. Why?"

"Just wondering."

After Gatlin left, Broussard popped a lemon ball into his cheek and briefly considered Gatlin's odd question. Then he rocked back in his chair, laced his fingers over his belly, and thought about how fine life had been before all this had begun.

18

This time, they'd put Teddy in the truck first, trying to be unpredictable, Kit thought. All day, she'd been wanting to talk to Larry without Roy around—to tell him Roy knew there was no money and that he was just playing Larry for a fool. But there'd been no opportunity.

Larry switched on the police scanner.

"Six eighteen, can you run a tag?"

"Go ahead."

"Tennessee plate four, two, seven, Lima, Victor, Delta."

"Roger, checking."

"Six twelve, we'll be special unless you get something that can't wait."

"Roger."

"Ochoa to six leader . . . silver Lexus approaching."

"Roger."

In Kit's courtyard, sitting on a chair he'd taken from the kitchen, Phil Gatlin lowered his radio and listened for the Lexus. A moment later, he heard it move into range. Most likely it was nothing; in fact, this whole idea that someone was picking up Kit's mail during the night was probably nuts.

The Lexus was directly in front of Kit's gate. . . The engine slowed. . . Gatlin slipped his 9-mm from his shoulder holster, hoping for the sound of a car door. But it didn't happen and the car continued past.

Larry turned the truck onto Dauphine.

"Fortier to six leader . . . Lexus clear."

Gatlin reholstered his gun and stood up. He adjusted his shorts and began a little stroll around the courtyard to get the stiffness out of his legs.

In the truck, Roy's mind replayed the exchange he'd heard on the scanner, splicing out the intervening transmissions. "Ochoa to six leader . . . silver Lexus approaching. . . . Lexus clear."

"Turn left on St. Philip and keep going," Roy said suddenly.

From where he sat in his car parked to their right on St. Philip, Sgt. Victor Ochoa watched them turn. He remained interested only until he was certain they didn't stop on St. Philip and send anyone back on foot. Then they were erased from his mind.

"Why didn't we stop?" Larry said.

"Did you hear that transmission on the radio about the Lexus?"

"I wasn't listening real close."

"She set us up. Those were cops waiting at her house for us."

"How'd she do that?"

"I'm not sure. But she's clever."

"Let's just kill them both and get out of here."

"We're not leaving. There's too much at stake."

"But we *are* gonna kill them. . ."

Kit could hear the eagerness in Larry's voice.

"We're going to keep them as bargaining chips in case we get into a tight spot. If they cooperate, when our business is done, we'll let them live. Did you two hear that . . . the part about cooperating? If you fail to meet your obligation in this arrangement, it releases us from ours."

In her imagination, Kit spit in his face. But even if she'd been able to, she wouldn't have actually done it. Better to let him think they believed his lie.

"So I guess we have to give up trying to get her money," Larry said.

"There never was any money," Roy said.

Kit was shocked to hear him admit it.

"Like I said, it was a setup. I didn't realize it until I heard it on the radio."

"There ought to be a penalty for that," Larry said.

"I agree."

They drove for quite a while; then the truck came to a stop and Larry got out. A few seconds later, there was a sliding sound. Larry returned to the truck, moved it a short distance, and cut the engine. Both men got out and the rear doors were opened. Kit felt a tug and some sawing at her ankles that freed them.

"Out," Roy said.

He helped her to her feet and pulled her by the arm, propelling her around the right side of the truck, over what felt like a dirt floor.

"Step up . . . about six inches," Roy said.

She did as he said and the dirt under her feet changed to something hard, definitely not wood—cement maybe.

There was a light switch thrown and Roy pulled her another ten feet or so. A door opened and another switch was thrown. Roy removed her blindfold. He stripped the tape from her mouth and plucked out the headband gagging her.

"Welcome home," he said. "It's not much, but we're simple people."

They were in a small windowless room with a cement floor and chipboard walls. Overhead, a naked lightbulb with barely enough wattage to illuminate the inside of a refrigerator threw ugly shadows over a stained mattress on the floor. Two grimy pillows on the mattress were the only other objects in the room.

"Down."

She got to her knees on the mattress and Roy pushed her over. It wasn't far to fall, but it still hurt when her shoulder hit. Roy left without bothering to retie her feet, shutting the door behind him and securing it with what she believed were two sliding bolts.

Her arms ached at the shoulders and her mouth was an arid country. The air around her smelled of mold and wine and unwashed body crevices, some of the latter most surely her own.

Where was Teddy? The thought they were preparing him for one of those damn penalties sent a wave of anger through her. Intending to check the door for a crack that would allow her to see into the adjoining room, she pushed herself up on one elbow and tried to gather her legs under her to stand, but there was no way to get any leverage.

She dropped back onto the mattress and used one leg to raise onto her left shoulder, but from there she could do nothing more.

Damn.

Heart pounding from the effort she'd exerted, she lay there, frustrated at her inability to get up. All she could do was wiggle on the mattress like an inchworm.

An inchworm . . .

She sat up and quickly discovered that by using her heels and knuckles, she could inch from one place to another. If she could get to a wall, she could put her back against it and maybe . . .

Slowly, she made her way to the chipboard wall. Now, back against it. . . Jesus, she was sweating like crazy, and now she was sure of it: She stank.

After a brief rest to gather her strength, she dug her heels into the mattress and pressed her back hard against the wood, hoping she could slide herself to her feet.

Uggggh.

Damn it. The angle was wrong, and all she did was press herself against the wall.

Suddenly, the bolts were thrown and Roy brought Teddy in.

"If you've hurt him again . . ." she began.

"We didn't," Roy said, pulling off Teddy's blindfold. He stripped the tape from Teddy's mouth and removed the headband gag. He brought Teddy to the mattress, swept his feet out from under him, and dropped him onto it, breaking his fall by holding on to his arm.

Larry had come in behind Roy and now they both came for Kit, picking her up by her arms.

"Leave her alone," Teddy croaked. "Or I swear you'll pay for it."

Ignoring him, they took her into the adjoining room and sat her in a white folding chair they must have brought from the trailer. Roy bolted Teddy's door.

There were no windows in this room, either, its illumination coming from a couple of fluorescent fixtures recessed into a drop ceiling liberally decorated with yellow water stains. The walls were painted plasterboard with saw-toothed raw spots where the facing had been peeled off. At least a dozen of the tile squares covering the floor were missing, revealing cement underneath.

To Kit's left, two more mattresses were pushed against the wall. In front of her sat an old oak desk; behind it, against the wall separating this room from the one where Teddy waited, was a six-foot wall of cubbyholes. Though she'd been in the room mere seconds, she had already noted the location of every additional door . . . one beside the mattresses, two on the opposite wall . . . one behind her . . . all of them closed. Reconstructing the path they'd taken coming in, she believed the one behind her led to the truck.

Larry dug in his pocket and came out with a half-dollar that he held up so she could see it. Reaching into a grocery sack near his feet, he produced a small self-contained torch and put it and the half-dollar on the desk.

And of course they'd brought the damn twine.

Larry got down in front of her with a length of it to retie her feet. Seeing him in such a vulnerable position, her resolve to give no indication of resistance disappeared and she lashed out with both feet, catching him in the face and toppling her chair.

The next thing she knew, Roy was straddling her and his belt was around her neck.

"I will not have this nonsense," he said, tightening the belt. His face was six inches from hers. She looked into his pale eyes and saw that his irises were abnormal—no striations or radiating rays of color variation, just a homogenous pale blue, as though they'd been cut from construction paper.

The belt was pinching and bruising . . . constricting . . . pain. Her head felt as though it were blowing up like a balloon. . . . The pressure . . . everywhere tight . . . air . . .

"It's death, Kit, so very close . . . just seconds away," Roy crooned. "Are you thinking of God and how you've ignored Him? Are you praying? Blink your eyes twice for yes and three times for no and maybe I'll stop."

Kit's head felt close to bursting and Roy's face was beginning to blur, obscured by the Kit Franklyn memorial fireworks display commencing behind her eyes. She wasn't thinking of God but, rather, was enveloped in hatred for Roy, the emotion pure and sharp, so strong it would permit no cooperation, regardless of the cost. Summoning the last of her waning resources, she poured them into the pathways controlling her eyelids, ordering them to remain motionless. It would have been so easy to close them and die, but that wouldn't show him how she felt.

"Do it," Roy ordered. "It could save you. Tell me. . ."

She saw his face dimly now, superimposed on a night sky filled with white starbursts, yet her eyes remained open. The aerial display in her head reached a crescendo; then suddenly, it was over. With the pyrotechnic arsenal expended, the night closed in upon itself.

She thought at first she was dead, but then, accompanied by the beat of a kettledrum, she faintly heard Roy say, "You are one crazy woman."

She was lifted from the floor and dropped in the folding chair. As the drumming in her ears began to subside, it was replaced by a horrid rasping sound, which she soon realized was her own breathing. Her vision cleared and there was Roy, sitting on the desk.

"You need psychiatric help," he said. "Anyone who would put defiance above self-preservation is very disturbed."

"You just bring out the best in people," Kit croaked.

"We're still gonna burn her, aren't we?" Larry said.

"There's no point. Get Ted in here."

Roy took Teddy's pistol out of his pocket and put the barrel behind Kit's ear. "I know this doesn't mean anything to you. . . . It's for Ted's benefit."

Larry pushed Teddy into the room.

"Give us any trouble and you both die," Roy said. "Larry, bring those chairs over here."

Larry picked up a straight-backed chair and carried it to Kit's side. "Where do you want it?"

"Right in front of her."

Larry put the chair down.

Roy looked at Teddy. "That one's yours."

His black eyes as cold as Roy's, Teddy stepped in front of Kit and sat down, his knees nearly touching hers. Larry arrived with the desk chair and Roy had him put it to Kit's right, so the three chairs formed a triangle.

"Tie his feet to the chair."

Larry did as Roy ordered, and when he was finished, Roy had him pass a length of twine around Teddy's waist and tie him into the chair. He then ordered the same treatment for Kit, threatening to kill Teddy if she resisted.

"We're going to free your arms now," Roy said, stepping back. "If either of you makes any trouble, I'll kill both of you." Roy nodded and Larry cut Kit's hands free.

"No quick moves," Roy cautioned.

The warning was unnecessary, for Kit's arms were loath to leave the tied-back position and sharp pains stabbed at her shoulders as she slowly brought her hands in front of her.

The procedure was repeated with Teddy.

"Both of you reach out and grasp the other by the wrists."

Though her shoulders ached when she lifted her arms and she and Teddy were both utterly under Roy's control, the feel of Teddy's fingers on her skin gave her renewed hope and she felt that somehow they'd get out of this.

"Tie their wrists together."

When Larry was finished with that, Roy had him run a length of twine from one pair of their joined wrists to the opposite leg of Teddy's chair. He repeated this with the other pair, effectively restraining any side-to-side or upward motion of their joined hands.

Kit saw that Teddy's lips were dry and cracked and seeing that reminded her how much she wanted a drink of water. For a moment, she lost her grip on reality and she was home in the shower, cool water pouring over her . . . enveloping her . . . water in her face . . . in her mouth . . . running down her throat.

Larry's voice brought her back.

"We doing him again?"

"She's given us no choice," Roy said.

Larry produced a cigarette lighter and thumbed the flint. He held the resulting yellow flame in front of the torch and turned it on, spawning an evil blue saber with a malignant whisper. He donned a single black glove from the bag that had held the torch and returned to the bag for a pair of pliers, which he used in his gloved hand to pick up the half-dollar and put it in the flame.

Roy sat in the desk chair and pulled it in close to Kit and Teddy. His face so close to hers she could see the pores in his skin, he said, "I think the problem with the way we did this last time was that it was all too abstract. Ted was in one room and you were in another. From your perspective, there was no immediacy to the situation.

You didn't hear or see any part of it, so it was relatively easy for you to wash it from your mind. But tonight will be different. I'm sure we won't hear Ted cry out. Even if he was the type to do that, his wish to appear strong in your presence would probably give him the resolve to stay quiet. But you may feel his palms sweat. Or are they already doing that?"

Teddy's hands did indeed feel moist against her skin. She was sure hers were no drier.

Seeing he would get no answer from her, Roy moved on. "His pulse will probably speed up as well, but I don't think your fingers are properly placed to detect that. Pay particular attention to his eyes, though. When the pain is greatest, we should see some change in his pupils. We may also hear and smell his skin cooking."

Kit's anger for Roy and her fear for Teddy filled her mind, making it hard to think. And she had to think, because the situation had become more complicated. Though she'd spent many hours reading and studying the motivation behind criminal behavior, Roy was a paper yet to be written. Her refusal to give him anything to feed on had been based more on pure stubbornness than insight. But now, she suddenly saw the choices before her and their consequences more clearly. If she denied Roy any emotional reaction to what Larry was about to do, he might raise the stakes, hurting Teddy even more the next time to force her to give him what he craved. On the other hand, if she gave in, it would show she could be broken, and that might bring him back for more, also with higher stakes.

In her heart, she believed there was no answer. Either choice would lead to more torture. The only solution was escape. Realizing it was a rigged contest, Kit chose the same route she'd traveled to this point. She'd give him nothing.

19

Kit stared at the rusty water in her cupped hands, then lowered her face and drank deeply, ignoring the rattling water pipes. No bubbling spring in the French Pyrenees could have been more satisfying. She refilled her hands and drank again . . . and again, then splashed water over her face and rubbed it in.

She turned off the water and dried ineffectually on a length of toilet paper from a limp roll sitting on the back of the toilet. Reluctantly, she looked in the mirror over the sink. The silver backing on the mirror had flaked away in blisters, giving her the appearance of having a pox. Between these lesions, she looked even worse than she imagined, like a prospector who'd been dragged facedown for miles by his horse. She craned her neck and saw that it still bore an angry red ring where Roy had tried to strangle her.

Unable to look at herself for another second, she turned her attention to the grimy toilet, whose rim was caked with yellow stains. Below the waterline, its bowl was pecan brown.

The paint on the seat was cracked and bubbled as though the material under it was disintegrating from being constantly wet. She'd have given anything she owned for a waterproof seat cover, but here again, she was trapped. The only option left was the obnoxious, barnyard curtsy. Envying for the moment the way males were plumbed, she tore off another piece of toilet paper and plugged the keyhole to keep Larry from looking in. Knowing he was also listening, she again turned on the tap in the sink. With the same determination that had seen her through Teddy's ordeal, she did what was necessary, all the while keenly aware there was no way to lock the door.

When she finished, she adjusted her clothing and shifted her attention to a hinged window on the wall next to the toilet. The glass was covered with yellow paint, so she couldn't tell what was on the other side. The latch, too, was encrusted with paint, but with a little effort she got it to work. The window, though, was firmly painted shut.

Larry pounded on the door. "You about done in there?"

She shut off the water in the sink, flushed the toilet, and opened the door.

Larry was waiting with the twine. "Come out here and put your hands behind you. Remember, Roy's watching Ted."

Kit stepped into the room and placed her hands in position. "Larry, Roy didn't learn from the radio tonight that there was no money," she whispered. "He's known it all along. He's been treating you like a fool."

"The spot you're in, you'd say anything," he said, tying her.

"It's true. He's putting you both at risk just to amuse himself."

"Roy's my brother. I'd believe him any day before I'd trust you."

Larry took her back to the room where Teddy and Roy waited and pushed her onto the mattress. After retying her feet, both of them took Teddy to the bathroom.

As they were leaving, Kit's eyes fixed on the sailor flap cut in Teddy's shirt. She could tell where he'd been burned the first time by the dried exudate staining the fabric. And soon, there would be another stain, most likely bigger, judging from what Larry had said about the torch being much better than the stove at heating the coin.

Roy had been right. With it all happening a few inches away, it hadn't been possible to insulate herself from it as effectively as when Teddy was in a different room. She'd managed as before to show no reaction, but she'd been all too aware of every second of his ordeal.

Through it all Teddy had been a brick, making no sound at all. But as Roy had predicted, the pain had caused his pupils to dilate. And even now, she could hear the frying-bacon sound the coin made when Larry had pressed it against his skin.

This must stop. It *must.*

In her desperation, she imagined that by now, Broussard had figured out what the glitter was on Burras's shoes. She pictured Gatlin and a bunch of other detectives lying in wait for Roy and Larry to return to the source of the glitter. But *had* he figured it out? Had the body even been found? These prickly questions showed her the odds were too long to rely on someone else rescuing them. She and Teddy would have to help themselves.

This brought her back to the bathroom window. If she could somehow open it and slip out . . . then what? If she tried that, Roy would probably kill Teddy. The glitter . . . Broussard had to figure out the glitter.

Teddy was back in less than five minutes. Then thankfully, Roy and Larry left them alone, but with the lights off.

Wincing, Teddy turned to face her.

"Does it hurt terribly?" she asked.

"I can deal with it. But we need to reach an understanding."

"About what?"

In the next room, Larry had turned on the police scanner. Teddy lowered his voice. "We both know they're not going to let us live."

"Yes."

"That means we have to take advantage of whatever opportunities are given to us and be willing to take some risks."

"I don't understand."

"I mean we can't let them use one of us to control the other . . . this idea that if *you* do anything to upset them, they'll kill *me*. You have to put that out of your mind. When Larry took you to the bathroom, did he stay outside?"

"Yes."

"Roy watched me, so I couldn't check it out, but there's a painted-over window in the bathroom."

"I saw it—the latch works, but the window itself won't budge."

"It's probably painted shut. If we can figure out a way to get it open, do you have the courage to climb through it and escape?"

"And leave you behind?"

"Every minute we stay with these psychotics, hoping for an easy solution, the less likely it is either of us will survive. You wouldn't be leaving me; you'd be going for help. Besides, I don't think they'll make good on their threat. If you get away, I'll be too valuable as a hostage for them to kill me."

"What if I try and fail?"

"Sometimes you have to work without a net. Can you do it?"

"I guess I'll have to. We'll need something to cut through the paint film. . . ."

"We won't find it sitting here in the dark. We'll have to get the lights on. Sit up and shift your body so your back is toward me."

Kit sat up and glanced at the door, worried that if they were able to reach the switch, Roy and Larry would see the light through the crack at the bottom. But even sitting there in total darkness, she could barely see the light from Roy and Larry's side. So chances were good they wouldn't notice.

She got her legs shifted around to her left and felt Teddy's back touching hers.

"Dig your heels in and push up. . . I'll do the same."

Working together in this way, they managed to get on their feet.

"The scanner will cover a certain amount of noise, but we still need to be as quiet as we can," Teddy said. "My boots will make a lot more noise on the cement than your shoes."

Kit began hopping toward the light switch, trying to stay on the balls of her feet. By the time she reached it, her thighs ached and she was breathing hard. It was a simple matter to nudge the switch on with her shoulder. Taking a deep breath, she hopped back to Teddy.

"Look for anything we can use as a scraper," he said. Together, they scanned the bare room, paying particular attention to the intersection of the walls and floor, where a useful object might nestle unobserved. But the room was swept clean.

Then Kit saw something. "What about that?"

Teddy turned to see what she'd found—a large nail sticking out of the wall about eye level.

"That'd be perfect," he said. "But it's too high to get at. Damn . . . so close."

They both stood looking longingly at the nail, trying to think of some way to reach it. But neither could. Finally, accepting that it was fool's gold, they continued the search.

When Kit saw the second nail—at waist level—she nearly whooped out loud. She pointed it out to Teddy and he hopped over to it. He turned his back to the wall and set to work on the nail with his fingers, leaning outward and shifting his body slightly from side to side.

The way things had been going, Kit was sure the nail would be seated so firmly, he'd never get it out. But maybe they could use it to abrade the twine around their wrists.

She was about to suggest this when Teddy lurched forward and took a short hop to keep from falling.

"I got it," he said. "I bloody damn well got it."

He hopped to the mattress, where Kit waited; then he turned and showed her the nail. It was not as large as the first one, but it was big enough that she'd be able to get a good grip on it when the time came.

"Come closer and I'll put it in your pocket."

Kit maneuvered herself around to where Teddy could slip the nail into the one pocket in her slacks.

"Let's get the light off before they notice," Teddy said.

Kit made her way back to the switch and found she had to use her chin to turn it off. She went back to the mattress and they got down on it by reversing the procedure they'd used to get up.

Their hearts were barely back to beating normally after all the exercise when the police scanner went silent. The door opened and Roy flicked on the light. He brought in a chair and two books, sat down, and resumed reading aloud *The Old Man and the Sea,* picking up where he'd left off earlier, acting as if this was the most normal thing in the world.

A couple of pages into the session, he crossed one leg over the other and Kit saw several flecks of glitter on his new shoes. He'd put the shoes on for the first time earlier that night, just before they'd all gone out in the truck. The fact the shoes now had glitter on them meant the source was some part of this building. Obviously, Broussard *hadn't* figured it out.

Roy soon finished *The Old Man and the Sea* and began to read them an Ed McBain novel. It was all wasted on Kit, though, because her mind was on their escape plan. She knew the window might be painted shut on the outside as well as the inside and that might keep it from opening. It might even be held in place by nails or screws she couldn't see. But then again, maybe neither of those problems existed. . . Maybe this *was* going to work. But if it did, she'd be leaving Teddy behind. And so it went.

Ready to put him away, Broussard reached for the zipper on the inner body bag containing the strangulation victim. With the *Schrader* lead dwindled away to the name C. F. Dumond and a hypothetical truck that might have picked the smuggled birds up at the dock, he'd gone over the body yet again, trying to link it to someplace other than where it had been found. And like all the other times he'd examined it, he'd learned nothing.

As the zipper meshed over the cadaver's chin, it stalled. Broussard shifted his stance and grabbed the bag below the jam. With his other hand, he managed to back the zipper up and free it.

Lord, but it was hot in here. He made a mental note to call Maintenance and have them check the morgue's climate controls.

Close inspection of the zipper revealed one slightly misaligned tooth. Not in the mood to shift the cadaver into another bag, he pulled the plastic taut so the two sides of the zipper were on the same plane and tried again.

And again it jammed.

Frustrated at being thwarted in his examination of the body and still plagued by the headache he'd awakened with two hours earlier, he was not about to let a zipper get the best of him. Grabbing the bag below the jam, he tried to work the zipper past the bad tooth. In doing so, the force he exerted on the zipper was transferred to the gurney and from there to the cadaver, whose head began to jiggle from side to side.

Out of the corner of his eye, Broussard caught a flash of reflected light from the rim of the cadaver's left nostril. Puzzled, he reached in and moved the cadaver's head from side to side.

There it was again. . . .

Bending for a closer look, he tilted his own head to get the image onto the bifocal part of his glasses, then moved the cadaver's head slowly from side to side.

There . . . a fleck of something shiny . . .

His heart tripping with excitement, he stripped off his gloves, threw them into the biohazard box, and put on a fresh pair. He then grabbed a long-handled cotton swab and a test tube. He moistened the swab with distilled water from a squirt bottle and returned to the body, where he carefully picked up the shiny fleck with the swab.

He put the swab into the test tube, broke off the protruding part of the swab handle, and capped the tube. The broken part of the handle went into the biohazard box and the test tube containing the swab went into another larger tube, which he likewise capped.

He put a biohazard label on the outer tube and slipped the tube into a clean beaker to hold it while he changed out of his morgue garb. Guy could deal with that balky zipper.

Two minutes later, he charged into the hall and practically ran for the elevator. Reaching his office, he went immediately to his desk and looked up the number of the Tulane Fine Structure Facility, which he knew had a scanning electron microscope fitted with a unit that could analyze solid samples by X-ray dispersal.

Mopping at the perspiration on his brow with some Kimwipes, head throbbing, he made the call and convinced the director of the facility that this was a sample needing top priority.

With the way cleared for its analysis, he grabbed the double test tube containing the swab and headed for the door. He was met there by the shadow of a visitor on the frosted glass. Whoever it was showing up without an appointment was just gonna be out of luck, he thought, throwing the door open before any knock came.

"You're not going anywhere until we've had a talk," Mark Blackledge said, pushing on Broussard's chest with his fingers. He crowded closer, trying to force Broussard back into his office, but Broussard held his ground.

"I'm the epidemiologist on this case, not you," Blackledge groused. "Where do you get off following up leads without consulting me?"

"I told you we should check out the docks, but you wouldn't listen."

"We'd have done that."

"Why are you so upset? By splittin' up, we maximized our effort."

"*We* didn't do anything. You went behind my back without authorization—just to humiliate me."

"I know you'll find this hard to believe, but your feelin's were way down my list of priorities. I've lost an assistant to that virus and there's no tellin' how many more people in this city are at risk. It's even reached to Natchez. I've also got two friends who are apparently in the hands of the murderous thugs who brought the virus here. I've got no time to coddle an egocentric, self-absorbed screwball. Now, get outta my way."

At that moment, Broussard heard a sound at his feet. Looking down, he saw the plastic test tube he'd been holding lying on the floor. Finally, he caught on and every sphincter in his body puckered. He looked imploringly at Blackledge, who took a step backward, pointing at the vicinity of Broussard's mouth.

"Andy . . ."

Broussard brought his hand to his mustache, where his fingers touched the blood seeping into it from his nose.

20

"Andy, I'm afraid you're in trouble," David Seymour said through his mask. He looked at the chart in his hand. "Your electrolytes and kidney function are still okay, but you've got a PT of thirty-five, a PTT of sixty-five, and your platelet count is only ninety K."

"Which means I'm probably in the early stages of DIC."

"I think so. You're also tachycardic and hypotensive and your hematocrit is thirty-two, so you're probably losing blood somewhere, most likely into your upper GI tract."

Broussard's headache had changed from feeling as though someone was traveling across his brain on a pogo stick to a diffuse ache that extended down his neck and across his shoulders. He lifted his arms from the sheet covering him and checked the backs of his hands. The sudden shift to a closer plane of focus sent his head spinning. His vision blurred. A table in his gut tipped and his stomach slid off it. Mercifully, the episode passed as quickly as it had come and his vision cleared. So far, there was no sign of bleeding under his skin.

"Our first priority is to get that bleeding under control. So we're going to start you on some fresh frozen plasma and platelets," Seymour said. "Since we'll also be drawing a lot of blood,

I've ordered the staff to rig you up with an arterial as well as a venous line."

Broussard groaned at the thought.

"I know it won't be any fun, but we also need a nasogastric tube so we can monitor your stomach contents. I don't think at this stage there's any blood in your lungs, but I'm having a portable X-ray machine sent up to get a chest picture just to be safe."

Standing next to Seymour, also gowned, gloved, and masked, Mark Blackledge said, "Andy, I'm really sorry this happened."

"So am I," Broussard replied. About all that was visible of Blackledge's face were his eyes, in which Broussard saw himself already in his casket.

"I believe he's a little jaundiced," Blackledge observed.

"I'm not dead yet, Mark," Broussard said. "And I'm still conscious. So don't call me 'he.'"

"Sorry. *You* look a little jaundiced."

Seymour tapped the chart. "With these LFTs, that's not surprising. Andy, we've got some ribavirin on the way, too. We'll add that to the mix and then . . ."

I'll either beat this or die, Broussard thought. Now that it was close at hand, Broussard found that death didn't frighten him. The prospect that there might soon be a Broussard-sized hole in the universe brought no terror or self-pity. It was where everyone was heading eventually, and it was, he believed, like falling asleep.

Of course, given the choice, he'd rather stick around awhile longer . . . haggle a few more times over the price of a painting with Joe Epstein, have afternoon tea again in Paris in the Salon Pompadour at the Hotel Meurice on the Rue de Rivoli. . . . He pictured the Meurice's crystal chandeliers, the Louis XV almond-tinted wood-paneled walls with their gilt garlands, the portrait of Mme de Pompadour presiding over the patrons. And he'd really love to have read all of Louis L'Amour's novels. But he'd had a fine, long life. Considering how many people younger than he had come through the morgue, and how many had showed up on the obituary pages of the paper, and how many friends he'd lost, he'd done all right.

On the other hand, departing this life hemorrhaging from every orifice wasn't the most dignified way to go. In any event, he wasn't going anywhere until he knew what that shiny speck was.

"David, I had a big test tube in my pants pocket when I came up here. Where is it?"

"Probably bagged with your clothes," Seymour replied.

"Would you run it down for me? I'm gonna have someone come by and pick it up."

"Sure. We should have it decontaminated, though."

"Will you see to it?"

"Of course. I'll leave it at the nurses' station."

"It's important, so put it in the care of somebody responsible."

"I'll give it to Doris Knight, the unit coordinator."

Despite his aching head and a touch of vertigo, he remembered her from when he'd visited Natalie. "I've got a banger of a headache and some nausea. . ."

"I can give you something for the nausea, but I don't want to be too aggressive with that headache. If you start bleeding into your brain, I don't want you so doped up you won't be able to tell me what's happening. But I think we can safely go with some Tylenol. I'll go and write the orders and check on that test tube. Meanwhile, get some rest and try not to worry."

Seymour left and Blackledge went with him. Through the glass in the door to the staging room, he saw Blackledge shake his head and say something to Seymour. Then they disappeared into the hall.

Turning to the nightstand, he picked up the telephone receiver, intending to call Charlie Franks, but his eyes were now functioning independently, so instead of one set of numbers, he saw two that slowly drifted toward each other until they almost touched before springing apart and beginning the cycle again.

He stabbed at the button for the operator and hit the faceplate. On his second try, he got it. He gave the operator the extension for the ME's office and had his secretary page Franks, feeling too rocky to get into a conversation with her about where he was.

Finally, Franks answered.

Too nauseated to sit up any longer, he slid down in the bed and closed his eyes. "Charlie, hi, it's me, Andy. I've got myself in kind of a spot and need some help."

"If I help you this time, how do I know you won't just get yourself in the same predicament again?"

"No games, please. This is serious. I'm upstairs in the TB isolation ward . . . as a patient."

"Oh my God. You haven't . . ."

"I'm afraid so."

"Yes, sure, of course I'll help . . . anything. God."

"I need you to take somethin' over to the Tulane EM facility for me."

"Where is it?"

Broussard took a breath to answer and realized he didn't know where the sample was.

"Andy . . . where is it?"

"I . . . It's . . ." He had the distinct feeling it was somewhere close . . . not in the office . . . The nurses' station. "At the Pulmonary Unit's main nursin' station. Ask for Doris Knight. She's got it. It's a sample of somethin' I found on the body of that strangulation victim. I've already told the people at Tulane it should be treated as infectious, but you should stress that again to 'em. And also remind 'em I need the analysis ASAP. Call me as soon as it's delivered. I'm at five-six-eight-three."

"How are you doing?"

"I'll be doin' better when I know what that sample is."

He then lay back to rest. With his eyes closed, he saw the image of Natalie sitting on the floor, her clothes covered with blood, her mind addled, unable to speak. If he didn't get the results of that analysis quick, he might be in no shape to deal with it.

Before he realized it was going to happen, he vomited, spilling black blood in a large sunburst on the white linoleum floor.

"GET ME ANOTHER CUP of unleaded, will ya?" Dilly Dillenhofer said, slipping another dripping spoonful of fried egg into his ugly kisser. He had a fat face and slack rubbery lips that made him look like a special-effects creation that had a hand up his neck instead of an esophagus, but the eggs kept disappearing.

On the table was his eye patch and the corset he wore to keep from looking so well fed when he hit the streets with his cup. When anyone was so unkind as to point out that the crutch resting against the chair next to him was an unoriginal idea, he'd always say, "So sue me for plagiarism," which he pronounced with a hard g.

Nick Lawson signaled the waiter for another cup of coffee. It was useless, he knew, to expect Dilly to tell him anything while he was eating.

Finally, when his plate was clean and he'd drained the last drop of coffee from his cup, Dilly let out a satisfied sigh. "Ain't nothin' like a big greasy breakfast to get the old ticker goin' in the mornin'."

"Talk to me, Dilly," Lawson prodded.

"What I got for you is sort of a referral," Dilly said, wiping at some egg yolk on his shirt and discovering it was from yesterday's breakfast.

"What do you mean?"

"I don't personally have any information relatin' to your problem, but I know a guy who might."

"Who?"

"I get to keep the fifty, right?"

"Only if this guy delivers. Otherwise, it goes on my account."

"Fair enough, I guess. Go over to the French Market and look for a guy sells straw hats."

"What's his name?"

"They call him Igor, on accounta he's got funny shoulders."

"How come I never heard of this guy?"

"Maybe you ain't as smart as you think."

"I HOPE THAT TUBE isn't too uncomfortable," David Seymour said through his mask. He was referring to the plastic fire hose running into Broussard's stomach via his nose.

They'd put the arterial line in at his right wrist and the venous line at the front of his left elbow. He also had cardiac monitor leads taped to his chest. Next to the bed on the side opposite the nightstand, four IV monitors slyly winked numbers at him. Overhead, his cardiac monitor showed his blood pressure and his heart waves.

The Tylenol hadn't done much good and he was having trouble concentrating, so that before he could formulate a reply, Seymour's question broke up and fell to the floor. Then he remembered . . . the ng tube.

"You couldn't find one a little bigger, could you?"

Seymour's eyes attempted a smile. "I'll see if we can find one," he said. "Maybe with a big brass nozzle on the end." He patted Broussard's shoulder. "That's good, Andy. Fighting back with humor . . . I've always thought that humor, even with a sarcastic twist, helps the immune system. I'll check on you later."

Lying there alone, plumbed and wired like a physiology experiment, Broussard didn't feel humorous. He felt lousy and defeated. With only machinery for company, he turned inward, imagining himself in the land of L'Amour, as a great black horse galloping alongside a herd of stampeding buffalo, the prairie stretching before them. The buffalo . . . so powerful, their onslaught unstoppable, their hooves shredding the turf . . . And while he was with the buffalo, their strength became his and he felt better, so that when the phone rang, he let the herd go on without him and he stayed behind to answer it.

"Broussard."

"Dr. Broussard, this is Monica Martin at the Tulane Fine Structure Facility. We have the results on that sample you sent over. It's an alloy of chromium, molybdenum, and cobalt, called F seventy-five."

"What's it used for?"

"Almost exclusively for making surgical implants and instruments."

"Okay. Thanks for respondin' so quickly."

He hung up and closed his eyes. Surgical instruments . . . That rang a bell, but the sound was muffled by his aching head. He let the thought go and rejoined the buffalo, which had merged with another herd, so they now spread over the prairie from horizon to horizon. Intent on overtaking the leader, the great black horse ran hard, his mane blowing in the wind . . . the smell of buffalo overpowering, the sound like ten Niagara Falls . . . so powerful, so strong, and their strength was his.

Broussard's eyes opened wide and the buffalo disappeared. Grinding wheels . . . the final polish of surgical instruments . . . the glitter . . . S and I Fabrication on N. Peters Street, out of business since John Cates died, but he was sure the building was still there.

He reached for the telephone and called Phil Gatlin.

"HEY, BUDDY, COME HERE."

Roy shifted his grocery bag to his other arm and studied the flea market vendor beckoning him.

The fellow was standing in a stall that sold huge straw hats with lots of floppy loose ends around the brim. He carried a disproportionate amount of his weight in his shoulders, which were lumpy, as though he'd stuffed his shirt with socks. His face was wide and he had stiff, dry hair that formed a corona around a circular bald spot on his crown, so that his head resembled the hats he sold.

Believing this was just a flea market come-on, Roy turned to go.

"Don't leave," the guy said. "I don't just sell hats; I also deal in information, and I have some that you very much need."

Roy turned, appraised the guy again, and walked to the stall. "What information?"

"No." The guy shook his head. "Payment on delivery."

"I don't have time for this."

Roy started to leave, but the guy grabbed his arm, quickly pulling his hand back to safety when Roy fixed him with a cold stare.

"It's about a warehouse," the guy said, "and something about to happen there."

That got Roy's attention. "How do you come by this information?"

The guy shrugged and glanced toward the gate that led to the trailer where Roy had kept Kit and Teddy. "I'm an observant guy and a good listener."

"How much?"

"Fifty."

Roy put his sack down on the edge of a table and got out his wallet. After buying the things they'd needed to make the warehouse semihabitable, only seventy-three dollars was left from the money he'd taken from Kit and Teddy's accounts. He withdrew two twenties and a ten and held them out. When the guy reached for them, he snatched them back and grabbed the guy's wrist. "I wouldn't proceed unless I was absolutely sure I was offering a product worth the price."

"It comes with my guarantee."

Roy let him go and handed over the money.

"There's a newspaper reporter on his way to your warehouse right this minute," the guy said. "Is that worth the price?"

"Why would he be interested in my warehouse?"

The guy lifted his eyebrows. "It's not so much the warehouse as what's inside."

"What does this reporter look like?"

He hesitated, as if he was thinking about asking for more money.

"I wouldn't press my luck," Roy said.

"He's blond and wears his hair in a ponytail."

Roy had more questions, but he could spend no more time asking them.

"I think I'll take one of your hats, too," he said.

Obviously puzzled, the guy reached for one on the table, but Roy stopped him. "One of those," he said, pointing at a pile in a box on the stall floor.

"They're all the same," the guy said.

"I like that one, on top," Roy insisted.

Shrugging, the guy turned and bent down to get the hat.

As Roy cut the vendor's throat, he made sure he severed his trachea so he couldn't cry out. He wiped his knife on the vendor's shirt, returned the knife to his pocket, and picked up his bag of groceries.

"CALL HIM," TEDDY SAID. "If he'll go for it, there'll never be a better time."

Breakfast for all of them but Roy had been a commercial packaged sandwich and a carton of orange juice. Wanting apple juice with his sandwich, Roy had gone out to find some, leaving Larry as the only obstacle to freedom.

Kit took a long look at Teddy and inhaled deeply. "Larry, I need to use the bathroom," she shouted.

The door opened and Larry said, "You'll have to wait until Roy gets back."

"I can't. I have to go *now.*"

Larry didn't answer, but his manner became hesitant and unsure.

"I'm not kidding about this," Kit said.

His face full of conflict, Larry walked to the mattress and helped Kit to her knees. "Wait there."

He went back into the other room, quickly reappearing with his knife in one hand and his gun in the other. Circling behind Kit, he knelt and cut the twine binding her feet.

"Okay," he said. "Take everything slow now."

From her kneeling position, it was a simple matter for Kit to get on her feet. Heart beating so hard in her ears she was sure Larry could hear it, she moved to the doorway, Larry following a few feet back.

At the bathroom door, he instructed her to swing her hands away from her body. He cut them free and quickly stepped back.

"I'm also going to wash my face," Kit said, going in without looking at him.

With the door shut behind her, Kit grabbed the roll of toilet paper, stripped off enough to reduce it to the proper size, and squeezed it as flat as she could before wedging it under the door, taking care that it didn't show on the other side.

Now, the nail . . .

She reached in her pocket . . . Where was it?

Her finger's scoured the pocket, digging at its corners. . . .

No . . .

Her fingers found a hole in the fabric.

Gone . . . it was gone.

NICK LAWSON EASED HIS car onto N. Peters and appraised the bleak landscape before him. On his right, a twenty-foot-wide strip of grass littered with blow-around led to a tall brick wall, over which he could see the superstructure of freighters tied up at the docks. To his left was a succession of dreary structures that began with a power substation and its Frankenstein movie-set clutter of high-tension electrical gizmos.

He gave the car some gas, aimed it between potholes big enough to swallow it, and went on past two men loading lettuce into an old pickup in front of a one-story wooden eyesore with the word PRODUCE fading into oblivion over the entrance.

Next was a fairly decent-looking brick building from which coffee was distributed; then came a large vacant lot that bordered Spain Street. On the other side of Spain was the place the hat vendor had told him about, a battered corrugated-metal warehouse with no windows.

He pulled onto the shoulder and studied the place, which actually seemed to be two warehouses joined at the back so that water from the peaked roofs of each would accumulate in a long trough between them. Or maybe the water was somehow directed to that little pipe he saw coming out the front on the right, where whatever had poured from it had made an orange stain on the metal. Next to the stain, in vertical lettering, he could make out S AND I FABRICATION. Access to the warehouse seemed to be through a sliding door facing the street. On the door, some moron with a can of blue spray paint had proven that he'd mastered the spelling of four-letter words.

Lawson doubted there was any place in the world that looked more abandoned. In the weedy strip bordering the warehouse and Spain Street, he saw a mop, a small pile of broken concrete, and a bunched-up piece of plastic sheeting. A little beyond the warehouse, between the old railroad tracks that ran in front of all the buildings on that side of N. Peters, was a rusting eighteen-wheeler trailer sitting like a mother hen over a clutch of old tires. Overhead, a jockstrap hung from the warehouse's power line.

It was only a quarter of a mile from the French Market, yet the whole area was practically deserted. Back at the produce business, he'd seen the two guys loading lettuce, and far ahead, where the street seemed to end, a big truck was backing up to a loading dock, but there was no other sign of human activity. Across the vacant lot, he could see a row of small houses lining the street, but no one was around them, either.

With the top down, he could hear a foreign language being broadcast from one of the freighters, mixing with the plaintive cry of gulls wheeling through the cloudless blue sky. A crow landed on one of the major power lines in front of him and added its voice to the others.

Could Kit really be in there?

Kit searched the bathroom for something else she could use to cut the paint seal, but there was nothing. Frantically, she looked under the sink for something she could pull loose and use. . . . Nothing.

Her eyes fell on the metal switch plate by the door. Its corners were very sharp and one of the screws that held it on was missing. She stepped to the switch plate, pressed her thumb against the remaining screw, and tried to back it out, but it wouldn't budge. Nor could she turn it with her fingernail.

Her search turned to something she could use on the screw. But the room was equally unproductive for that. Without a plan in mind, she took the lid off the toilet tank and looked inside. Her eyes traveled over the contents—to the flush lever, the float, the flapper valve . . . the metal clip that held that little tube to the overflow. . . .

The metal clip . . .

She removed the clip, intending to use it as a makeshift screwdriver, then realized its corners were very sharp, too. Afraid to believe she'd found the answer, she turned on the cold-water faucet, setting the pipes vibrating. Under cover of their rattle, she began raking the edge of the clip along the paint sealing the window.

And it seemed to be working. But was it going deep enough?

By the time she'd made her way along the entire bottom of the window and had gone as high as she could reach vertically, her finger was aching from the pressure of the thin edge of the clip. To reach the upper part of the window, she got on the toilet and stepped across to the sink, praying it would hold her weight.

It was nearly impossible to use the clip in any manner but the way she'd been using it. And she couldn't change hands. Ignoring the pain in her finger, she went back to work.

Two minutes later, with six inches of the horizontal seam still to go, the sink shifted under her, dropping slightly. Whatever was holding it to the wall was giving way.

Nick Lawson considered his options. He could drive to a phone, call the cops, and let them handle it. But there was no assurance the hat vendor knew what he was talking about. He hadn't dealt with him before, so the guy had no track record. Considering all the cops who'd love for him to fall on his face, he couldn't risk turning in a false alarm. Besides, backing off wasn't the Lawson way.

He looked over his shoulder to make sure he wasn't about to jump into the path of a vehicle coming up from the rear, but his view was blocked by a brown paper bag three inches away. At the same instant that he heard the sound of the gun firing, his face was speckled with hot gunpowder and a bullet ripped through his cheek, came out his neck, and penetrated the passenger seat and floorboard before skidding off the pavement into the grass.

At last, the paint seal was fully scored. Kit reached down, disengaged the latch, and yanked on the handle. The window didn't budge. She yanked again, nearly pulling her arms out of the socket, but the window remained stuck.

Gathering her strength, she gave another mighty tug. The seal broke with a loud crack and the window swung open, so unpredictably, she nearly went over backward off the sink.

Looking out the window, her heart sank. She'd assumed the meal they'd had was breakfast, but there was no sunlight beyond the window. To the contrary, it was so dark, she could see nothing.

Suddenly, through the bathroom door, she heard Roy's voice.

"Get her out of there. We're leaving . . . for good."

As Larry tried to open the door against the toilet-paper roll wedged under it, Kit went through the window.

21

Kit landed in a crouch on a cement floor thick with dust, which went up her nose in clouds. Stifling a sneeze, she heard a grunt and the heavy thump of a shoulder being thrown against the bathroom door.

The small square of light spilling through the open window left the limits of the room in darkness, so she could tell very little about her surroundings. As the bathroom door took another hit, she spotted, to her left and about ten feet ahead, a grid pattern glowing weakly near the floor.

Remaining in a crouch, she scuttled in that direction. Reaching the spot, she looked through the grid and saw the back of the white panel truck.

"She got out the window," Larry yelled from the bathroom.

Realizing the grid was a ventilator panel in a door, Kit jumped up and twisted the doorknob.

Locked.

Instinctively, she kicked at the panel, but it was made of a stout material that hardly rang with the blow. The bathroom window closed and she heard the latch being thrown. The room now was in utter darkness.

Were they just going to leave her here? Highly unlikely. They were probably coming around to get her.

She fumbled for the light switch, praying there was one, and even while that prayer was still on her lips, she found it. But when the light came on, she was stunned and sickened to find herself in a room that, except for a wall of metal shelving, was bare.

She dashed to the shelves and pulled on the framework, hoping to find a loose member she could use as a club, but everything was securely welded together. Her mind raced, escape now appeared hopeless.

Her thoughts locked on what she'd heard Roy say: "Get her out of there. We're leaving . . . for good."

Something was obviously about to happen. Maybe help coming . . . But they all might be gone when it arrived . . . or Roy and Larry would be gone and she and Teddy . . .

She ran to the door, dropped to one knee, and looked again at the truck. Returning to the shelves, she wrote her name in the dust on one of them and added, HELP WHITE TRUCK and the truck's license number, which she'd seen through the vent.

Footsteps coming . . .

She looked at the floor and could clearly see her footprints going to the door and then to where she stood. In the last seconds before Roy and Larry reached her, she crisscrossed the room, obscuring the path to the message she'd left.

The door flew open and Roy and Larry came for her.

"THERE'S NO ONE HERE, Lieutenant," Sergeant Tapp, head of the NOPD Tac Unit said.

Gatlin turned from the cages holding what he estimated as two hundred screeching parrots. "I was afraid of that. Not much doubt it was that reporter Lawson who spooked them. Never did like that guy."

Tapp lifted his eyebrows in surprise at his comment, their movement causing the overhead lights to reflect off a fleck of glitter he'd picked up in his search.

"Awright, I'm not happy he took one in the face. But he's why we're standing here looking stupid." The discomfort of his own mask and the short crotch on the jumpsuit he was wearing over his clothes did nothing to help Gatlin's foul mood. "The medics say how it looks?"

"Not good, but he was still alive when they left with him. You want us to stick around?"

"No. These bottom-feeders won't be back. I'm gonna take a quick tour of the place. Then I'll probably check on Lawson, see if he can tell us anything."

"I wouldn't count on that. Least, not right away."

"Why don't you go over to the orphanage and tell all the kids there's no Santa Claus."

"I think they already know."

"Go on, beat it. Make sure you all check yourselves for ticks before you leave. If you find any, don't touch them with your bare hands. And incinerate them with a cigarette lighter."

Tapp left and Gatlin returned to the room with the desk and the refrigerator. He strolled over to the two mattresses on the floor and threw their pillows aside. He then picked up the end of one mattress and looked under it. Seeing only the floor, he let it drop, producing a whoosh of flophouse air. He did the same to the other mattress.

He approached the fridge and opened the door. Seeing no kidnapper's itinerary inside, he closed it and went to the desk, where he briefly examined a copy of *The Old Man and the Sea*, then ran all the desk drawers. This phase of his investigation produced some thumbtacks, three paper clips, and a cardboard cylinder of dried roach bait. Near the desk, he knelt and examined some small pieces of twine. Moving into the adjacent room, he found more pieces of twine, more pillows, and another mattress, which he also lifted.

It didn't take a twenty-year man to figure out this was where they'd kept Kit and, most likely, Teddy, if they were both still alive.

And he believed they were, because the kidnappers had made no effort to hide the body of the strangulation victim, suggesting that if Kit and Teddy were dead, their bodies would probably have already been found. The Franklyns had still received no ransom request, so the reason for Kit's abduction remained unexplained.

He stood for a few seconds, absorbing the room, then left and went to examine the bathroom.

The first thing he noticed was the immobile door, stuck in a half-open position. Sucking in his gut, he squeezed inside and saw the toilet paper jammed between the door and the floor. He turned and his eyes locked on the window and the paint chips on the sill. He opened the window and looked into the next room, whose light was on. Getting a distinct picture, he turned to the toilet, whose tank top was sitting on the seat. It took no more than a few seconds for him to notice that the clip for the overflow pipe was missing.

He turned and looked on the floor under the window—more paint chips . . . and . . . there was the missing clip. Someone had gone out that window.

He left the bathroom, crossed the room with the desk, and went into the garage portion of the building, where he found the door he'd seen from the bathroom. Opening it, he stood on the threshold and looked at all the footprints in the dust. Paying careful attention, he saw three sets. Those in greatest number were also the smallest.

"Lieutenant?"

Gatlin turned, to see one of the uniforms assigned to the operation.

"We just got word there was a murder committed in the French Market that sounds like it happened about the same time the reporter was shot."

"Who was killed?"

"Some guy that ran a hat concession. His throat was cut."

"Thanks. I'll check it out. Now get out of here."

The French Market, in broad daylight . . . an unlikely place and time for a murder. This new connection called to him and he was eager to learn the details and question the vendors whose stalls bordered the victim's. Someone had to have seen the killer.

He left the warehouse, pulled off his mask, and walked over to where the uniform who'd told him about the hat vendor was sitting in his patrol car.

"I'm going to the French Market. How about keeping an eye on this place until I can get someone over here to take care of things?"

"Be glad to."

He warned him about going inside again and had him get out of the car. After checking each other for ticks, Gatlin suggested that the uniform give the patrol car's interior a thorough search to be sure he hadn't brought one into it from the warehouse. They discussed what he should do if he found one; then Gatlin went to his own car and shucked the jumpsuit and his rubber gloves before heading to the French Market.

As he passed the coffee dealership, he thought about how the small footprints in the dusty room were most likely Kit's. Opposite the produce business, he remembered how resourceful Kit had been in other situations. At the electrical substation, he turned the car around.

"My face hurts," Larry said, gently touching the fiery chevron where Kit had scratched him during the scuffle in the dusty room.

"She got you pretty good," Roy said from the passenger seat. "Now slow down. I don't want to get stopped for a traffic violation."

On the floor between them, the police scanner provided background noise for the drive. In the back, bound, gagged, and blindfolded, Kit and Teddy lay in their usual positions. They'd been under way for perhaps ten minutes.

"What are we gonna do for money?" Larry asked.

"The Lord will provide," Roy told him.

"What hurts even more than my face is what we left behind," Larry said. "All that work for nothing."

"Look at all the experience you got."

"And I'm tired of hauling those two around."

"Won't be necessary for much longer."

Then, from the scanner came, "All cars . . . Be on the lookout for a white truck, make and model unknown, license, Sierra, two, two, five, eight, eight. Occupants believed armed and dangerous and may have hostages. Number and sex of suspects are unknown. Hostages may be one male and one female."

Kit's spirits practically lifted her off the truck floor. Gatlin had found her message.

"That's us," Larry whined. "How'd they know?"

"Secrets, it seems, are difficult to keep here," Roy replied, opening the glove compartment.

Kit heard the rustle of paper and assumed Roy was unfolding a map.

"We've got to get off the road and hide out for a while," Roy said. "Fortunately, Jack was prepared for this. And so was I. That's why we came this way. If we can make it another twenty miles or so, we'll be fine."

For the next twenty minutes, Kit listened hard for the sound of a siren, but apart from Roy occasionally telling Larry where to turn, there was only the low hum of the tires against the pavement when it was on solid ground, the change in pitch when they passed over water, and the constant cop chatter on the scanner.

Finally, Roy said, "There . . . that's it. That's what we want."

The truck slowed and Kit felt it make a right turn. The road became bumpy. One second, she was rolling against Teddy; the next, he was being thrown against her.

This went on for quite a long time. Finally, Roy told Larry to stop the truck and get out.

Kit heard the doors open, and the truck rocked as both men left their seats. Kit was well aware what this could mean. A bumpy road was certainly an unpaved one, and that meant they were now somewhere in the boondocks. She thought about crime-scene photos she'd seen of abduction victims who'd been driven to remote areas and murdered. And when Larry had complained about hauling them around, Roy said it wouldn't be necessary much longer.

Thinking it might be the last time she'd be able to feel his touch, she shifted her body so she lay against Teddy and then waited for whatever was about to happen.

And waited . . . and waited.

What were they doing?

She pictured them digging . . . a shallow grave big enough for two. The cruelty of it was that she and Teddy would die without being able to say anything to each other. There was also cruelty in the waiting, lying there with her heart pushing on the headband in her mouth.

Then the rear doors opened and the truck rocked as one of them got in. Hands grabbed at her shoulders and her ankles and she was slid from the truck.

Outside, she was stood on her feet. One of them put his shoulder against her middle and lifted her like a big sack of dog food, which made her think of Lucky and wonder if Bubba would keep him when she was gone.

She could tell from the way she was shifted about that the terrain was irregular. In the distance, birds chirped, oblivious to what was happening to her. She imagined them stopping briefly at the sound of the gunshot that would end her life and then picking up again a few seconds later as though it had meant nothing. Or maybe Roy planned to strangle her, which wouldn't disturb the birds at all.

She heard the rustle of weeds and felt them brush her face at the same time that she became aware of a moist algal odor. The terrain seemed to grow unstable and she could feel whoever was carrying her struggling to keep his balance. His footsteps now had a hollow sound.

She was dropped—not onto hard dirt, but a piece of hard wood—a boat seat. The chirping birds now seemed happy for her. Roy wasn't going to kill her, at least not right now.

The boat continued to rock as whoever had been carrying her went back onto shore. A few seconds later, she heard the truck being started and then it drove away. She'd begun to think they'd all left her, when she heard the rustle of weeds. Accompanied by the sound of scuffling, the boat began to rock again. It shuddered as something hit down hard.

The boat rocked and hollow footsteps came toward her. Her blindfold was stripped away. In the glare of light so bright she could barely keep her eyes open, she saw Roy standing over her. He pulled the tape from her mouth and removed the headband gagging her. Squinting from the light, Kit leaned to the side to see around him.

She was sitting in the stern of a boat with three other seats. In the second from the small one in the bow, Teddy sat facing forward, still blindfolded.

"Where's Larry?" she croaked, sounding like Janis Joplin after a two-hour set.

"He took the truck back up the road so if anyone finds it, the swamp won't be the first place they think we went."

"How about taking off Teddy's blindfold and gag, too?"

"He'll probably just use the opportunity to show us how angry he is."

"Isn't he entitled?"

"So we're back to the concept of fair play. Listen to me." He leaned down and squeezed Kit's chin between his fingers.

"Fair play exists only in prep school mottoes and crocheted onto doilies. It's a myth. Stop pretending it isn't."

He let her go and turned his back.

She considered throwing herself at him, then realized all it would accomplish would be to tip them both into the brown water, where he would simply scramble to shore and she'd drown.

After his tirade about fair play, Kit was surprised to see him remove Teddy's blindfold and gag.

"Angry?" Teddy said, his voice only slightly more normal than Kit's. "You bet. The word doesn't do justice to my feelings about you. We need a new word for that. And you're wrong about fair play. You'll realize that before this is over and you're on the other side of things."

"Sounds more like retribution than fair play," Roy said.

"Don't talk to him," Kit said. "He's enjoying it."

"I was rather," Roy admitted, straddling the seat between Kit and Teddy so he could see both of them. Kit saw on the front seat a couple of books Roy had brought.

They sat without talking, waiting for Larry's return, the only sounds the distant chirping birds, until high above them, a shrill *kee-you, kee-you* signaled the arrival of a red shouldered hawk. It circled twice, then flew away on wings that made Kit hugely envious.

A short time later, well before Larry himself appeared, Kit heard the sputter of the police scanner, faint at first, then louder. Larry's head and shoulders came into view over the tall grass lining the bank. He dipped to one side and a flat piece of metal sailed over the swamp, hit the water, and sank—the truck's license plate, Kit assumed.

There followed some rearranging, during which Kit was moved to the next seat up and Larry took her position in the stern, along with the scanner, which he put on the seat. Roy passed Larry a long pole, then put a canoe paddle in the boat. He pushed the boat away from the bank and hopped in.

Using the paddle, he turned the boat around and consulted a piece of paper from his shirt pocket. He brought the bow in line with a point he'd apparently determined from his map and motioned for Larry to get to work with the pole.

They were in an open stretch of water decorated with clots of floating duckweed, but soon entered a mass of water hyacinths that pressed against the boat, slowing their progress toward the cypress forest thirty yards away.

Some minutes later, they passed to the left of a grotesquely shaped cypress tree ten feet thick but only thirty feet tall and entered a world that, despite the circumstances, Kit found eerily beautiful.

The cypress trees were massive, their thick trunks forming great fluted wedges rising from the water, so close together the sun could find its way through only in patches, backlighting the gray shrouds of Spanish moss flourishing in the branches. Scattered between the trees were walls of cypress knees four feet high, woody stalagmites that together with the trees divided the water into a myriad of intimate rooms.

"Turn off that radio," Roy said. "If there's anybody else in here, I don't want us announcing ourselves."

Roy consulted his map, then pointed to a gap between trees. The boat moved forward.

As they penetrated deeper into the forest, the water changed from tan to black. To be in the midst of such beauty and at the same time be in fear for your life seemed positively surreal. Adding to this incongruity was the comfortable air temperature and the absence of mosquitoes, as if this were some kind of ultimate ride at a demented Disney World where the price for the experience was death.

They picked their way between trees for perhaps thirty minutes, seeing no wildlife along the way. Then, as they passed a knot of cypress knees, a bird with a bright orange head and beak landed on the knees and burst into song, programmed no doubt by the engineer who'd designed the ride.

A few minutes later, they were all startled by a drumming sound, as though someone was hitting one of the trees with a stick. This proved to be only a black woodpecker with a bright red topknot and a startling white stripe down the side of its head.

Then they came to the snakes—gray, thick-bodied, evil—two or three on nearly every clump of cypress knees and sometimes coiled on the lowest branches of the trees. Kit wasn't the only one disturbed by them.

"Roy . . . I don't like it in here," Larry whined.

"They're not poisonous," Roy said.

"He's lying," Teddy said. "If one of them bites you, you'll be dead in five minutes."

Kit thought Teddy was just saying that to get Larry even more upset, but it did the same for her.

Roy looked at Teddy. "It's very difficult to talk without a tongue. One more comment and you'll see that for yourself."

Kit continued to watch for snakes long after they'd been left behind, until she saw a peculiar scalloped membrane sticking out of the water a few yards ahead. When they drew near, the water erupted and they were all soaked as a spike-nosed garfish nearly as long as the boat headed for the bottom.

BROUSSARD WAS ONCE MORE on the plains, but all that remained of the immense buffalo herd were a few pitiful groups standing in twos and threes, their heads bowed, too listless even to feed. The great black stallion was breathing hard and bloody foam bubbled from his nose and mouth.

David Seymour stood beside Broussard's bed, silently cursing the virus consuming the old pathologist. It had taken him like a raging forest fire that had leapt the medical firebreaks they'd put down as though they weren't there. Now, he was in multiple organ failure. And, simply put, he was going to die.

ROY HELD UP A cautioning hand and ordered quiet with his finger to his lips. Larry eased up on the pole. Roy used the paddle to change their direction and signaled for Larry to move the boat forward.

Roy guided them into a position where the stern was flanked on the right by a string of tall cypress knees and the bow by a huge tree trunk. He signaled again for quiet and motioned for Larry to grab the cypress knees.

Leaving his seat and moving carefully in a crouch to where Teddy was sitting, Roy whispered, "There's an old man ahead of us fishing from a small boat. I don't want to kill him, but I will if he sees us. So if you two don't want his death on your heads, keep quiet. And you"—he motioned to Kit and Larry—"bend down."

Kit considered her options. Maybe the old man had a gun, too, and wouldn't be so easy to kill. He surely knew the forest better than Roy, and his smaller boat would give him better mobility. And this might be her last chance.

But if Roy did kill him because of something she did . . . No. She couldn't take that. She bent down and hoped Teddy had made the same decision.

She listened hard for some sign of the old man's approach and finally heard something plop into the water not far off. All was quiet for a few minutes and then she heard the old man's bait break water and another plop as he tried a new place.

Then it grew quiet.

Seconds ticked into minutes. Wondering if he'd gone, she decided to sneak a look. She rose slowly, until her eyes cleared the wall of cypress knees blocking her view.

And there he was—not twenty feet away, looking right at her—a grizzled old man in a dirty yellow cap and a checkered shirt, his mouth slightly open, showing an expanse of bare gum line.

Cursing her curiosity, she ducked behind the cypress wall and held her breath. Roy had his pistol ready.

But there was no shout from the old man, no greeting, no accusations, no questions. Soon, Kit heard another plop, farther away than last time.

Roy peeked from behind the tree, looked back at the others in the boat, and nodded, making a gesture that the old man was moving off in a different direction.

Eventually, they resumed their own trip.

After a time, Larry said something Kit, too, was thinking. "I'm thirsty."

"Unless you want to drink swamp water, there's nothing I can do about it," Roy said. "There'll be water at the shack."

"How much longer?"

"We're about halfway."

"Jesus, it's far."

"That was the idea."

As the day wore on, the temperature climbed a bit. If you were merely riding in a boat, it was still comfortable, but Roy and Larry both began to sweat. Larry bore his discomfort silently and did not speak again until they saw a large ball of what appeared to be caviar floating a few feet from the boat.

"What the devil's that?" He lifted his pole from the water, got a short grip on it, and sent the tip toward the ball.

When the pole made contact, the caviar exploded into a wiggling mass, part of which came up the pole with incredible speed. And Kit saw what they were—fat black-bodied ants.

Larry watched them running toward him as though he was hypnotized.

Then the first wave reached his hands. Screaming in pain, he dropped the pole in the water and began dancing and slapping at the ants, which were now seething up his arms. This set the boat rocking so violently, Kit lost her balance and tumbled to one side, nearly taking a header into the water.

Hanging precariously over the side, she tried to throw herself in the opposite direction, but, bound as she was, she could get no leverage.

The boat dipped again and she felt her legs lifting. She was going over. . .

22

Seeing they were about to lose Kit, Teddy threw himself at her feet, pinning them against the seat. Then Larry jumped out of the boat. He went under in a mass of bubbles.

Despite her close call, Kit had the presence of mind to hope he couldn't swim. But his head popped to the surface and he grabbed for the boat.

Roy scrambled past Teddy and Kit and helped Larry in.

"They were so fast," Larry complained. He looked at his hands, which were pocked with white welts. "Look what they did to me."

"You shouldn't touch things you don't understand," Roy said. He glanced at the ant colony and saw that it had been pushed a safe distance away by all the ripples Larry had caused. He pointed to the pole floating nearby. "Pick up your pole and let's get moving."

"The radio," Larry said. "It's gone."

"When you don't think before you act, bad things happen," Roy said.

They reached their destination an hour later. It was nothing but a shabby corrugated-metal box on stilts. Though Kit would have preferred room service at the Hilton and a nice bed with the covers turned down and a mint on the pillow, the shack looked mighty good.

Roy tied the boat up at a rickety ladder leading to a dock that was equally suspect and told Larry to wait there until he had a look around. He climbed the ladder, walked to the front door, and opened the padlock securing it. He then went inside.

While they all waited for him to return, a small lizard the same color as the weathered dock came out from a crack between one of the pilings and a stringer and studied them with evident curiosity. Roy's footsteps when he emerged from the shack and returned to the boat sent it back into hiding.

"The place has been ransacked," Roy said flatly. "They got in through a broken window. Most of the food is gone, but they left the water and a few cans of beans. They also took the propane tank for the stove."

"We can't stay here without food," Larry said.

"Not for long, but we can get by tonight. We'll figure out what to do in the morning. Let's get them inside."

Roy carried Teddy into the shack on his shoulder. Larry did the same with Kit. They were deposited on an artificial brick floor, next to the sink in a room whose walls were paneled in rough-cut cypress. Against the wall to Kit and Teddy's right was the gas stove, with pale images on the cypress above it the only evidence of the pots and pans that had once hung there. Next to the stove was the broken window. There were two metal cots with thin bare mattresses in the room, one on each side of the front door, which was directly opposite Kit. To her left, a blanket bearing an Indian design curtained off a small alcove. Through the crack where the blanket didn't touch the door frame, Kit saw a raised platform with a hole cut in it—the toilet, obviously open to the water below. A circular table and four chairs that looked as though they might have been made during the Crusades sat in the L formed by the sink and stove. Kit could see a gallon jug of water, a kerosene lamp, and three cans of beans on the table.

Larry grabbed the jug, unscrewed the cap, and tilted it to his lips.

"Give them some water, then get the glass from that window cleaned up," Roy said, motioning to the shards scattered over the linoleum.

"I'm hungry."

"Do what I say."

Roy went out the door, leaving it standing open. He walked onto the dock and studied their surroundings.

Larry brought the water jug to Kit.

"You want some of this?"

Right now, there was nothing Kit wanted more, but she wasn't going to beg. "Roy said give it to us. So don't play games."

"You think I do everything Roy says?"

"Like a trained gopher." It wasn't smart to antagonize them, she knew, but it was all she could do.

Hearing Roy's footsteps as he headed back to the shack, Larry put the jug to Kit's lips and tilted it acutely, giving her more than she could handle, so the excess ran down her chin, soaking her blouse.

"I'm gonna enjoy killing you," Larry said.

He moved over, put the jug to Teddy's lips, and did the same to him.

Roy came inside with the two books he'd brought and glanced their way. Ignoring what Larry was doing, he went to one of the beds and put the books on the floor beside it. Then he lay down and closed his eyes, hands folded on his chest. His expression when he'd looked at Kit and Teddy had been as stony as always, but there was something in his manner that made Kit believe he'd reached a decision out on the dock. He had, she feared, lost interest in them.

Larry set about gathering up the broken glass and throwing it out the window. When he finished, he went over to Roy.

"The glass is all cleaned up."

Without opening his eyes, Roy said, "Make sure they're not sitting on any or have any in their hands."

Larry went over to Kit first and rolled her onto her side. He inspected her hands and did the same with Teddy. He then went back to his brother.

"Now can I eat?"

"Go ahead."

Larry found a can opener and a spoon in a drawer by the sink. He opened a can of beans, dropped into one of the chairs, and dug in. Seeing Kit and Teddy watching, he paused, his spoon halfway to his mouth. "Roy didn't say to give you any."

Larry finished the can and took a long drink from the water jug. He eyed another can but left it alone. He stood, fished the gun from his pocket, and sat down again.

He popped the cylinder and shook the bullets into his hand. Snapping the cylinder back in place, he pointed the gun at Kit and pulled the trigger. He shifted his attention to Teddy and did the same thing.

Satisfied that the gun was still functional after going into the water with him, he reloaded, got up, and put it on the unoccupied bed before going through the rest of the drawers in the sink cabinet.

He brought a deck of cards back to the table and began a game of solitaire.

After a while, he got up, looked behind the Indian blanket, and went into the alcove, where his activities there couldn't be ignored. Kit felt the call herself but found the bathroom situation so repulsive, she was able to resist it.

"You okay?" Teddy whispered.

She wanted to be strong and optimistic, but she was so tired of being dirty and sore and thirsty and tied up that she couldn't help saying, "Not really."

"It's going to be okay, I promise. Just hold on a while longer."

She nodded listlessly.

Somehow, she managed to doze off. When she woke, Larry was asleep on one bed and Roy was sitting on the other reading the Ed

McBain book. He glanced at her, then went back to his reading. Through the open door, it appeared dusk was falling. She looked back at Roy, who seemed fully absorbed in his book and had no intention of reading it aloud.

She was now sure that in the morning, before leaving the swamp, he was going to kill both of them.

CHARLIE FRANKS LOOKED OUT the window for the fifteenth time. Beside the window, Bubba Oustellette sat hunched forward, his elbows on his knees, staring at the speckles in the terrazzo floor. Next to him, taking up the other two seats on the sofa, sat Grandma O, the fire in her dark eyes banked, her head moving almost imperceptibly from side to side. Across from her, Guy Minoux sat like a statue, one leg crossed over the other, a paper cup of cold coffee in one hand.

David Seymour appeared in the doorway and everyone came to life, their collective hope for good news so intense that, like every other time he'd had to do this, it made him hate his job.

"I wish I had happier news," he said, and it seemed like the lights in the room dimmed. "But he's simply not responding. We're doing all we can, but it's basically his fight now." Having learned that it's best not to linger after delivering bad news, Seymour turned and walked briskly away, hoping no one would follow.

"We got to stay hopeful," Grandma O said. "He don' need no negative energy from us." She got up, a black taffeta mountain that dwarfed its surroundings. "Le's all hold hands an' form a mental picture of dat ol' rascal doin' a jig in his hospital gown."

Franks and Minoux looked at each other, their discomfort at this suggestion obvious. Knowing she meant business, Bubba was already on his feet, with his hands out.

"Don' stan' dere, you two. Grab on." She took Bubba's hand and reached for Guy, who was too intimidated to refuse. Feeling like a fool, Franks completed the circle.

They stood quietly for what seemed to Franks and Minoux like an hour. Just as Phil Gatlin entered the room, she terminated the exercise.

"I don't like the looks of that," Gatlin said. "How's he doing?"

"Not well," Franks replied, his face flushed at being caught in such an absurd activity.

"But we're all stayin' positive," Grandma O said in a warning tone to the others.

"That's important," Gatlin said, meaning it.

"Any progress on findin' Kit?" Bubba asked.

"Actually, there is . . . a great deal. We almost had the kidnappers this morning, but they got away minutes before we arrived at where they were holding Kit, and most likely Teddy LaBiche."

"They got Teddy, too?" Bubba said.

"I think so. Kit left us a message written on a dusty shelf telling us they left in a white truck, and she gave us the plate number. An hour ago, the truck was found abandoned about thirty miles from here. The plates were missing, but we found pieces of twine in it that matched twine found at their hideout. Not far from the truck, there was evidence a boat had been stashed in the brush for several weeks. We also found a lot of trampled weeds and grasses on the edge of a nearby swamp. So we think that's where they are. It's too late to get a search started tonight, but first thing in the morning we'll be out there in force."

"Where exactly was da truck found?" Bubba asked.

Gatlin told him and Bubba said, "Dat's a big place."

"We've got plenty of help lined up. But I'll tell you, it's hard to concentrate on anything with Andy lying in there so sick. I liked things the way they were and I don't want to have to get used to somebody new running the ME's office." He looked at Franks. "I didn't mean . . ."

"I know," Franks said.

Gatlin stood sucking his teeth, thinking about all the years he and Broussard had been friends—the times the two of them had chartered a boat and gone deep-sea fishing; the arguments about who was the better writer, Louis L'Amour or Zane Gray; the look on Broussard's face when he'd given the old pathologist a box of thin macaroni slices labeled as fish assholes for his birthday; Broussard's irritating habit of asking a question and then answering it before you could say a word; the fine poem Broussard had written for them when little Andy died, two lines of which they'd put on his gravestone.

Then police business intruded on his memories, forcing him reluctantly back to his office.

Shortly after he left, Grandma O wandered down to Broussard's room and went into the staging area, where she looked at him through the glass. It was the first time she'd seen him in the hospital, and the sight of all those wires and tubes coming out of him and his face covered with an oxygen mask hit her like a pickax. Murmuring encouragement to him, her hand went to the locket hanging on a chain around her neck. Inside the locket was a four-leafed clover, the locket and clover a gift from Kit to celebrate the opening of the restaurant.

As her fingers rubbed the locket, she was staggered by the strongest premonition she'd ever had.

Hurrying back to the waiting room, she drew Bubba aside. "If dey wait until mornin' to start a search for Kit, it'll be too late. You got to help her tonight."

"David."

David Seymour looked up from Broussard's chart and some very dismal data to see Mark Blackledge, his right hand resting on the counter, fingers curled around a small piece of Styrofoam bearing three plastic test tubes.

"I want you to inject Andy with the contents of these tubes," Blackledge said.

"What is it?"

"Three monoclonal antibodies I just picked up at the airport. They've all been shown to react with CCHF virus in ELISA assays."

"Are they neutralizing antibodies?"

"Nobody knows."

"Are they safe?"

"Don't know about that, either. This is all cutting-edge stuff. They were only isolated a week ago."

"And you want to experiment on Andy?"

"What's his prognosis now?"

"Suppose they're like the antibodies produced in response to rheumatic fever strains of streptococcus. *They* cross-react with cardiac muscle . . . destroy normal tissue."

"What's his prognosis now?"

"It stinks."

"So there's really nothing at risk, is there? Without these antibodies, the virus kills him. With them, he might live."

Seymour waited until a nurse walking by was out of earshot, then said, "But if they damage him and he dies, somebody might say we killed him."

"Damn it, David. Be a man. I'm giving you a chance to save him."

"I don't want that responsibility."

"Then I'll do it," Blackledge said. "Are there syringes on the isolation cart?"

"Yes. But if he dies, we've never had this conversation."

BUBBA JOCKEYED HIS PICKUP so that the lights were directed into the swamp. Leaving the ignition on, he got out and went around to the back. The cops at the site where the kidnappers' truck had been found had turned him away, as though there was only one way to get to the water.

He pulled his pirogue from the bed of the pickup and carried it to the water, where he launched it. He returned to the truck several times for the things he'd need—his cell phone, a paddle, his shotgun, a thermos of chicory-laced coffee, his frog-gigging helmet with the miner's light on it, and something in a long white box.

With the pirogue loaded, and it was a full load indeed, he put on the helmet and returned to the truck to shut off the lights and the engine and lock up. Then he turned on the helmet light, made his way back to the pirogue, and shoved off into the darkening night.

In the shack deep in the swamp, Roy was reading at the table, the kerosene lamp duplicating him on the wall. Larry was asleep in his bed. The door was closed, but the frog chorus outside was so loud it could have been heard even if the window wasn't broken.

Kit's bladder was calling so urgently, she was just going to have to lower her standards. "I need to use the bathroom," she said.

Without looking up from his book, Roy said, "Sorry, you can't be trusted. You've already proven that."

"I'm serious. I *have* to use it."

Roy didn't respond, but he shifted in his chair, so he was facing away from her.

Outraged, Kit held it as long as she could, but then the inevitable happened. Embarrassed and humiliated, she began to cry. She didn't want to, God knows, but she couldn't stop. And from that moment, she was beaten.

Kit slept, mostly because sleep was the only escape open to her. Sometime during the night, she was awakened by the creak of a floorboard. The lamp was still on and in its light she saw a figure on the other side of the table moving toward Larry's bed. For a moment, she was sure she was hallucinating. She glanced beside her. It *was* Teddy. Somehow he'd freed himself.

All this happened in a space of time far shorter than it takes to tell it. There was another creak—from Roy's bedsprings as he sat up and quickly raised his hand. A gunshot rang out.

Caught in the open, Teddy spun to his right and threw himself at the broken window, disappearing through it as a second bullet thudded into the wall beside the window.

Kit heard Teddy hit the water; then there was a hideous reptilian roar and more splashing. Roy grabbed the lantern and rushed to the window, Larry close behind. Roy leaned out, holding the lantern above his head and searched the darkness.

After a minute or so, he pulled his head and the lantern back inside and walked over to Kit. "Looks like Ted's been taken by an alligator. It's probably best if you don't think too hard about what that's like." He lifted the lantern and inspected the floor where Teddy had been sitting. He bent and picked up a piece of glass that he showed to Larry. "He cut himself free with this. Where do you suppose he got it?"

Larry looked at the floor.

"You've got to be more careful." Roy rolled Kit to the side and looked for glass behind her, under her, and in her hands, exposing the still-damp stain on her slacks.

When she'd seen Teddy across the table, Kit had felt hope, but again it had led nowhere, except to Teddy's death. It was too much; there was no emotion left. She'd been manipulated until, like Roy, she was empty. Making no attempt to sit up, she again fled into sleep.

She woke in a sitting position, to see Roy and Larry eating the last two cans of beans. Larry finished first and tossed the can in the sink. "Now what?" he said.

"Kill her," Roy replied. "Then we're leaving."

Larry's face radiated pleasure. He picked up his gun from the table, walked to Kit and, with his foot, rolled her onto her side, facing away from him. She felt the barrel of the gun pressing behind her ear.

Drained as she was, she still wanted to live, and that translated into a fear that made her tingle. She closed her eyes and tried to follow the hawk she'd seen the day before, but the way was blocked by the image of the frightful damage a head shot causes when the bullet exits. Then she heard herself crying. . . No . . . *not* her . . . a child.

Larry and Roy heard it, too. Larry removed the gun from Kit's head and listened hard. "It's out front," he said, going to the door.

He opened it and saw at the end of the dock a large stuffed rabbit with long, drooping ears and wearing a tiara of fabric roses and a purple velvet dress trimmed in lace. Clothespinned to a string around its neck was a white envelope.

Before Roy could stop him, Larry stepped out onto the dock and headed for the rabbit.

"No," Roy yelled. "Get back in here."

Larry hesitated.

"Eh bien, mon cher," a voice shouted from Larry's right. He looked that way and saw Bubba standing in his pirogue, a shotgun to his shoulder.

"Eh bien."

Twenty yards from Bubba was another pirogue and another shotgun, held by the old man they'd seen fishing.

"Eh bien."

Another pirogue and another shotgun.

"Eh bien."

And another.

Larry threw his gun onto the dock and raised his hands.

In the shack, Roy turned and made a step toward Kit, obviously intending to use her as a hostage. But he was stopped from a voice at the window.

"You're finished, Roy. If you so much as blink, I'll send you to hell."

Teddy . . . with a shotgun.

His eyes fixed on Kit, Roy's gun hand came up. The shack was rocked by an explosion and then another. The bird shot from Teddy's gun ripped into Roy, turning the side of his face to hamburger and driving him off his feet. Teddy came through the window and pumped another shell into the gun. He walked over to Roy, looked at him, then knelt and felt the undamaged side of his neck for a pulse. He fished in Roy's pants for his knife, picked up the chrome pistol, and went to Kit. Setting the guns on the floor, he grabbed her in his arms. "It's over, baby. It's all over."

"Untie me," she said against his ear.

Teddy released her and cut her loose. He helped her to her feet and tried to put his arms around her again, but she pulled free and went to Roy's body. Dropping to her knees, she slapped the side of his face that still looked human, then began to sob into her hands.

A CURSORY INSPECTION WOULD not have found the black stallion, for he lay quite still, hidden by the tall prairie grass, unable to rise, his eyes open but sightless. The crushed grass on which he lay kept him from the ground, insulating him from the faint vibrations passing through it.

Gradually, the vibrations grew stronger. Soon, even the grass was set aquiver. A muscle on the stallion's flank quickened. One staring eye twitched in its socket.

The earth strummed the grass and the stallion's nostrils flared.

The tremors in the dirt became sound in the air, like the rumble of a distant storm. The stallion lifted its mighty head and its ears swiveled toward the thunder.

Over the horizon they came, muscle and sinew, a juggernaut sweeping over the prairie. The great stallion struggled to rise, its feet kicking at the air.

On they came, thousands upon thousands, their eyes wide and determined, driving startled insects from the grass until the musky air was thick with them. On his grassy bier, the stallion kicked and squirmed and gained his knees . . . and then his feet.

The first wave of buffalo rolled past, mere yards away, coaxing the stallion after them in a trot. Then, as his blood began to flow and his muscles loosened, he broke into a gallop. In the TB isolation ward of Charity Hospital, Broussard's fever broke.

23

"The alligator roaring after I went out the window . . . that was me," Teddy said, taking another sip of iced tea.

"It certainly made Roy think you'd been eaten," Kit said, scratching Lucky under the chin and withholding the admission that she, too, had believed it.

After their rescue, Kit and Teddy had been taken to the hospital, where they were given a thorough physical examination and Teddy's burns had been treated. Concerned that they'd been exposed to the virus, David Seymour checked them for tick bites and samples of their blood had been sent to Blackledge for viral analysis.

While waiting for the results on their blood test, the public health people thought it best that they both be socially isolated, a decision Kit welcomed, as she was in no mood to talk to anyone, not even Teddy. So they'd remained apart.

In her time alone, which Kit spent in her own house, she fulfilled a fantasy she'd had in the shack, taking the longest shower of her life. Afterward, she'd slept for twenty-four hours straight, so exhausted not even the specter of hemorrhagic fever disturbed her slumber. She'd been awakened by the telephone, bringing news that there was no sign of the virus in either her blood or Teddy's. Nor was Roy or Larry infected.

Free now to have visitors, she'd agreed to receive them, even though she still felt too shattered to be sharing herself. The still-vivid memory of being forced to live for days without changing clothes or bathing and that supremely humiliating moment in the shack had dictated Kit's attire, turning her from her usual slacks and blouse in favor of a paisley print red silk dress with an English tan belt and matching Italian calfskin pumps. At her throat was a double-linked gold necklace; at her ears, ruby earrings. And still she felt dirty and unattractive.

She looked at Bubba. "If you hadn't arrived when you did, I'd be dead. What can I possibly say to express my thanks?"

Bubba blushed and studied the ice in his tea. "You could say you're not mad at me for gettin' your rabbit dirty."

"I'm sure it can be cleaned."

Bubba looked up and grinned—a Cheshire cat with a bushy black beard.

"I heard there was an envelope attached to the rabbit," Phil Gatlin said. "What was inside?"

"Nothin'. We weren' plannin' on lettin' anybody get close enough to open it."

"Clever."

Bubba looked at Kit. "But it was Gramma O who tol' me you needed help right away. She should get da credit."

Kit turned to Grandma O, whose dress practically covered the upholstered chair in which she was sitting. "How did you know?"

"Cookin' ain't my only talent."

"I can sure vouch for that."

"Which reminds me, it's time Ah got back to da restaurant. No tellin' what kin' of goofy things dat knucklehead who's been runnin' it for me has been up to."

She rose from her chair, bringing everyone else in the room to their feet. Losing the lap he was in, Lucky jumped to the floor.

"Kit, honey, you come by and Ah'll cook you somethin' special to make you forget what you been through. An', Teddy, dat goes for you, too." She looked at Gatlin. "You ain't been through anything, so you got to eat from da menu."

Kit saw Grandma O and Bubba to the door, kissed both on the cheek, and fondly watched them cross the courtyard and disappear into the parking alcove. When she returned to the living room, Gatlin and Teddy were still standing.

"When do you think Andy will be able to have visitors?" she said to Gatlin.

"I think he can have them now. There's no longer any sign of virus in his blood and he's awake and talking . . . still weak, of course, but coming right along."

Kit felt an intense longing to see and touch the old curmudgeon, partly to comfort him, but also to seek his help in finding herself again.

"I know your parents are gonna be here any minute and you're anxious to see them," Gatlin said, "but I'd like to ask you a few questions before they arrive."

"Of course."

"Andy traced the kidnappers to the warehouse where you were being held—by some metal specks he found on the body of a strangulation victim that was dumped on Frenchmen Street. He also found a wrapper from a lemon ball he gave you in the victim's pants cuff. Did you actually witness that murder?"

"Yes. It was Roy. He strangled him with his belt. The body fell right on top of me."

"Did you see Roy shoot Nick Lawson?"

"Nick Lawson . . . This is the first time I've heard about him."

"He was shot in front of the warehouse shortly before the kidnappers took you two and fled. In fact, he may be the reason you all were gone when we arrived."

"I did hear a shot just before Roy came in and said we were leaving. How is he? Lawson, I mean. He's not . . ."

Gatlin swished the thought away with a wave of this big hand. "Naw. Like most of life's irritants, he'll be back."

"What was he doing there?"

"Thinking about trying to rescue you."

Their conversation was interrupted by the sound of the bell at the front gate. Going to the door and seeing her parents on the TV monitor, Kit buzzed them in.

Her mother came out of the parking alcove first. When she saw Kit, she froze and her hands went to her face. Over her fingers, she drank Kit in, then, crying, she ran to her and wrapped her in her arms, enveloping her in the aroma of Red Door and cigarette smoke. Over her mother's shoulder, Kit saw her father, handsome as ever, hurrying across the courtyard, a grin on his face.

"We were so worried," her mother said into Kit's left ear. "At first, they said you might be ill and then that you'd been kidnapped."

Kit's father arrived and, being unable to get any closer because of her mother, cupped the back of Kit's head and rubbed it. Her mother drew back and looked at her. "Did they hurt you?"

Of course they hurt her. . . . She hurt still. But that wasn't what her parents wanted to hear. "I'm fine. It's over and I just want to put it behind me."

"Kitten . . . they didn't . . . force themselves on you, did they?" Howard asked. "Sexually, I mean." A faint flush spread over his face. It was the first time in Kit's entire life that he'd brought sex into a conversation with her. "Because I'd kill them if they did."

She reached up and laid her palm against his cheek, which was hot to her touch. "No, Daddy. They didn't. And one is already dead. Teddy shot him."

"Then I'd like to shake his hand."

"Well, you can—he's inside."

They all went into the house and Kit took her parents back to where she'd left Gatlin and Teddy.

"I guess you both know Lieutenant Gatlin," Kit said.

They said they did.

"Kit tells us you shot one of the kidnappers," Howard said to Teddy.

"I'm not proud of it, but he gave me no choice."

"I'll be proud for you," Howard said, extending his hand. Somewhat reluctantly, Teddy shook it.

When he'd first met Beverly, Gatlin had been struck by her resemblance to Kit. Now, as they stood side by side, he was reminded of that.

Kit offered her parents a glass of tea, but both declined. They did accept seats on the Russian settee.

"So these guys were parrot smugglers," Howard said to Gatlin.

Gatlin nodded. "Retail value of the birds we found was around two hundred K."

"Do you know for a fact my brother Jack was involved in that?" Beverly asked, leaning forward.

"Larry, the kidnapper we've got locked up, says Jack was the leader of it. The buyer up north had apparently paid him twenty-five thousand down when the birds arrived, the balance to be paid when the buyer arrived for the pickup."

"That must have been the money Roy and Larry thought Jack gave *me*," Kit said. "Though I still have no idea why they believed that. Did the money ever show up?"

"We think it got spread around to the captain and crew of the *Schrader*."

"If he was involved in the smuggling, why wasn't there any glitter stuck in the sludge on the soles of his shoes?" Kit asked.

"He was the idea man," Gatlin said. "He left all the physical work to Roy and Larry. He never set foot in the warehouse."

"Surely Jack wasn't part of the kidnapping," Beverly said.

"No, he wasn't. That was Roy's idea, the one Teddy shot."

Gatlin watched relief spread across Beverly's face as she leaned back on the settee. "Larry's being very cooperative. He gave the fish and wildlife people the name of the buyer up north who contracted for the birds and the middlemen involved in the smuggling operation."

"Sounds like you've got it all wrapped up," Howard observed.

"Yeah, pretty much," Gatlin agreed. "But there is one thing that's been bothering me."

"What's that?" Howard said.

Gatlin looked at Beverly. "Mrs. Franklyn, you don't have a brother."

The blood drained from Beverly's face, leaving it the color of skim milk. She stood, wringing her hands, her eyes darting around the room. Howard, too, rose and put his arm around her shoulder, his brow worried.

All this brought Kit to the edge of the tiger-striped chair where she sat.

Howard leaned down and gently said to Beverly, "We've got to tell her."

Her face an emotional collage, Beverly looked at Kit.

"We have to," Howard repeated.

Now Kit got up. "What, Mother? What is it?"

Beverly turned to Gatlin, a tiny muscle at the corner of her mouth twitching. "I . . . Everything I told you was true except the parts about him being my brother and stealing from my parents. I gave you his real name and where he was living the last time I heard from him. . . . That's all you needed. I was sure he didn't have anything to do with Kit's disappearance, but even if he did, you didn't need to know the other. . . . It wasn't anything that would help you find her. And I couldn't tell you that because . . . when she came back to us, she'd . . ." Beverly looked at Kit.

"Mother, what *are* you talking about?"

"Jack was—" Beverly began, but her hands went to her face and she moaned into them. Her breathing grew heavy and ragged.

Howard reached out and took Kit's hand. "Kitten, Jack was your father."

Kit heard the words but thought it was a joke. She looked from face to face for a suppressed smile, a too-innocent expression, anything to support her belief this was a prank in monstrously poor taste. But she found no such evidence.

"We should have told you, I know," Beverly pleaded. "But at first you were too young to understand. Then, when you were older, it seemed like we'd waited too long."

Shivering, Kit pulled her hand from Howard's grasp and hugged herself with both arms.

"Please, Kitten, try to understand," Howard said.

"Jack was so irresponsible," Beverly said. "We never had any money because he was always losing what we had on wild get-rich-quick schemes. And he'd disappear for days at a time, telling me only that he couldn't be caged. It was one thing when it was just the two of us, but then you came and I told him he'd have to change . . . that I wasn't going to have you doing without because of him. But he didn't change. So when you were three months old, I threw him out. And a short time later, I met Howard."

"Who named me Kitten?"

"Jack," Beverly said.

"Did he ever write to me?"

"I've received only three letters from him since you were born, all of them many years ago, and all requesting money."

"And he never asked about me?"

"He did ask each time."

"Did you send him the money he wanted?"

Beverly averted her eyes. "Yes . . . but only with the understanding that he never try to contact you."

"Does biology really matter all that much?" Howard said. "I'm the one who loved you . . . the one who pushed your carriage and wallpapered your room . . . made you kites and bought you dolls . . . the one who showed your report card to the other employees down at the bank. I kissed your bruises and worried about the boys you dated. You *are* my daughter and have been for all but a tiny part of your life."

Kit stared at Beverly and Howard, seeing them almost as strangers. Finally, she said, "A lie . . . my whole life is a lie. I'm not who I thought I was and neither are you."

"We're all the same, baby," Beverly said, tears welling in her eyes, "Nothing has changed."

"*Everything* has changed," Kit shouted. "I trusted you and you betrayed me."

"Kitten, please," Howard said, reaching out for her.

"Please leave . . . *now.*"

Kit turned and ran from the room, Lucky at her heels. It was too much. After what she'd just been through, this was too much.

Gatlin, too, was surprised at Beverly's admission. If he'd known that's who Jack was, he'd have handled things differently for Kit's sake. When the time was right, he'd apologize. For now, he'd just leave with the Franklyns.

Kit went to her bedroom, shut the door, and threw herself across the bed, feeling as though everything beneath her skin had been scooped out of her. With Lucky stretched out beside her, his chin on the bedspread, she lay there, her mind filled with white noise, too frightened and confused to turn it off.

There was a tapping on the door and Teddy came in and joined her on the bed. Needing him as she never had before, she sat up and threw herself into his arms.

Teddy held her for a while, then separated from her so he could look into her eyes.

"I know this is a lousy time for this, but it's been in the back of my mind from the moment I realized we both might die. And since this seems to be the day for truth telling . . ." He drew a deep breath. "That friend of mine who owns this house . . . There is no friend. I own it."

Kit's jaw dropped. "You own it? How is that possible? When Roy checked your bank account, it was as depleted as mine."

"That was only one of my accounts. I'm a bit better off than you've been thinking. In fact, I guess you could say a lot better off—okay . . . wealthy. I knew you needed a place to stay and were hurting financially after selling your house and I also knew you'd never accept this house as a gift or rent it from me at a bargain price. So I made up the story I told you. I just wanted to help."

What little fabric still remained of Kit's life unraveled. "Get out," she screamed. "Get out."

Sensing he should take Kit's side, but confused because the target of Kit's anger was old Teddy, Lucky managed a few half-formed barks that sounded like *brrrf*.

Teddy slowly got off the bed. "There was no malice in this. Can't you see that?"

Lurching to her feet, Kit pushed him toward the door.

"Kit . . ."

She pushed him again.

Stumbling under her onslaught, he threw open the door and escaped.

BROUSSARD HELPED HIMSELF TO one of the lemon balls Guy Minoux had brought by a half hour earlier and he tucked it into his cheek. He was not feeling so chipper he could get up and go home, but he was well enough to have finished the L'Amour novel he'd found at the parking lot and which Phil Gatlin had picked up and delivered to him. But now, boredom was beginning to set in, so it was with more than his usual enthusiasm that he received his mail, which Charlie Franks had sent up and which the nurse had just given him.

On top of the pile was an envelope the size and shape of a card, addressed in a flowing feminine hand to him in his hospital room. He tore it open, briefly admired the glossy reproduction of a Dutch flower painting on the front, and turned to the inside, where to his surprise there was a lengthy message.

Dear Dr. Broussard,

I was so pleased to hear you are recovering from your recent illness. You no doubt are aware that the antibodies that made your recovery possible were provided by Dr. Mark Blackledge, who received them from a colleague in another state. What you probably do not know is he was forced into a trade by what I can only describe as a selfish individual who puts his own welfare above even the life of others. This man, whom I shall not name, demanded that in return for the antibodies you were given, Dr. Blackledge give him the remaining antibodies to a rare viral protein it took Dr. Blackledge three years to make, and will take another three years to replace, severely damaging his research and putting a considerable portion of his funding at risk. I am sure Dr. Blackledge would be furious at me for telling you this, but I felt that such generosity should not go unnoticed. Please don't tell him about this card.

Iva Eastman, Administrative Assistant,
Tulane Center for Viral Studies

Broussard was replacing the card in its envelope when the door opened.

"Hello stranger," Kit said. "Come here often?"

"Second time this year, so it sure seems that way," Broussard replied, his pleasure at seeing her openly displayed.

Kit walked over and took his hand. "I hear you had a rough time."

"Guess we both did. I can see you're physically okay. But how's the head?"

"Not good."

She was about to pour her story out to him when the door opened and a male voice said, "Well, you're looking a lot better than the last time I saw you."

"Feelin' better, too," Broussard replied.

Mark Blackledge approached the opposite side of the bed from where Kit stood.

"Do you two know each other?" Broussard said.

"Haven't had the pleasure," Blackledge replied.

Broussard introduced them, placing each of them in context and mentioning that Kit was the one who'd been kidnapped by the parrot smugglers.

"Glad to see you're unharmed," Blackledge said, offering his hand across the bed.

It was true they hadn't met before, but Kit knew his name and his history with Broussard. That and his interruption of their conversation caused her to dislike him. Rather than make an issue of it, she shook his hand and thanked him for his concern. Meanwhile, Broussard hid the card from Blackledge's secretary under some of his other mail.

Blackledge turned his attention to Broussard. "Odd how things'll surprise you. I would have bet my ass that the vector we were after was an Ioxid tick, but they were Argasids—soft ticks, for God's sake—the absolute worst kind, considering how frequently they feed."

"Was I bitten?" Broussard asked.

"There was no evidence of it."

"I didn't cut myself workin' on any of those bodies, either, and it doesn't seem to travel in the air . . . so how'd I get it?"

"I noticed that you have cracks in the skin on your feet. . . ."

"Happens every year at this time."

"Following a hunch, I went to your house and took a look around. I found an Argasid tick crushed on the bathroom floor. My guess is you accidently flattened it when you were wearing shoes, then a short time later stepped on it with your bare foot and became infected through those skin fissures. I cleaned it up and decontaminated the area. I also fed your cat."

"What *haven't* you done?" Broussard said. "David Seymour says it was you who saved me."

"Yeah, well, I guess now we're even. How about when you're up to it, you and I get together for dinner—no agenda, just sort of catch up on each other?"

Bewildered at Blackledge's congeniality, Broussard said, "Sure. But you've got to let me pick the restaurant."

"Done," Blackledge said. He glanced at his watch. "Sorry for the brief visit, but I've got to get back and interview a prospective Tropical Medicine fellow. I mean it about dinner. This isn't just Calspeak."

"I know."

"Okay, long as you do. Kit . . . good to have met you."

When he was gone, Broussard looked at Kit. "I don't know what *that* was all about. He sounded like he wanted to be friends again."

"He does."

"Why? Because I almost died?"

"No. In a way, because you didn't. Remember him saying, 'now we're even'? I think after you rescued his career for him, he felt humiliated and inferior every time you'd meet. And that translated into animosity. Now he's saved *your* life, so you can be equals again."

Having it laid out like that made it all seem obvious. And Broussard was ashamed he'd been so small and self-centered that all these years he'd responded to Blackledge in kind. It was a flaw he vowed to correct. "I see you haven't lost your skills."

"I don't know why I still have those. It seems like I've lost everything else."

"What do you mean?"

"I was taken away from my home as one person and have come back another. Everything has turned inside out." Then, damn it, she felt her eyes fill. Embarrassed, she pulled her hand free and turned her back so he wouldn't see.

Shielding the movement, she wiped at her eyes and ordered herself to stop acting like a child. When she'd regained her composure, she turned again to face him. "After what you've been through, I shouldn't be bothering you with my problems. It's just that . . ."

"What's happened?"

"That man who sent me the roses . . . He was my . . . my real father."

"But your mother said he was her brother."

"She lied. All those years thinking Howard was my father . . . and they didn't tell me. How could they do that?"

"If someone had asked you before this happened if Beverly and Howard had been good parents, what would you have said?"

"That they were, but . . ."

"Would you have said you'd felt wanted and protected?"

"Yes."

"And loved?"

"Yes, of course."

"Then what's the problem?"

"The lie . . ."

"Forgive me for buttin' in, but you're makin' entirely too much of that. People make mistakes. To expect otherwise is unrealistic."

"*You* don't lie."

"Lord, don't look to me. I've got plenty of faults. You just showed me one with Blackledge. As for lyin', I might do it, if the stakes were high enough—if, for example, I thought the truth would upset someone I cared for. I might very well lie . . . and so might you. None of us knows what we'll do in a tough situation until we confront it. Don't set such high standards for other people. Our friends and loved ones deserve better."

"I'm not even sure what love means anymore."

"Now you're pushin' me into an area I have some trouble with myself. If I could get to my 'cyclopedia of practical quotations, I might be able to say somethin' memorable. Without it, I'm pretty limited. Can't even think of anything useful Babe Ruth ever said. I do know, though, that now I've been given a few more years, I'm gonna try to be less judgmental and make sure I enjoy every day left to me. And I'd like to see you do the same. What do you say we make a pact to do that . . . you and me, right now."

"I appreciate what you're trying to do, but I didn't just dent a fender on my car. I found out half my DNA came from a con man. What does that make me?"

"Nothin' more or nothin' less than what you were before you found out."

Kit had come hoping Broussard would say something to make sense of all that had happened. A better person would have come to comfort *him*. Suddenly, she felt too ashamed of her behavior to remain.

"I'm sorry, I have to go. Forgive me for being so self-centered. I love it that you're getting better. It shows that sometimes the right things happen." She leaned down, kissed him on the forehead, and hurried to the door, where she paused, her hand on the pull. Looking back at Broussard, she said, "Where's Jack's body?"

"Still in the morgue."

"Do you think I could have it released to me?"

"It's infectious, so I expect the Health Department will order it cremated."

"Would they let me arrange a place for the ashes?"

"Don't see why not. I'll mention that to 'em."

A few minutes after Kit left, Broussard received another visitor—Ruth Lamm, the hospital infection-control officer, wearing a frilly pink dress, her gray hair perfectly coiffed. She was holding a small azalea whose flowers matched the color of her dress.

"I thought this might brighten things up," she said, putting it on the window ledge.

"And so it does," Broussard said.

"How are you feeling?"

"I'm startin' to hate this room."

"That's good. It means you're getting better. I heard how you tracked down the source of the virus. That was fine work."

"I was lucky."

"I doubt that." There was a pause, during which she began smoothing her dress and fidgeting with her hair, obviously uncomfortable over something on her mind. Finally, she said, "I was wondering if . . . That is . . . Oh, hell, I might as well say it straight out. There's a tractor pull and a monster truck show at the dome two weeks from Saturday night. Would you like to go, assuming you're feeling up to it? If you've never seen a monster truck crush cars in person, it's something you really should try."

There wasn't a defense counsel in the country who could trip Broussard up with an unexpected question. Even when students asked him about things he hadn't considered in years, the answers came without effort. The juxtaposition, though, of monster trucks and Ruth Lamm cast him adrift.

The event, of course, was one he wouldn't even *think* of attending, and she sure wasn't what he was looking for in a woman, not that he was looking at all. At least those were positions held by the *old* Broussard. But as he'd told Kit, he was no longer that man. And to prove it, he said, "Sure, why not."

"Good," she said. "We can firm up the details later. Now I've got some work to do." She went to the door, then turned around. "By the way, if you don't want people at the tractor pull staring at you, you might consider leaving at home the string on your glasses and that goofy bow tie you usually wear."

KIT WALKED TO THE elevators and got on. Howard was her *step-father* . . . and he and her mother had kept that from her for decades. It was impossible. Broussard was asking too much to expect her to understand. He'd feel exactly as she did if it happened to him. No . . . it was too much.

Kit rode down two floors, where she got off and made her way to the room number she'd been given by hospital information. Inside, she found Nick Lawson, propped up in bed, reading a paperback copy of *Deliverance*, surgical bandages covering his left cheek and most of his neck.

"You don't look so bad," she said, walking to the bed.

Lawson put his book down and picked up a stick of chalk and a small slate on which he wrote, "Where are my flowers?"

"I thought a real man like you wouldn't want any."

With an eraser from the nightstand, he wiped the slate clean, so the dust fell into a shallow plastic container lying beside him. He pecked at the board with the chalk and turned the message toward her.

"Explanation accepted."

"Will you be able to talk again eventually?" she asked.

He erased the board and wrote again. "Able now. Doc says not to."

"I hear you were responsible for scaring the kidnappers off just when the cops were on their way."

The chalk clicked over the board. "I had a bad day. Surprised to see you."

"I'm sorry you were hurt."

He used the chalk again. "How about a pity date?"

Kit hesitated, wavering, Broussard's advice chipping away at the anger she still felt at Teddy's confession, reminding her of all they'd gone through together with Roy and Larry and all the good times before those two had come along, and how Teddy had not only saved her life there at the end but had long ago given it a center.

"Tell you what . . . you get better and I'll take you to dinner at a place that serves a very tasty white shark special. They'll even let you get in the tank and catch the one you want. Not a date, just a thanks for trying to help."

Lawson wrote again. "Want to get in here with me?"

Before Kit could reply, a nurse came in with a tray of materials. "I'm sorry to interrupt your visit, but it's time for me to change Mr. Lawson's dressings."

"I have some things to do, anyway," Kit said. She looked at Lawson. "Let me know when you're ready for that shark."

She then went to her car and returned home, where she left a message of apology on Teddy's answering machine in Bayou Coteau, then picked up the paper to look for a new place to live.

About the Author

Photo by Jennifer Brommer

I grew up in Sylvania, Ohio, a little suburb of Toledo, where the nearby stone quarries produce some of the best fossil trilobites in the country. I know that doesn't sound like much to be proud of, but we're simple people in Ohio. After obtaining a bachelor's degree at the U. of Toledo, I became a teacher of ninth grade general science in Sylvania, occupying the same desk my high school chemistry and physics teacher used when he tried unsuccessfully to teach me how to use a slide rule. I lasted six months as a public school teacher, lured away into pursuit of a Ph.D. by Dr. Katoh, a developmental biologist I met in a program to broaden the biological knowledge of science teachers. Katoh's lectures were unlike anything I'd ever heard in college. He related his discipline as a series of detective stories that had me on the edge of my chair. Stimulated to seek the master who trained Katoh, I moved to New Orleans and spent five years at Tulane working on a doctorate in human anatomy. Stressed by graduate work, I hated New Orleans. When Mardi Gras would roll around, my wife and I would leave town. It wasn't until many years later, after the painful memories of graduate school had faded and I'd taught microscopic anatomy to thousands of students at the U. of Tennessee Medical School in Memphis (not all at the same time) and published dozens of papers on wound healing that I suddenly felt the urge to write novels. And there was only one place I wanted to write about . . . mysterious, sleazy, beautiful New Orleans. Okay, so I'm kind of slow to appreciate things.

Practically from the moment I decided to try my hand at fiction, I wanted to write about a medical examiner. There's just something appealing about being able to put a killer in the slammer using things like the stomach contents of the victim or teeth impressions left in a bite mark. Contrary to what the publisher's blurb said on a couple of my books, I'm not a forensic pathologist. To gear up for the first book in the series, I spent a couple of weeks hanging around the county forensic center where Dr. Jim Bell taught me the ropes. Unfortunately, Jim died unexpectedly after falling into a diabetic coma a few months before the first book was published. Though he was an avid reader, he never got to see a word of the book he helped me with. In many ways, Jim lives on as Broussard. Broussard's brilliant mind, his weight problem, his appreciation of fine food and antiques, his love for Louis L' Amour novels . . . that was Jim Bell. When a new book comes out, Jim's wife always buys an armful and sends them to Jim's relatives.

My research occasionally puts me in interesting situations. Some time ago, I accompanied a Memphis homicide detective to a rooming house where we found a man stuck to the floor by a pool of his own blood, his throat cut, and a big knife lying next to the body. Within a few minutes, I found myself straddling the blood, holding a paper bag for the detective to collect the victim's personal effects. A short time later, after I'd listened to the cops on the scene discuss the conflicting stories they were getting from the occupants, the captain of the general investigation bureau turned to me and said, "What do *you* think happened?" The house is full of detectives and he's asking *my* opinion. I pointed out a discrepancy I'd noticed in the story told by the occupant who found the body and next thing I know, he's calling all the other detectives over so I can tell them. Later, we took this woman in for questioning. I wish I could say I solved the crime, but it didn't turn out that glamorous. They eventually ruled it a suicide.

Made in United States
Orlando, FL
22 November 2021

10644833R00152